SALVATION'S INFERNO

INFERNO, BOOK ONE

KAT MIZERA

AUTHOR'S NOTE

Dear Readers:

The Inferno series was born from two general ideas: the first was simply that Dante needed a book of his own and that led to the others. However, the second inspiration came from the simple need to promote acceptance. These books are fictional, and as authors we often push the envelope with things like insta-love, travel times, locale and more. We know they aren't always realistic but we hope that you enjoy them for what they are—escapism entertainment based on reality.

In the Inferno books, I deal with issues that are prevalent in today's society: Hate crime, the struggles within the LGBTQ community, divorce and blended families, and the many, many differences in how people from all walks of life live their lives. I don't promote nor condemn any of them, but I hope that you can discern the distinctions in these scenarios I've created. Not all of them are realistic and they truly aren't meant to be; these are fictional depictions of potentially real people and situations.

I don't in any way want anyone to assume that all BDSM clubs are like Club Inferno—because Club Inferno doesn't exist and is simply a place I created in my mind that these specific characters might enjoy. Not all bisexual people live like Jamie and Viggo. Not many divorced couples can have a relationship like Viggo and Emilie.

The liberties I take with the BDSM lifestyle are not meant to portray it in any way other than the way that fit with this series—fun and sexy and occasionally over-the-top with both good and bad people involved in it, just as there are in real life. They are in no way meant to be realistic from the perspective of romantic fiction--just good fun, good sex and happily-ever-afters.

All the best,

Kat

Please note: No characters were harmed in the creation of these books (except maybe the bad guys).

PROLOGUE

Five women on their knees. Five women ready to suck him off. Five hot, sexy, naked women with their hands tied behind their backs, blindfolds over their eyes, mouths open, ready for action—and Dante was staring at them with a scowl. Two blondes, two brunettes and a redhead, all for him, and his cock hadn't even stirred. Reaching for the nearby bottle of tequila, he took a swig and then reached down to grab one of the blondes by the chin.

"Drink!" he snapped, pouring some of the liquor into her mouth. She swallowed greedily, as if she loved tequila, and licked her lips.

He rubbed his thumb along her full lower lip and watched her chest start to rise and fall a little faster in anticipation; she wanted him even though she'd been blindfolded before he entered the room and had no idea whose cock would wind up down her throat. The thought of these women wanting to suck a cock, any cock, made his dick jolt just a little, showing the first signs of life in months and he released it from his leathers. Pushing it into the blonde's mouth, he closed his eyes, willing his dark thoughts to fade into the even darker recesses of his mind. The warm wetness her lips and tongue provided gave him only momentary relief; instead of physical pleasure, all he felt was the draw back toward the mindlessness of the black abyss in his soul.

Grunting in irritation, he dug his fingers into her hair and rammed his cock deeper into her throat. He heard her gag and a tiny prick of guilt caused him to ease back, though his grip on her hair tightened in frustration. He didn't want this one or any of the others; all he wanted was a mind-numbing release so he could go back to drinking. Pumping faster, he willed himself to get lost in her rough warmth. Relentless as he fucked her mouth, he finally felt the first spasms of ecstasy and allowed himself to spurt deep into her throat. She coughed but caught herself, swallowing as quickly as she could even though some of it dripped down her chin.

Dante looked down in disgust, stuffing himself back into his pants with disdain. He was about to tell them to get the hell away from him when he heard the door open and the click of high heels behind him. He turned, his face dark with annoyance at the interruption.

"That's enough." A tall, pissed-off blonde folded her arms across her chest and glared at him. "Let's go! Now."

He made a face. "What are you doing here?!"

"I said we're going home," she hissed. "Or I call Kate."

He narrowed his eyes. "Dammit, Emilie, I'm not your—"

"You're about to be my bitch if I have to ask again!" Though she was four months pregnant and probably no more than 110 pounds, even at five feet nine inches, his friend Emilie Martensson didn't look like she was kidding. An experienced dominatrix, Emilie could kick ass and take names, and the look in her eyes told him he needed to tread carefully. A hormonal Emilie could be dangerous, even if they were just friends, and he made a spontaneous decision to give in, though there was a fierce look on his face.

"Fine," he snapped. "Let me get my things."

Fifteen minutes later they sat in his plush limousine heading through the empty predawn streets towards his estate just north of Manhattan. Emilie was still glaring at him and Dante simply stared out the window. For a while she just watched him before finally scooting over so she was right next to him, one pale hand on his arm.

"Dante?" Her voice was much softer than it had been at the club. "You can't keep doing this to yourself. It's not going to make the pain go away."

He grunted.

"Why do you even bother going to those places?" she asked. "You don't enjoy yourself and you come home feeling more frustrated than before you went."

"How the hell do you know what I feel?!" he growled, his eyes darkening dangerously.

"Because I'm your friend." She laced her fingers through his, her sad blue eyes imploring. "Dante, please. It hurts me to see you doing this to yourself."

For a moment, the harshness in his eyes faded and he gently touched her face. "Emilie, I don't deserve your friendship. I'm in the deepest kind of hell right now—you shouldn't be around me."

"We live together." She chuckled. "Where shall I go?"

He sighed, looking away. "This is the only relief I get, Em. It's the only time I can get away from my demons."

"You didn't kill them," she whispered. "It's not your fault they died. You have to stop blaming yourself."

"I brought that bitch into my home!"

"But you didn't know she would turn on you." Emilie stroked his muscular arm with slow, comforting movements. "You have to let go of this. You're only hurting yourself, and while I don't care what Larissa would have wanted, I know Trey loved you and wouldn't be happy with you right now. Please, Dante. It's hard to watch you self-destruct. I care for you, and I *will* call Kate if you don't stop."

He held up a hand. "Fine. Leave Kate out of it. She went through a lot last summer—she has a hard enough job being my publicist. She doesn't need personal aggravation too."

"She's your friend and she's worried about you, just like I am. How do you think I knew where to find you tonight?"

"She didn't know where I was!" he muttered.

"No, but Jamie did, and he told Karl." Karl was Emilie's brother, as well as Kate's husband, and Jamie was one of Karl's teammates.

Dante made a face. "A man has no privacy."

"A man like you has no reason to go to places like that! What do you get out of it? It's not about sex for you and we both know it."

"I don't fucking know, Emilie," he muttered after a moment. "But it's all I've got right now."

"You have to stop the behavior," she said finally. "The sex clubs, the hookers, the drinking… I know it's the off-season, but it will be time for baseball again before you know it and you're not going to be ready. None of this is going to bring them back."

"I know that!" he shot back. "But sex clubs and alcohol make me miss them less!"

"You have to learn to live with missing them," she whispered, resting her head on his shoulder. "We all miss people."

"Ah, *querida*." *Sweetheart*. "So much loneliness in the house, yes?"

"No." She shook her head. "We have each other and friendship makes up for a lot."

"Friendship definitely makes up for a lot."

"Promise you'll move past this, Dante."

"Emilie, I—"

"Promise." She put his hand on her tiny stomach. "I need you to be the man I know you can be; both of us can't be a mess."

"You're not a mess." He sighed and softly kissed the top of her head. "But I promise."

1

It was raining. Again. Dante stared out at the blackened sky that seemed to match his mood and downed the tumbler of whiskey in his hand. It burned its way down his throat and he turned to stare at the flames sizzling in the fireplace. The crackling of the burning wood was the only sound in the house right now, and though he normally relished his privacy, tonight it was making him crazy. The silence was louder than any noise the TV or radio could make, and he exhaled with a loud, frustrated breath.

It had been a rough few months since the death of his fiancée and their unborn child. He hadn't loved Larissa, but he'd been over the moon at the prospect of having a son. So over the moon he'd let her manipulate him into moving into his home and nearly ruining his life. In the end, she'd died, their child had died and his best friend and agent, Trey Montoya, had died as well. Now he was left with memories and regrets that did nothing to fill the emptiness of both his house and his life.

His phone buzzed in his pocket and he took it out grudgingly; he really didn't want to talk to anyone, but it was Kate. She was someone he would almost always talk to. "Hello, Kate." His voice was deep, offering no trace of his Cuban accent when he only said a few words.

"Where have you been?" she demanded. "I've been texting and calling but you don't call back."

"Is everything okay?"

"Yes, but I'm worried about you!"

He smiled faintly. "I'm sorry. I've been hibernating."

"You've been moping." She knew him well.

"The house is empty without Emilie here." Kate's sister-in-law, Emilie Martensson, was living with him while she went to design school in Manhattan. It had worked out well since she needed a place to live and he hadn't wanted to be alone after moving to New York.

"She's already left?" Kate knew Emilie was going home to Sweden for the holidays.

"Today."

"Dante, come to Vegas and spend Christmas with us."

Dante sighed. "I'm not good company, *querida*." *Sweetheart*. His heart lurched as he thought of another woman he'd used that term of endearment with. Damn, he wanted to call her, see her, touch her. But he'd promised her anonymity, and he wouldn't break that promise. Their night together had been stolen time; a handful of hours that had meant more to him than any other time spent with any other woman. He'd had a pregnant fiancée at home then, though, and the woman he'd been with had a job that made sleeping with bad-boy baseball players taboo. Now it felt like he had nothing and his memories of her were often the only thing that got him through each day.

"We want you anyway." Kate's voice was soft, knowing how much he was hurting. "It's our first Christmas in the new house and you would—"

"I would be in the way."

"Bullshit. You're a part of our family, Dante. We want you here."

"Are you sure your husband feels the same?"

"Of course! Look, neither of our parents are coming and it'll be good to just hang out. Come on, you know you want to. You love Vegas."

"I do." He sighed, closing his eyes. *She* lived in Las Vegas. *She* was a friend of Kate's. Running into her would be inevitable if he went for the holidays. The only problem was that if he saw her, he didn't know if he could keep his promise; he hadn't been able to stop thinking about her since the night they'd spent together nearly six months ago.

"Please come, Dante. You shouldn't be alone at the holidays. You need to be with people that love you, and frankly, Trey was my friend too. You're not the only one who misses him."

"I know." He nodded even though she couldn't see it. "All right, I'll come. I'll book a hotel—"

"You will not," she huffed. "I have five goddamn bedrooms and you need to sleep in one of them!"

He laughed. "Okay, don't get your feathers ruffled. I'll sleep in your guest room."

"I'll book your flight." She disconnected before he could protest, but he was smiling as he put the phone back in his pocket. In addition to being his friend, Kate was also his publicist, so she often made travel arrangements for him. She knew his preferences and had access to his credit card, so it was just as easy for her to make the plans. Even if she had him on a flight in the morning, it wasn't like he had anything else to do. He would go to Las Vegas and spend time with some of the only friends he had. It would be good to see them and let the women make a fuss over him. They were all married, but that was okay; he liked their husbands and though he wouldn't say it out loud, he liked being part of their close-knit group. God knows, he'd never had those kinds of friendships in his own life. Except for Trey, of course, but Trey was dead.

S pending time with Kate and her friends was wonderful. Dante couldn't remember the last time he was so relaxed—or so pampered. The funny thing was, at home he did very little in the way of work or chores. He had a cleaning service that came twice a week, and maintenance people and secretaries to do almost everything else. He concentrated on staying in shape and playing baseball. Here at Kate's, he helped set the dinner table, load the dishwasher and take out the garbage. He hadn't done any of those things in years. Hell, he'd never loaded a dishwasher. They didn't have one growing up, and as soon as he'd gotten his first major league contract, he got a housekeeper who did things like that. It was strange that doing these types of menial tasks actually relaxed him, and he'd been sleeping better since he got here.

The only problem with being in Las Vegas was knowing that Becca was close by and not being able to reach out. She'd been clear that she didn't want to be associated with a guy like him, and he didn't blame her. His life was in a constant state of chaos and she deserved someone who would be good for her; that definitely put him out of the running because he was a disaster waiting to happen. No matter how hard he tried, he always fucked up. The only place he was consistently good was on the baseball field, but one injury could end his career at any time.

"What should I make for dinner?" Kate asked, coming in from the grocery store, her hands full of bags.

Dante took them from her and put them on the counter.

"I don't care."

She made a face at him. "You're impossible." She moved away, her long ponytail swinging behind her.

He watched her walk back out to the garage, her round ass swaying in a pair of tight jeans. They were good friends and business associates, but there had been a time when he'd thought he could fall in love with someone like her. She'd never had eyes for anyone but her tall Swedish husband, though, and then he'd met Becca. Apparently, he liked women with curves, even though he'd never dated women like that in the past. He had a thing for brunettes too, though many of the women who'd been in his bed over the years had been blondes. He didn't know what had happened to him in the last year, first becoming attracted to a curvy publicist who was in love with someone else and then a sexy Head of Media Relations who didn't want his crazy life to ruin her career. Somewhere along the way he'd lost his taste for models and socialites, leaning towards more wholesome, *normal* women.

He'd thought it was because he'd gotten his on-again, off-again girlfriend, Larissa, pregnant. Being engaged to a woman he didn't love didn't bother him until he was living it. Suddenly it was a huge pain in the ass and she'd only gotten more and more demanding as time went on, making him desperate to get away from her. If Kate had been willing to give him a chance, he knew without a doubt he would have ended things with Larissa, but that never happened and he'd been resigned to his fate. By the time he'd met Becca, Larissa was six months pregnant and they knew it was a boy. They'd decorated a nursery and picked out a name; he wasn't in a position to bring Becca into his life as his mistress. It wouldn't have been fair to any of them. Then Larissa and the baby had been killed and he hadn't thought rushing to Becca while he was grieving was appropriate. Besides, she'd made it clear that though she had feelings for him, he wasn't the kind of guy she wanted in her life.

"Dante, how do you feel about grilling steaks tonight?" Kate asked, coming in from the garage.

"Whatever works for you," he smiled.

She paused, eying him carefully. "What's going on in your head, big guy? You seem different. Is there a new woman in your life?"

He shrugged. "I seem incapable of finding a nice girl who wants to take a chance on me. It's new, this inability to attract a woman I want, but it's happened twice in less than a year."

"Okay, I know I was one, but I also know that we never got close enough for me to break your heart. Who is it that has you acting so strange?"

"It's best if you don't know," he said softly.

"Is it Tiff?" Tiffany was the widow of Dave Marcus, a Sidewinders coach who'd passed away last June.

Dante shook his head. "Tiff is my friend, just as you are, but no. There was never anything between us but friendship."

"So there's someone else, that I obviously know, that you don't want to talk about." She nodded. "Okay. But understand that I *will* figure it out."

"I'm sure you will," he said. "And when you do, I would appreciate it if you would keep it to yourself."

Kate frowned. "Dante, I would never do anything to hurt or embarrass you."

"I know that. If I didn't, I wouldn't be here."

2

____

ORGASMS. REBECCA HERNANDEZ HAD SPENT MORE THAN HALF OF HER twenty-seven years alive thinking about what it would be like to have one. Actually having one had been better than anything she'd imagined. The fact that it had been induced by the hottest, most notorious, bad-boy baseball player in the world might have had something to do with it, but the fact remained that she'd finally had one. Five or six, actually, but who was counting?

Rolling over, she squinted at the clock on the nightstand. It was almost five in the morning and there was no way she was going back to sleep now. Instead she would lie here and think about the man of her dreams. She saw him regularly on magazine covers and on TV, always the center of attention, always strikingly hot, but nothing had prepared her to be with him. Naked, hot, open for him to do anything he wanted to her. That possibility had never even occurred to her when she'd drooled over him from afar.

Seeing him at the bar that night had been a surprise. It had been an even bigger surprise when he'd joined her and struck up a conversation. It was probably the alcohol that made her tell him the truth about why she was at a sex club even though she had no idea what to do there. She'd never had an orgasm, couldn't even seem to do it on her own, and she'd been hoping one of the experienced men at that club would be able to help her. Somehow, a man she'd always lusted after, Dante Lamonte, had taken it upon himself to show her the way. And damn, he'd shown her things she couldn't even think about without blushing. She could still picture the discarded remnants of their lovemaking scattered around them: vibrators, dildos, lubricant, condoms, restraints. Even the damn blindfold.

She'd gotten dressed as quickly and soundlessly as possible afterwards. Her dress had been on the other side of the room and she'd tiptoed over to where it was, sliding it over her head. Her shoes had been by the door, but she hadn't put those on until she was in the elevator; she hadn't wanted to wake him. Saying goodbye would have been too awkward, too gut-wrenching, for her already aching heart. She'd never believed in love at first sight, but the moment Dante's lips first touched hers she'd known she was gone. He wasn't just a famous celebrity athlete with gorgeous eyes, the kind of body you wanted to lick from head to toe and tons of money—he was the absolute epitome of a bad boy with a heart of gold. In a different time and place, she knew instinctively that he would have fallen in love with her too. A time and place where he wasn't engaged to another woman already carrying his baby.

Becca had taken one long, last, steadying breath. She'd gone there to figure out why the pleasure of sex had always eluded her; she'd left with a new appreciation of her body but a stupidly broken heart. He'd been gentle when telling her he had no choice but to go home to the woman having his child, and honest when admitting that he didn't love that woman but had a responsibility to her.

"Here," he'd told her, bringing her hand to his chest. "You'll always be right here."

In his heart, just not in his life.

"Thank you," she'd whispered in the darkness as she'd opened the door and slipped out. She didn't know what she'd been thanking him for, though.

Life had been lonelier than ever since then, but her work kept her too busy to dwell on it and the personal tragedy that had befallen him not long after their night together had kept her from reaching out even though he was single now. It had been big news that his pregnant fiancée, Larissa, and his best friend and agent, Trey, had been murdered. The killer had also attempted to murder Karl Martensson, one of the players on the Las Vegas Sidewinders, the team for which Becca worked. Karl's wife, Kate, was Dante's good friend and publicist, and since Becca knew her as well, she'd been kept apprised of what was going on in his life, though she'd opted to keep her distance. She hadn't known what to say when she'd heard about it, and all these months later, she still didn't know any details. She didn't even know if he was interested in seeing her again, and she'd rather die than face any kind of rejection from the man who owned her mind, body and soul. Most of the time, she just tried not to think about him.

There were a hundred things on her to-do list, but the one Becca had to do now was a huge disappointment, and she tapped her fingers on her desk as she waited for her friend to answer the phone.

"Kate Martensson."

"Kate, it's Becca."

"Hey! What's up?"

"Busy, as always."

"I hear you." Kate also worked as a publicist, although she had her own firm, with a plethora of famous athletes as clients.

"Listen, I'm probably not going to be able to come on Christmas Eve. My mom said something about going away and I guess I have to go with her."

"Oh, bummer. It's going to be fun! *And*…Dante is coming."

Becca was quiet for a moment. "Dante Lamonte?"

"Do we know any other Dantes?" Kate laughed.

"I guess not." Becca was quiet again.

"What's the matter with you?" Kate demanded.

"Just a little distracted—sorry. I've got a million emails to send and I have to travel with the team on this next trip. Anyway, I'll see you this weekend for yoga, right?"

"I'll be there! Maybe I'll bring Dante with me…"

"Men aren't allowed!" Becca protested, trying to hide her dismay at the idea of seeing him at yoga.

"It's Dante Lamonte—they'll take one look and beg him to stay."

"I have to go." Becca chuckled weakly. "See you Friday."

Becca stared at the phone for a long time after she hung up. *Damn.* Dante was going to be here over the holidays. How was she going to hide her feelings if she was actually in the same room with him? She had no doubt she would see him; he and Kate were extremely close and he was friendly with Karl and some of the other guys on the team as well. Staying away from him would be impossible unless she stayed away from her friends, but there would be no way to avoid him if he attended one of the Sidewinders' games. She had to be there, of course, and he was always a VIP when he visited. The likelihood that they would run into each other was high, and though he'd kept his promise to keep their night together a secret, she had a feeling everyone would know there was something between them the moment they were in the same room together. Her feelings were still raw, even after nearly six months, and the thought that he might reject her was more than she could bear.

Closing her computer, she got up and started packing up her things. The team was leaving town tomorrow and they wanted her to go along this time because of some television appearances several players had agreed to make, so she needed to pack and make sure everything was taken care of at home. She usually liked traveling with the team, but she had no desire to go to Detroit in December. Christmas was a week away and she hadn't finished shopping or decorating the tree, and her mother was insisting they do it together.

Sighing, she grabbed her laptop bag, threw her purse over her shoulder and headed out to her car. If she could get her suitcase packed quickly, maybe there would be time to finish the tree before bed. Then her mother wouldn't be on her case the whole time she was gone. It was only three days, but when her mother nagged, it could feel like an eternity.

Generally, she and her mother were close. Her father had walked out on them when Becca was fourteen and they'd had to find a way to make it on their own. Her mother had taken a job as a housekeeper and didn't make a lot, so they'd moved to a tiny apartment and Becca got a paper route to supplement their income. Luckily, she'd gotten scholarships that allowed her to go to college. When she graduated, she'd gotten a job right away and that had been a big help. The Sidewinders organization had moved her and her mother to Las Vegas when they hired her, and after less than a year she'd been able to buy them a house. Her mother had a decent job now, managing the housekeeping department at a small hotel and casino, so life was better than it had been in a long time. Except for her personal life.

She'd never been the kind of girl who dated a lot. Not only was she what most people would call chubby, she was half-Hispanic and found she didn't fit in with other Mexican girls thanks to her silver-blue eyes, but she hadn't been accepted by white girls either. Besides that, she'd had to work and make sure she got good grades because she'd known the only way she would be able to go to college would be with a scholarship. Dating had been so far down on her list, she hadn't even lost her virginity until she got to college. That had been a spectacularly underwhelming experience and the two other men she'd had sex with after that hadn't been much better.

Then she'd met Dante. It had been a fluke. The one and only time she'd ever been to a sex club, and there he was. She'd been searching for her seemingly nonexistent libido and he'd simply been at the right place at the right time. What they'd done wasn't just sex, it was *sex*, the kind that made your toes curl and your stomach flip over every time you thought about it. She'd never imagined anything could feel like it felt when Dante touched her. The things he'd done to her made her flush even now, but she would do it again in a heartbeat. They'd spent maybe five or six hours together, but he knew more about her than anyone else in the world did. Maybe not the details of her life, but he knew her heart, her fears and her feelings of inadequacy. He also knew how to make her come apart in his arms, and that was more powerful than anything she'd experienced with other men.

She'd ached to reach out to him when she'd heard about the deaths of his fiancée, their unborn child and his best friend, but she hadn't known what to say. She'd been the equivalent of a one-night stand and they'd both been firm in their promise to never, ever acknowledge the night they'd spent together. He was engaged at the time and trying to clean up his bad-boy image; she was the newly appointed Head of Media Relations for the Sidewinders after her boss left unexpectedly. A tryst at a club known for being a playground for some of the kinkiest people in the world wasn't something either of them wanted people to know about. Mostly Becca, though. Dante would get through a sex scandal like he got through everything else, but she could potentially lose her livelihood and that simply wasn't an option.

Sighing, she realized she'd driven home on autopilot and she walked into the house calling out to her mother. "Mom?"

"Hi, honey!" Donna Hernandez wore her forty-eight years well. Her honey-blond hair was layered and fell to her shoulders and her blue eyes sparkled when she laughed. Though she'd had a hard life since her husband had left, she'd never looked back. Becca was the best daughter in the world, and though she worried about her sometimes, she was proud of her.

"What smells so good?" Becca put down her bags and walked into the kitchen.

"I made tortilla soup—seems like a good thing for December and I can take the leftovers to work."

"Mm." Becca sniffed the pan. "I'm starving."

"Sit down. I'll get you a bowl."

"Mom, you worked all day too." Becca smiled at her, shaking her head. Her mother still tried to take care of her, even though Becca was an adult.

"I came home early and it's—" she glanced at her watch. "After eight. You work a lot more hours than I do, sweetheart."

"Thanks, Mom." Becca sank into a chair and pulled out her phone. She'd already gotten a few dozen emails from work and she sighed as she scrolled through them.

"So you'll be home Friday?"

"Yes." Becca was immersed in her emails.

"Becca."

"Hm?"

"Would you put the phone down, please?"

Becca glanced up at the seriousness in her mother's voice. "Of course—what's wrong?"

"We need to talk."

"About?"

"Christmas. You. A lot of things."

Becca narrowed her eyes. "What are you talking about?"

"Honey, you are the best daughter in the world. When your dad left, you just stepped up to the plate. You never asked for help, you never hesitated, you just stepped in. I don't know what we would have done if you hadn't." Donna fought the tears that threatened. "But you're a woman now, and it's not your job to take care of me. It's time for you to live your own life. And for me to live mine."

Becca frowned. "What? Mom, would you just tell me what's going on?"

"I want to go away at Christmas," Donna said quietly. "Without you. I'm going away with a friend. A man."

Becca's mouth fell open. "You're dating someone? Why didn't you tell me?!"

Donna looked away. "Because I met him through you."

"Through me? Who would you have met through me? I mean, the guys on the team are a lot younger than you and—" She stopped short. "Wait. Please tell me you're not dating Coach Gagner."

Donna laughed and shook her head. "No. He's in his sixties, and while I'm no spring chicken, I'm interested in someone a little younger."

"Pierre Bouchard." Becca's heart hammered against her ribcage; Pierre Bouchard was the General Manager of the Sidewinders and, even worse, he was her *boss*.

Donna flushed as she nodded. "I'm sorry I kept it from you, Becca. I thought it was going to be a one-night stand, and then he kept calling and now…" Her face was bright red. "We love each other and we're tired of hiding."

"But, but, he's my boss!" Becca sputtered, trying to contain her fury. "I could lose my job, my career, everything. Because you're fucking lonely?!"

Donna gaped at her daughter but then narrowed her eyes. "You think I'm so lonely that I would jeopardize my daughter's future? I'm sorry you think so little of me. I thought I'd raised you better than that." She gracefully got out of her chair, her dinner untouched, and headed out of the kitchen. She paused and turned back, her blue eyes shrouded with hurt. "I've been alone for a long time. I spent my whole life making sure you were okay. Yes, you helped financially, but I married your dad right out of high school and had you at nineteen. I never had the chance to go to college like you did. When your dad left, I scrubbed toilets and cleaned up strangers' vomit so we could eat. I'm forty-eight years old and yes, I'm *fucking lonely*. I know forty-eight seems ancient to you, but trust me, it sneaks up on you. One day you'll be here too, Becca. I just hope you're not still a workaholic who puts your career before everything else."

"My career is why we live the way we do!" Becca spat angrily, tears burning her eyes.

"I know that, and I appreciate it. But at what cost, Becca? Look at you. You're exhausted. You work eighty-, ninety-hour weeks during hockey season. You've never had a serious boyfriend! You never even date. If I hadn't pushed you, you wouldn't have made friends with Kate. She's the only girlfriend you've had in years, and that's not healthy. I understand your need to be able to provide for yourself—watching your father leave when you were so young had to be hard—but what are you working for? Don't you want someone to share that money and success with? Don't you want someone to curl up with in the middle of the night? Don't you like sex?"

Becca felt like her mother had slapped her, and she turned away, squeezing her eyes shut.

"I'm sorry if that hurts you, but it needed to be said." Donna left the room and Becca heard the door to her bedroom shut a moment later.

She buried her face in her hands. Her mother was dating the General Manager of the Sidewinders, *her boss*, and this could be just as much of a disaster as people finding out she'd been at a sex club with Dante Lamonte.

3

BECCA STARED AT THE CEILING IN HER ROOM FOR WHAT SEEMED LIKE HOURS. She'd cleaned up the kitchen and packed for her trip. Then she'd just lain on the bed thinking. Her mother was forty-eight, divorced, and had a boyfriend; Becca was twenty-seven, single and didn't have anyone. Her mother also had a rich, successful boyfriend, who was pretty good-looking for a guy in his fifties.

Of course, Becca never really thought about him like that, but there was no denying those striking blue eyes or that thick silver hair. She wondered if they had sex like she and Dante had—she grimaced. That wasn't something she wanted to think about, but dammit, it was so unfair! She groaned, burying her face in her pillow.

"Becca?" Her mother's soft voice called to her and she sat up.

"I'm awake." She pulled her knees up to her chest, meeting her mother's gaze guiltily.

"I'm sorry we fought." Donna sat on the edge of the bed.

"Me too." Becca put her chin on her knees. "I guess I'm a little jealous."

"Oh, sweetheart." Donna moved closer to her, running her fingers through her daughter's hair. "You're beautiful, intelligent, hard-working... you just need to—"

"I'm a chubby girl with brown skin and light eyes," Becca sighed, closing her blue-gray eyes. "Most guys don't even notice me."

"Becca, you *push* men away. I've seen guys flirt with you and you give them that look, the same one you give me when I nag you about working too much or not going out enough. You're strong, successful and stubborn. Sometimes you need to let loose, give in to the moment. It's okay to let it all hang out sometimes, you know."

Becca turned bright red, covering her face, and Donna's eyes widened. "Wow, what did I say to embarrass you like this?"

"I'm not good at sex!" she blurted out.

"What? Who told you that?" Donna demanded.

"You don't understand." Becca rubbed her eyes. "I never enjoyed it. I couldn't, you know, *finish*."

"Never?" Donna brushed her daughter's hair out of her face, looking at her intently.

"Not until last summer."

"What happened last summer?"

"I met someone."

"Who?"

Becca took a breath and told her about her night with Dante, leaving out the details of the incredible sex they'd shared. The way he'd tied her up. The way he'd made her scream his name. She didn't know if she would ever tell anyone about *that*, but she had no one else to talk to and now he was coming to town.

"Dante Lamonte? Really?" Donna's eyes were glittering with delight. "Becca, that's incredible. Was he good?"

Becca flushed, but a dreamy smile crossed her face. "Like nothing you can even imagine. I'd never, you know…"

"You'd never had an orgasm before?"

Becca shook her head.

"And then you had a bunch with him?!" Donna was giggling and Becca couldn't help but giggle too.

"Oh, yeah. So many I couldn't move."

"Last summer." Donna squinted, thinking back. Dante's name had been all over the news last summer. "Was this before or after his girlfriend died?"

Becca sighed. "Right before. I asked him if he loved her, and he told me he wasn't capable of love. But he is, Mom. I saw it—I felt it. Or maybe not, because he knows how to find me, and he's never reached out."

"He's probably had a rough time," Donna said gently. "But honestly, even though the sex was hotter than hot, what did you think was going to happen with a guy who cheated on his pregnant fiancée?"

"He wasn't planning to cheat! He was just there because it was a place where no one bothered him. It wasn't until I told him why I was there…" She hated turning red so often.

"Wait, where were you?"

"It was a sex club."

Donna cocked her head. "You went to a sex club to try to have an orgasm?"

Becca blinked back tears, nodding miserably. "We started talking and then he said he would help me if I trusted him."

"And you…let him?" Donna looked mystified since they both knew Becca didn't have an adventurous bone in her body. The idea that she'd told a sexy professional baseball player like Dante Lamonte that she couldn't have an orgasm was completely out of character for her.

"It wasn't what you're thinking." Becca pulled her knees closer to her chest. "We were just *talking*, and when I told him I was going to find someone at the club to do it, he got really possessive. He kissed me and told me if I wanted him to, he would help me. I was so desperate, so anxious to figure out what was wrong with me, it just kind of happened."

"And it was good?"

"Good?" Becca smiled. "It was so much better than good, I'm not sure how to explain it. He was—gentle and wild and sexy. I didn't know it could be like that."

"And then that was it. You both walked away?"

"I wanted to call after I heard about what happened, but what would I say? Hi, I'm the girl you fucked at the sex club a few months ago and I'm really sorry your fiancée died—hey, wanna fuck again?"

Donna snorted. "No! You could have sent flowers or a card, expressing condolences."

"He knows where I work. I figured if he was interested, he would have called."

"And you've been pining for him all this time?"

"I don't have time to pine for anyone," she muttered. "The thing is, Kate is his publicist and he's coming to town for the holidays. He's going to be at that Christmas party I told you about."

Donna's eyes widened. "Then I guess it's a good thing you're going to be there."

"Mom, I can't!"

"Why not?"

"I'm too dumpy for a guy like him."

"He obviously didn't think so."

"He was being chivalrous. He met a nice girl at a bar who told him she couldn't have an orgasm—what else would a macho Cuban guy do?"

"Buy her a drink and wish her luck. Don't be silly, Becca. If you had a connection like you think you did, he's thought about you too."

"Maybe we didn't have a connection. Maybe it was just really good sex. It's not like I have any other experiences like that to compare it to."

"You're a smart girl. I think you would know the difference between good sex and something that touched you emotionally."

"He definitely touched me emotionally." Becca met her mother's eyes. "I'm sorry I was a bitch earlier. The last few months have been hard, and hearing that you're dating my boss freaked me out."

"Don't worry—we talked about it long before anything happened. He knows our relationship is separate from anything that goes on at work."

"I hope so. I love my job."

"I know that, sweetie. I would never let him put you in the middle. I promise. Besides, he's a really great guy. He's good to me."

"Do you love him?"

"I think so. I mean, that's why we want to go away together. We've spent so much time sneaking around, we don't get to spend much time alone. Two days in Reno will be a good way to figure it out."

"I'm really happy for you. He's rich and good-looking—I just want him to treat you well."

"So far he treats me like a princess."

"And the sex?" Becca blushed but couldn't resist asking.

Donna grinned. "The sex is hot! Maybe not in-a-sex-club-with-Dante-Lamonte-hot, but we're not in our twenties anymore!"

Becca chuckled. "Dante is thirty-two."

"You two would make some beautiful babies," Donna sighed.

Becca rolled her eyes. "Okay, we're not having the grandchildren conversation. I have to go to bed."

"I love you, Becca."

"I love you, too, Mom."

Becca dressed carefully on Christmas Eve. She'd known what she was going to wear the moment she'd decided to go to Tiffany Marcus's Christmas party. Though the thought of seeing Dante again made her a little sick to her stomach, she couldn't help but hope that he'd thought of her at least a little since their night together. She knew he'd felt guilty about cheating on his fiancée with her, but he'd told her he didn't love the woman carrying his child and that he wasn't even capable of love.

That, she thought to herself, was a lie. The man she'd been with back in June had been much more than a magnificent lover; he'd been gentle, attentive and completely in tune to her needs. The way their bodies had come together had been soul stirring, and she knew he'd felt it too. She'd known he wasn't in a position to be with her, not while another woman carried his child, but she'd seen the regret in his face when he'd apologized for not being able to see her again.

She hadn't worn the little black dress since that night and she pulled it out of the closet now with a small smile. Same dress, same high heels, same bright red lipstick. Maybe he would remember how good it had been. Maybe he'd never forgotten. She had to try, because she knew she wouldn't be able to hide her feelings once they were in the same room together. Kate would undoubtedly pick up on it right away; they weren't best friends, but they were pretty close and Kate knew she'd had a one-night stand last summer that had rocked her world. She didn't know who it was, of course, but she would put two and two together quickly.

Pulling up to Tiff's house a little early, it felt safer to be there early and find somewhere to hang out instead of arriving late and having everyone looking at her. She wasn't shy, and she knew everyone who would be at the party, but knowing Dante would be there was different.

She'd worked with the team for eighteen months now and was friendly with all the players and coaches, as well as many of the wives and girlfriends. The only person that would make her nervous was Dante, and there was no help for that now. If he was going to shoot her down, she wanted to get it over with. Maybe if she saw him again, and he was uninterested, she'd be able to move on. *Maybe.*

"Hey!" Tiff called out to her warmly and Becca walked in with a smile.

Someone whistled and Becca flushed as one of the guys from the team, Zakk Cloutier, gave her a cheeky grin. "Who knew you had legs under those stuffy suits you always wear!" he chuckled, leaning over to kiss her cheek.

"Merry Christmas, Zakk!" She smiled and put the casserole of chicken enchiladas she'd made on the counter.

"My favorite!" Zakk said, putting his hand over his heart. "Are you sure you won't marry me, Becca?"

"You would weigh 5,000 pounds and not be able to play hockey!" she laughed.

He sighed, his green eyes twinkling with mischief. "But it might be worth it, the way you cook!"

She rolled her eyes. "Would you go make yourself useful?"

"Fine!" He headed out to the garage to get more ice and Becca grinned after him.

One of the things she loved about her job was her relationship with many of the guys on the team. They were like big brothers in a lot of ways, and she had a good time hanging out with them. Zakk was probably one of the best looking guys on the team, as well as the largest at six-foot-seven, and he'd been asking her to marry him since the first time she'd cooked for him. Even though she knew he wasn't serious, it felt good to have someone that looked like him flirt with her.

"Merry Christmas!" Kate leaned over and kissed Becca's cheek, grinning broadly. "You look gorgeous!"

"Thanks—Merry Christmas to you too!" Becca put down her purse just as Tiff put a glass of wine in her hand.

"Figure you guys should start drinking now," the tall woman said.

"Works for me!" Becca took a sip, hoping a glass of wine would help relax her before Dante arrived.

"Where are the guys?" Tiff asked Kate.

"Karl and a few others went Christmas shopping at 10:00 this morning," Kate chuckled. "Last I heard, they were still at the mall and were trying to get out so they could get home, shower and come over. We'll see them around midnight!"

The girls laughed as Tiff put out more wineglasses.

"It's your first Christmas together," Becca said to Kate. "Did he really wait until the last minute to go to the mall?"

Kate shook her head. "No! I found two bags from Tiffany's in his underwear drawer and a sealed box from Amazon in the toolbox in the garage. I'm thinking he got a last-minute idea or he went to keep the other guys company."

"What did you get him?" Tiff asked her.

"A bunch of stuff," Kate grinned. "Some tools that he wanted, a state-of-the-art grill—it cost a fortune so it better do the shopping *and* the cooking—and a bunch of lingerie that's technically for me, but he gets to enjoy it."

"You two still all into bondage and stuff?" Tiff asked with a chuckle.

"Oh yeah!" Kate smiled. "I mean, not all the time—we only do that about fifty percent of the time. Hell, even standard missionary position sex with him is so hot I can't even think about it without getting a little turned on!"

Becca chewed on her lip. "So you and Karl…are into bondage?"

Kate laughed. "Now don't go putting out a press release!" she said. "And don't get the wrong idea. He ties me up a few times a month, I tie him up once in a while, and when we bought the new house we got a swing, but we're not super kinky or anything!"

"A swing?" Becca felt her cheeks get warm. "What do you do with that?"

"He puts me in it and then he fucks the hell out of me!" Kate giggled as Becca's face turned bright red.

"Are you restrained?" Becca was trying to act nonchalant since she had no idea how a swing worked and memories of her night with Dante made her curious.

"Usually, but you don't have to be. The thing that makes it fun is that the swing holds my weight and he can adjust the height and position to exactly the way we like it, so it can be really intense. He doesn't have to hold either of us up, he just stands there and uses the momentum of the swing to make it as hard or as easy as we want."

"Sounds amazing…" Tiff sighed. "Dave and I never used one of those."

"I've never had a steady boyfriend," Becca admitted. "Not one that lasted long enough to try anything like that."

"It's fun," Kate said, "but it's not necessary. I don't think I could be with someone who only wanted to have sex if I was tied up. I love the nights we just curl up together and barely move—you know, where it's more about being intimate than having an orgasm? Those times are the best, but I've had some crazy orgasms doing the other stuff!"

"Dave and I had some awesome sex when we first got together," Tiff said. "He was a lot older than I was, but he was forty-one when I met him so we had a few good years before he got the prostate cancer."

"That must have been hard," Becca said softly.

"Yes and no." Tiff paused, looking at them. "He still took care of me, if you know what I mean. We just had to do things a little different. When you really love someone, you can work around the sex. Plus, we had the twins by then, so it's not like we had a lot of time!"

"Hello, hello!" Guests started to arrive and Becca was glad to get away from the conversation about sex; she was nervous enough as it was. Instead, she moved into publicist mode, working the room as she talked to the guys on the team and their wives or girlfriends. She knew everyone and was grateful to have been included. Despite her nervousness at seeing Dante again, she genuinely liked these people and was happy to spend the holiday with them. The people were a big part of the reason she loved her job so much. She couldn't imagine working anywhere else.

4

DANTE TOOK A DEEP BREATH BEFORE WALKING INTO THE PARTY. NOT BECAUSE he didn't want to go, but because he was a nervous wreck. No woman had never made him feel like this before and he was beginning to wonder if he was going to make a fool of himself tonight. Not for the first time since Trey's death, he missed his friend. Although Trey had been gay, they'd lost their virginity together to the same girl, and Trey had promptly confirmed that he didn't think pussy was for him.

Though Dante was a hundred percent heterosexual and Trey was not, he and Trey had been through almost everything together, sexually and otherwise. When MLB scouts came calling, Trey stepped up and became his manager, learning everything he needed to know in record time so that Dante didn't get screwed. And Dante never did. Not financially anyway. Trey made sure of that, and together they'd amassed a fortune.

Even though his agreement with Trey had been a flat ten percent of everything Dante made, Dante had given him a hell of a lot more than that. In fact, Trey had lived with him for most of the last fifteen years, so he'd put a lot of money away. Not that it would do him any good now. Dead at thirty-three, with no children and no relationship with his family, all of Trey's money had come right back to Dante. The irony didn't escape him and he hated it. He would give up everything he had to have his friend back. Instead, he was richer than ever, but the loneliest he'd ever been too. Hopefully, that would change as soon as Becca arrived.

And he spotted her immediately.

Even with her back turned, he recognized the curve of her ass, the shape of her calves in those stupidly high heels, and that damn black dress. Exactly what she'd been wearing the night they met. Except tonight her hair was curled and it bounced as she laughed at something Zakk was telling her. He felt a moment of jealousy before remembering that this woman didn't belong to him. They'd agreed not to see each other again and to keep their one-night stand a secret, so he had no right to be jealous; the tightness in his chest told him he was anyway.

"Dante!" Tiff saw him and headed for him with her arms outstretched.

He pulled her close for a tight hug, kissing her cheek and wishing her a merry Christmas.

"I'm so glad you're here!" She squeezed his arm. "We should do lunch before you leave—it's been too long since we talked."

"Absolutely." He smiled at her before turning his head. His gaze instantly met Becca's, her silver-blue eyes hooded and hard to read.

"Dante." She spoke his name casually, her hips swaying slightly as she walked towards him.

"Becca." Instead of hugging her, he reached for her hand, bringing it to his lips and letting them linger for a few seconds before pulling away.

"It's nice to see you again. Merry Christmas."

"Merry Christmas." He didn't break his gaze as he stepped back, noting that her hand shook slightly as she pulled it away.

"You look beautiful tonight," he said in a voice that he hoped no one else could hear.

"Thank you. You look very handsome as well."

"I hope you'll have a drink with me later," he said, starting to move past her. "We can talk."

"I'd like that." She nodded and turned in the other direction, heading for Kate and a group of women.

Dante watched Becca from across the room for a long time. She talked and laughed with her girlfriends, but he knew her body language well enough to know she was nervous and uncomfortable. *Because of him.* He knew it as surely as he was standing there, but he didn't know what to do about it. She had to know he wouldn't embarrass her; if he'd been so inclined, he would have done it by now. No, this was something else. He'd caught her gazing at him a few times but pretended not to notice. She was keeping her distance and he was trying to respect her wishes. Even though it was killing him, he wouldn't break his promise to keep their history a secret.

He wanted to find a way to talk to her, but she was making it hard. She stayed in groups and didn't wander off alone. If it wasn't for the looks she kept sneaking in his direction, he would have thought she was completely uninterested.

"What's with you and our little PR cutie?" Karl Martensson leaned his six-foot-four-inch frame against the wall and looked at Dante curiously.

Dante's head snapped up and then he forced himself to shrug. "Pretty face. Nice ass. Doesn't seem interested."

The goalie snorted. "She hasn't been able to keep her eyes off you," he said. "The question is, why are you two dancing around each other? She's smart, sexy and single—what's the problem?"

"We've met professionally in the past," he said lightly. "She never showed interest. I don't think I'm the kind of guy she dates. She seems like the kind of girl who wants the white picket fence and 2.5 kids."

Karl arched his eyebrows. "Becca is the kind of girl who wants someone to love her. Trust me—she's a lot like Kate. Smart, successful, independent—and really fucking insecure in the romance department. She works ridiculous hours for the team and helps take care of her mom too. I think Dante Lamonte is exactly the kind of guy she needs. Go talk to her."

Dante glanced at her again, and this time their eyes locked. She gave him a soft smile before turning away and he sighed. "I don't want to make her uncomfortable."

Karl rolled his eyes. "Listen, she and Kate are friendly. She's been over to the house a few times and I heard her tell Kate she met some guy in New York last summer who broke her heart. She hasn't been able to look at another guy since and it's killing her. I think you're the kind of guy who could make her forget about some douche who didn't know what he had."

At that moment, Dante was grateful for spending so many years in the spotlight; it was the only reason he was able to keep from showing any reaction to what Karl had just said. *Some guy in New York had broken her heart last summer?* There was no way in hell that was a coincidence. How had he broken her heart? He wouldn't deny there'd been something special between them that night, but aside from the fact that he'd been engaged, she'd also been insistent that her job was too important to her to take a chance on a bad boy like him who was always in the tabloids. Hadn't she?

Or had that been his lust-filled interpretation of the things she'd said? *Had he hurt her?* It seemed unfathomable that he'd caused any kind of pain to the beautiful, sweet little temptress who'd twisted his heart like a corkscrew when she'd snuck out of the club and his life.

Feeling like an idiot now, he nodded at Karl. "Maybe I will talk to her."

"Attaboy!" Karl clapped him on the shoulder and moved towards one of his teammates.

Dante walked over to the group Becca was standing in and gave the ladies his most charming smile.

"Hey, Dante." Tiff smiled at him. "Having a good time?"

"Yes, thank you for having me." He nodded at her. "It would have been a difficult year to be alone at the holidays."

"Tell me about it." Tiff glanced behind her. "I need to get more wine. Excuse me."

"I'll help." Kate followed her.

Now that they were alone, he it was obvious that Becca was definitely nervous. "You've been avoiding me," he said quietly, opting to be direct.

"Have I?" She widened her eyes innocently. "I've just been mingling."

"That's a lie," he said, his voice barely a whisper against her ear. "I know everything about your body. How it reacts to sound, touch… even feelings. Tonight your body has been reacting to my presence. The tightness in your shoulders, the way you keep chewing your lower lip… I wish you would tell me why."

"You need me to tell you why?" Her eyes met his heatedly.

"You're fighting your attraction to me—and that's unnecessary. I am well aware you're attracted to me."

She swallowed, as if trying to keep her emotions under control. "You've seen me naked. You've touched me everywhere. You did things to me that still make me blush. Yet I have to sit here in a house full of our friends and pretend like we barely know each other. It's *hard*."

"I didn't think our history would make you so nervous." He was thoughtful as he watched her. "But it appears that it does."

"Maybe the things we did are what you do with everyone," she said under her breath. "But they were special to me. That whole night was special and you're acting like, like…" With a barely perceptible cry, she turned and fled from the room.

S he slipped into Tiff's downstairs guest bathroom and locked the door behind her. Resting her hands on the sink, she took a few long, deep breaths and forced herself to look up. She could do this; she had to. He wouldn't humiliate her in front of their friends. If he was no longer attracted to her, she would get through the evening and be okay.

There would be someone else out there for her. *Right?* She almost laughed at how ridiculous it sounded, even in her own head. There would *never* be anyone like Dante Lamonte. Not in her eyes, not in her bed and definitely not in her heart. All she could do was hang on to her dignity and try to get out of here before she embarrassed herself.

It wouldn't be easy, though. As always, Dante looked incredible. With tawny skin the color of desert sand and eyes that resembled buttered caramel, she'd been drawn to him the first time she saw him on a magazine cover. Up close, he was even better. Those caramel-colored eyes were framed by the longest, curliest eyelashes she'd ever seen on a man, and she knew first-hand how wonderful his perfectly formed lips felt when they touched her.

His straight, patrician nose and masculine chin undoubtedly came from his French father while his eyes, skin, and the dark hair that was cropped close to his head most likely came from his Cuban mother. His body, however, was a toss-up. He was six-foot-three, nine inches taller than her five-foot-six, and though she couldn't see it, she knew every inch of his abdomen was cut and rippled. His thighs were like steel and if she had one regret about their night together it was that she hadn't had a chance to take a bite out of his perfectly shaped ass. God, the spot between her legs got a little damp just thinking about it. How the hell was she going to get through this?

S he stepped out a few minutes later, surprised to see him standing there. Hands in his pockets, leaning against the wall, she nearly stumbled as she took in the long legs and broad shoulders she remembered so well.

"Are you okay?" he asked, gripping her arms to steady her as she lurched forward.

"You startled me," she murmured, trying not to focus on the way it felt to be so close to him.

"I'm sorry, *querida.*" *Sweetheart.*

"Don't call me that!" Her whimper was barely audible but she couldn't hide the hurt in her eyes.

"Why not?"

"Because you don't mean it and it's not fair to tease me."

"Tease you?" He cocked his head. "I thought you liked it when I called you that."

"That was then." She was on the verge of tears again as he moved closer. He touched her cheek, causing her eyes flutter closed as a soft moan escaped. She pushed the side of her face against his warm palm and couldn't help but sigh, the pleasure unmistakable.

"So sweet…" he murmured, curling his fingers against the soft skin of her face.

"Shit." Her eyes popped open and she moved away slightly. "I didn't mean to do that."

"Do what?" He rested one hand on the small of her back, not allowing her to move any further away.

"Show you how weak I am. Let you see how much I still want you."

His eyes darkened, glittering with pure desire. "Has no one else been able to take care of your needs?" he asked in a throaty whisper.

Her breath caught and she shook her head. "I work sixty-, seventy-, sometimes eighty-hour weeks. I don't have time to look for a man, and to be honest, after you…" Her voice trailed off.

"After me?"

She sighed when she realized he wasn't going to let her off that easily. "What could possibly ever be as good as that night?"

He used his thumb to trace the line of her cheekbone, apparently taking his time as he thought about what to say. "You haven't been with anyone else?"

She slowly shook her head.

"Well, I've thought about that night a lot too."

"You have?" She was shocked.

"More so lately, now that the grief isn't as overwhelming."

"I wanted to reach out," she whispered. "But I didn't know what to say. Hi, remember me? We had great sex—I'm really sorry your friend and your baby died—should we have sex again?"

He smiled. "I understand. It probably would have been a little strange."

"I thought sending flowers to a man like you would be…weird?"

He smiled. "My friend who died, Trey, loved flowers. I had an amazing garden at my house in Philadelphia because of him. Flowers would have been okay, but you had no way of knowing that."

"I'm truly sorry about what happened. It must have been a terrible time for you."

He nodded. "For sure, the hardest thing I've ever gone through."

She didn't say anything at first, but then whispered, "I hoped you would call. After."

"You did?" His reaction made it seem as though she'd caught him off guard.

"You told me I would always be special to you…" Her voice trailed off and she looked down.

"You are."

"Then why didn't you call?"

"You told me not to."

"I did?" The look in her eyes changed to confusion as she met his gaze.

"You said being seen with me could cost you your job."

"I said being seen with you *at a sex club* could cost me my job."

He didn't say anything, just stared into her beautiful silver-blue eyes. "Perhaps we were so overwhelmed by the emotions of that evening we misunderstood each other."

"I didn't misunderstand you," she protested. "You were engaged and having a baby—you didn't have the option of dating me, even though I think you wanted to."

He nodded slowly. "Maybe I heard what I wanted to hear, so that walking away from you would be easier."

"Maybe."

"But now we're here and I'm no longer engaged."

"We're no longer at a sex club either."

"Ah, *querida*, I've missed you."

5

DANTE'S LIPS GRAZED HERS AND HE LET HIMSELF ENJOY THE WAY IT FELT TO taste her again.

"I think maybe it was better this way, us keeping our distance for a while. I was a mess. Larissa, the baby…and Trey. He wasn't just my agent. We were brothers, you know? First friend I made when I came from Cuba. I had no idea how hard it would be to get over losing him."

"I wish I could have been there for you."

"It was probably better that you weren't. I had very dark days."

"It didn't show on the field."

"You watched me?"

"Every game I could find on TV."

"Do you like baseball?" He seemed skeptical.

She smiled sheepishly. "Not particularly, but there's a shortstop who plays for the Bandits that I really enjoy."

A smile tugged at his lips. "Why is that? What's special about *him*?"

"I love the way he plays up the middle." Her eyes twinkled.

"I would love to play up your middle," he chuckled.

"What's stopping you?"

The flirtatious look on her face made Dante growl, deep in his chest, and he pulled her against him roughly. "I wasn't planning to do this here," he rumbled, bending his head towards hers.

"I seem to recall you saying you weren't interested in sex the night we met, too."

His lips claimed hers in one swift dip of his head and she moaned against his mouth just as Kate came around the corner.

"I knew it!" Kate cried, hands on her hips. "I *knew* the two of you were hiding something from me!"

Dante and Becca jumped apart like teenagers caught by their parents and Dante scowled at Kate.

"Kate." He hoped the look in his eyes would make her understand she needed to tread carefully and luckily, she seemed to understand.

"Sorry!" She held up her hands. "But there are about forty-five people in the house—someone else is going to come around this corner any minute now." She turned and disappeared the way she'd come.

Dante ran a hand over his face. "I'm sorry, Becca. I know you didn't want anyone to know."

"Kate is my friend," she shrugged. "Probably my only female friend that isn't someone I work with, so chances are I would have told her eventually."

"All of it?" he asked playfully.

She blushed. "Maybe not *all* of it."

"You still blush." His fingers were gentle on her face. "Will you blush if I tie you up again?"

"Without a doubt."

There was laughter in her eyes and he desperately wanted to kiss her again but restrained himself. "Becca, tell me what happens next."

Her lips parted slightly, her gaze meeting his in confusion. "What do you mean?"

"It's going to be impossible for me to spend the evening in your presence without touching you. Can I touch you? Can I hold your hand? Would being my date tonight embarrass you?"

She stared at him. "Why would it embarrass me?"

"Come on, you two!" Tiff peeked her head around the corner. "Everyone already knows you were sucking face back here so come join the party."

Becca smiled faintly and leaned up to press her lips against his, whispering against his mouth, "There is no universe where being with you would embarrass me. We just have to come up with a different story about how we went from being strangers to kissing."

"We met in New York during the *All Sports Magazine* Awards. We had drinks at the hotel one evening but I was engaged at the time so nothing happened. Now that I'm single, something is happening."

She laughed, her arms looped around his neck. "I like that plan."

"You're going to like my plan for later much, much more."

The evening's festivities were in full swing and Becca felt a little tipsy as the night wore on. Tiff kept her wineglass full and Dante's presence at her side kept her edgy and thinking about sex. Though they'd received a few curious glances, almost everyone here was a friend and seemed to accept the idea without much thought of Becca and Dante hooking up. They weren't actually a couple, though, and Becca desperately wanted to ask him what they were doing.

Being together in public meant there would be questions and she didn't know how she would answer them if this was going to be nothing more than sex. How did she explain going from a platonic attraction to sleeping together in one night? She had no experience with things like this and it made her nervous, but every time he looked at her she forgot everything except him.

"You are a terrible friend!" Kate hissed in her ear at one point. "I can't believe you and Dante had a thing for each other and you didn't tell me!"

"He never called," Becca said softly. "I thought it was my imagination. I mean, why would someone like him be interested in a regular girl like me?"

"Because you're special and he desperately needs someone special to take care of him."

Becca met her friend's eyes. "Kate, we had a one-night stand last summer. It was more than just talking at the bar, but please keep that between us."

Kate's big brown eyes rounded in surprise. "Of course I'll keep it between us, but *really*?! That's the hook-up you told me about?! Oh my God!"

"I don't know how I'm supposed to act!" Becca whispered. "I mean, he never called, even after he was single again. You think he's just interested in getting laid? I have no idea how to read him…the sex was so good I might not be thinking straight."

"He's been in a bad place, but he's a really good guy. Be patient. Let him get used to the idea of having a nice girl in his life. Be gentle but persistent, if you know what I mean."

"But we've already slept together—how do we start over?"

"*Tell him* you want to start over. Tell him you want to go out on a date and get to know each other. You can even use the whole 'you're still grieving so we should go slow' excuse."

Becca nodded. "I'm sorry I didn't tell you, but we made a deal we would never, ever tell anyone. He was worried about looking like an asshole for cheating on his pregnant fiancée and I was worried about my job. I'm not supposed to sleep with athletes!"

"You're not supposed to sleep with athletes from the *Sidewinders*," Kate grinned. "Other athletes are fair game."

"God, I hope so." Becca looked across the room to where Dante was laughing with Karl and Zakk. He was so good-looking she couldn't think about anything except being close to him again. She wanted him so much she wasn't sure she could keep it platonic, even though she knew it would be better if they took things slow. He'd awakened her sexual desires and she'd been forced to go without for six months; she didn't know how she would resist doing anything he wanted.

"I t's late," Dante whispered in her ear sometime after midnight. "I think Karl and Kate are leaving soon."

"I can take you home if you want to stay later." Becca met his eyes.

"I want to do whatever you want to do," he said, his hands at her waist.

"I want you to take me out on a date!" she blurted out. If she didn't let him know what she wanted, she would probably start ripping her clothes off any minute now.

A small smile played on his mouth. "Do you?" His lips grazed hers. "Is that your way of telling me I'm not getting any tonight?"

She let out a nervous sigh. "I'm so turned on being this close to you, I'm afraid it's going to start dripping down my leg, but after everything that's happened, I don't know if we should just fall into bed right away."

He ran a hand over the curve of her ass, remembering what it felt like to be inside her and how she'd looked when she'd had her first orgasm. He wanted her as much as she apparently wanted him, but he recognized her need for him to respect her. She needed romance to go along with the sex, something he'd already sensed about her, and he was fine with that. The only problem was that she'd been without sex for a long time and was obviously torn about satisfying that need.

"Have you forgotten what I told you that night?" he asked finally.

She looked away. "Men say a lot of things right after sex. Especially the kind of sex we had, where you were basically teaching me *how* to have sex! I thought maybe you were just being kind, since you were kicking me to the curb."

"Do you really believe I would tell you something so intimate if I didn't mean it? I told you I would hold you close to my heart—is that the kind of thing men say after a casual fuck?"

"I thought maybe it's the kind of thing you'd say to a woman who just had her first orgasm and who let you tie her up and do really embarrassing things to her—so she wouldn't be *as* embarrassed." Her eyes were shadowed, barely looking at him.

"Silly girl." He tilted her face up to his. "If that was the case, I would have thanked you for giving me the honor of your trust. I would have told you that you were sweet and that I hoped you found a wonderful man who would take care of you in the future. I would have kissed your cheek and put you in a cab. I would *never* have put your hand on my chest and told you that you would always be inside my heart."

Her eyes glistened with tears. "I just thought… I guess I picture you with someone more exciting."

He laughed. "That isn't possible, baby girl. You are the sexiest, most exciting woman I've ever met. Thinking about the way I took you that night is the only way I can jerk off anymore."

"You haven't been with anyone else either?" Her eyes rounded with surprise.

"Not intercourse," he murmured, embarrassed for the first time in his life about some of his behavior. Did blow jobs count? Technically, oral sex was sex, but she was the last woman he'd made love to and he figured that had to count for something. "Larissa died soon after we were together and I couldn't even think about that kind of intimacy. It took three therapists and every ounce of self-control I had to get up and play ball. I was also focused on getting myself traded to the Bandits, packing up the house in Philly, moving to New York and helping Emilie get settled and past the humiliation of what happened to her."

"She moved to New York with you but you still haven't sold the house in Philly?"

He shook his head. "I could only handle so many things at that point and selling the house could wait. Once the season ended, I allowed myself to fall apart. The month of November was Dante having what we'll call a minor nervous breakdown."

"And the month of December?"

"I hope it's the month Dante takes Becca out on the most romantic date of her life and then makes passionate love to her."

"Does tonight count as a date?" she asked, moving against him. "Because I don't think I can wait much longer for the other part."

"Shall we go?" was all he said, one arm around her waist.

"Yes."

6

Becca had never dreamed she would bring Dante Lamonte to her modest little house. She'd been cooking for the party all afternoon, so the kitchen was a mess and she hadn't made her bed. There were shoes in the entranceway and three discarded outfits on the floor of her room. She scooped them up self-consciously, throwing them in the closet and shutting the door.

"I don't care if your room is messy," Dante said, casually leaning against the door.

"I'm not usually a slob, but with my mom out of town and me working half a day, I didn't have time to do anything but cook when I got home."

He walked towards her, shaking his head. "You work too many hours, Becca."

"It's my job," she said, looking up at him.

"Tonight your job is to relax and enjoy."

She reached for his hand and put it against her cheek. "I know we were together just that once, and it seems silly, but I missed you; your touch, your voice, everything."

"I missed you as well." He met her eyes. "So it's not silly at all. I'm very glad you came to the party tonight. Did you know I would be there?"

She nodded. "Kate told me. Initially I said no, because my mother wanted to go out of town for Christmas, but then she told me she was going away with a man." She paused. "I guess you wouldn't know—my mother is dating my boss."

Dante frowned. "Your boss? Isn't that the GM—what's his name?"

"Pierre Bouchard." She sighed. "I was furious at first, but we talked about it and she promised it wouldn't affect my job. It's just weird; my mom is forty-eight and has a boyfriend. I'm twenty-seven and can't even get a date."

"Not true." He pulled her against him. "You had a date tonight, didn't you?"

"I didn't give you much choice," she chuckled.

"*Querida*, I know you read the tabloids—you're aware that I can be a complete prick when I want to be, yes?"

"Yeah, but you wouldn't do that with me." She paused. "Would you?"

"Not on purpose, no, but I'm not perfect. I screw up sometimes even when I don't mean to."

"We all do."

"If I didn't want to be with you, tonight definitely wouldn't have been a date."

"I had a feeling about that."

He just smiled, his fingers toying with the fine hairs at the base of her neck. "So your mother went away with your boss and you decided to seek me out?"

"I decided this was the perfect opportunity for me to find out if what we shared last summer was a fluke or if there was more than an orgasm or two between us." She shivered against his touch.

"Or four or five." His eyes sparkled with humor. "So, what did you find out?"

"That you missed me too."

"I did."

"Then why doesn't this feel real?"

"Because you're still uncertain."

"I've never brought a man home with me."

"Are you nervous?" he whispered, leaning over so his mouth was close to hers.

"Only because I don't know what I'm supposed to do. Last time, I didn't have to do…anything."

He smiled. "I'd like to think you'll find my lovemaking pleasurable even if you're not tied up and blindfolded."

Heat rushed to her face and moisture gathered between her legs. *Again.* Just thinking about him doing those things to her made her yearn for them.

"Thinking about what we did that night still turns you on," he chuckled, his thumb sliding across her nipple, making it pucker into a hard point. "And we'll do that again. But not tonight."

"Okay." Her breath quickened.

"But you like when I'm in control, don't you?" His voice was rough but playful, his eyes studying her intently.

"Y-yes." She appeared as excited as she was nervous.

"So I'll give instructions and you'll do as I say?"

She nodded.

"Get on your knees."

She instantly slid down, looking up at him expectantly, but he seemed hesitant.

"Did I do it wrong?" she asked in confusion.

"No, baby girl." He gently stroked her chin. "I'm sorry, I was just thinking: where do you keep the lipstick you were wearing earlier? In your purse?"

She nodded again.

He disappeared and came back a moment later, her purse in his hands. "I don't like to go through a woman's purse. Get it out, please."

"You can go through my purse," she chuckled. "Are you going to steal something? I think there's twenty dollars in there."

He chuckled too. "Larissa didn't like—" He stopped abruptly.

"I am not Larissa," she said easily, digging into her purse as though talking about his ex was something they did all the time. "I have no problem with you going in my purse. I don't have secrets and I'm confident you're not a thief. If you're interested in my two credit cards and fifty thousand lipsticks, pens and flash drives, you're welcome to rummage to your heart's content." She pulled out the red lipstick she'd worn earlier and held it out.

"Put it on," he said quietly. "I know all women do it differently and I'm not much of a makeup artist."

She laughed, applying the lipstick without even looking at a mirror. She put it aside and glanced up, waiting for instructions.

"Now I want you to wrap those perfect red lips around my cock," he said, tugging off his shirt and unbuckling his pants.

"Dante?" Her voice held the slightest tremor.

"Yeah, baby girl?" He frowned as he looked down into eyes that were now filled with trepidation.

"I don't know exactly how to do…that."

"No?" He ran his hands along the tops of her shoulders. "I'll teach you—don't worry."

She reached for his boxers and slowly slid them down. She waited as he stepped out of them and then drank in every inch of him with her eyes.

He was absolute perfection. His torso was lean and tan, with muscles that cut through his stomach and led a perfect path down from his hips. He gave new meaning to six-pack abs and she traced a finger from his navel to the thatch of black curls around his cock. Last time they'd been together she hadn't been able to explore his body like this so she studied him carefully now. He obviously believed in manscaping, since everything was neatly trimmed and cut back, but still masculine and downright sexy.

"Touch the studs," he suggested, referring to the piercing in his penis. "I know you were intimidated last time and I want you to feel comfortable with it."

She reached out her fingers, touching the two small silver balls, one on each side of his shaft, attached by a rod of some sort, underneath the skin. The piercing was just below the head, on the bottom of his penis, with the studs approximately an inch apart.

As he grew fully erect, she figured he was ten or eleven inches and she felt a flutter of excitement when she thought about how good it was when he was inside of her. He was so thick she couldn't close her hand around him. She attempted to do so now and gave him a quick grin when her fingers didn't quite touch. He was smiling too when she glanced up and she couldn't help but laugh.

"Stop stalling," he chuckled. "Go on—give it a try."

She sighed, meeting his eyes. "I really, really don't want to be bad at this."

"Not possible," he said, running his hands through her thick hair. "Keep your lips around your teeth for the most part, although a little bit is okay. The only bad thing you could do is bite down, and I'm assuming you have no desire to dismember me."

She giggled. "No way. I want this inside me again." She gripped him in her hand, holding him up and staring at the vein pulsing along the top. She put a tentative tongue on the tip, curious what it felt and tasted like. Though his penis was hard, the skin was soft and the tip slid between her lips effortlessly.

For now, she avoided going any further, concentrating on keeping her teeth out of the way and using her hands to stimulate him as she got familiar with doing this. One finger traced a line along the bottom, pausing at the studs and rubbing the skin that covered the rod that connected them. She felt it just below the surface and it was an odd sensation, the hard metal of the rod against the softness of his skin.

His moan brought her eyes up to his and he was smiling. "Very nice. Try taking a little more."

She did as he asked, bringing him further into her mouth.

"Close your lips around me tightly."

Again, she did as he requested and felt him throb against her tongue.

"Remember what it felt like when I licked your clit?" he asked. "It's the same movement. Circle, suck, lick, flick. No rules. What feels good to you will feel good to me."

More confident now, she worked him a little deeper into her mouth and closed those red lips around him, about halfway down his shaft. He would be all the way down her throat if he had anything to say about it, but he was patient. She wasn't quite there yet, and anyway, just having her mouth on him like this was absolute heaven. Her careful, tentative moves were sexy simply because she trusted him, and he was happy to enjoy having her learn her way around his body.

"What makes this really good for you?" she asked, suddenly pulling away.

"It might be a little much for you the first time, baby."

"You want me to deep throat you," she said knowingly.

He simply nodded.

"Will it make me gag?"

"Do you gag easily?"

"No."

"Then maybe not. Are you sure about this? We can work up to it."

She nodded. "I really want to."

"Okay." He took a breath, trying to wrap his mind around this incredible woman who seemed willing to do anything he wanted. "First, I need you to put your hands behind your back and clasp them together. No matter what, you keep them there, okay?"

She nodded, putting her hands behind her.

"I'm going to do the moving, so all you have to do is open your mouth and keep contact with your teeth to a minimum—a light grazing is sexy, so don't stress about that. Once I start going deep, relax your throat. If you tense or try to swallow, you'll gag. I won't go all the way until I'm just about to get off and I'll warn you."

She just smiled and opened her mouth.

"God, you're fucking gorgeous." He paused, leaning down to kiss her before straightening again and sliding his cock between her waiting lips. He dug his fingers into her hair and used his hands to hold her still as he began pumping in and out. She swirled her tongue along the bottom of his shaft and he groaned, his eyes closing at the sweet torture. This was as good a blow job as any he'd had, and he'd had a lot of them.

Opening his eyes again, he wanted to watch her face when she took him all the way in and he slowly began to slide deeper, just a little more with each thrust. His balls were already drawing up tight in anticipation of release and he would have been embarrassed at his nonexistent stamina if she had anything to compare it to. Since she didn't, his fingers dug into her scalp harder, moving her against him as he fucked her mouth. This was so good he never wanted it to end; it had become much more than a simple blow job. The chemistry they had when they touched was spectacular, like nothing he'd felt with anyone else.

"Relax now," he said gruffly. "Let it slide back."

She did exactly what he suggested and when he thrust into her, she took him all the way to the base of his shaft, her eyes closed, face completely at ease.

"Fuck, Becca!" He shot off deep in her throat and it was only then that she coughed. He held her fast, unwilling to pull out in the midst of such ecstasy, but he slid out just enough to keep her from choking. Finally, he pulled free and grabbed her under the arms, lifting her against him. "God damn, baby girl, that was fucking awesome!" His lips found hers and she curled into him, a newfound sense of confidence shining in her eyes.

"It was okay?" she whispered against his mouth. "You're not lying to make me feel good?"

"I've never come that fast, ever," he said, arms closed around her tightly. "It was magnificent—*you* are magnificent. Just like last time."

She closed her eyes, smiling against his shoulder, and he was content to let her stay there. This was new to him, so much intimacy, and he felt just as uncomfortable as she'd probably felt when he'd asked her to suck him. She hadn't hesitated to do what he wanted, though, and now he wouldn't hesitate to follow her lead either.

Eventually, he pulled away and looked down at her. "You're wearing far too many clothes."

"Should I strip or do you want to undress me?"

The look on her face was playful, almost easygoing, and he felt a surge of pride that she still trusted him. The first time he'd asked her to undress he'd had to threaten her with punishment before she would do it. Now she wanted to know which way would be best and he loved it.

"How about you undress for me?" he suggested, lying back on the bed and putting his hands behind his head. "Last time you were so nervous I didn't get to fully enjoy it. Can you do it without being nervous?"

She bit her lip. "I think so. You already know how fat I am."

He sat up in a flash and yanked her against him, his eyes dark, almost angry. "I don't ever want to hear you say that again! You hear me? You're not fat. You're curvy and sexy—a real woman with boobs and hips and a beautiful ass. I can have almost any woman I want and you're all I've thought about for months. So unless you want me to put you over my knee and spank your sweet ass until it blisters, don't ever let me hear you talk like that again."

Her eyes were wide with surprise and maybe a little bit of trepidation, but then she looked away.

"What?!" he demanded, grabbing her chin and forcing her to look at him.

"I'm okay with who I am. Really. I'm healthy and energetic and active. I generally don't give a shit what people, even men, think of my body and I have no problem being me. But you…" She touched his lower lip with her finger, tracing it lightly. "You're something different altogether. You're not a regular guy, with regular needs or regular anything. Being with you means I have to be something I'm not, and I don't think you understand that. *Because* you're you."

He scowled. "What does that mean?"

"It means that being with you would make me an automatic celebrity, someone the whole world is going to judge. What I wear, how much I weigh, what my makeup looks like. Everything I do will be scrutinized, carefully and publicly, and there aren't a lot of people who can live with that long-term."

"What does that have to do with anything?"

"You have to be prepared for me being fat—what you think of me personally doesn't matter. The moment you take me out in public, the whole world is going to have something to say about Dante Lamonte's *curvy* new girlfriend."

His jaw worked angrily for a moment, his eyes narrowed as he glared at her. But instead of focusing on any of that, something she'd just said clicked and he smiled despite his annoyance, bringing her face close to his. "Does that mean you're my girlfriend now?"

She rolled her eyes. "I'm talking about going forward."

"I'm talking about right now. You wanna go steady?"

She burst out laughing. "Dante! I'm being serious!"

"So am I."

"Um, we just, I mean, we barely know each other." He'd definitely caught her off guard.

"If you're already thinking about how the press is going to judge you, it should be official, right?"

She cocked her head. "Are you trying to distract me?"

"No. I asked if you wanna go steady. If you don't, say so and we'll just go back to the club and fuck once in a while."

"Do people our age go steady?"

"I just asked you to, didn't I?"

She shook her head. "You're impossible, Dante."

"Is that a yes?"

"Yes."

He kissed her. "You know what happens when you go steady with Dante Lamonte?"

"I'm sure you're about to tell me."

"Ain't nobody ever going to call you fat. Not the press, not our friends, not anyone. Know why?"

"Because you're Dante Lamonte?"

"Exactly." He found her mouth hungrily; she was his now. End of story. All that other stuff was just bullshit.

7

"Can we get back to the part where you undress for me?" he asked after he'd kissed her breathless.

"Of course." She smiled and pulled her dress over her head, letting it fall to the floor.

"We need to go lingerie shopping," he said, taking in her round hips and the swell of her breasts.

"You don't like what I've got on?"

"I like it very much, but it seems to be the same bra you wore six months ago."

She laughed. "We already discussed how many hours I work every week —I have the opportunity to wear a black strapless bra maybe three times a year. Why would I need more?"

"Because now you have a horny boyfriend who will want you to wear sexy bras three times a day—maybe more."

She flushed. "Then I guess we can go lingerie shopping."

"Leave the shoes on," he said as she started to step out of them.

"They're starting to hurt," she admitted.

"Your feet are going to be in the air a few minutes from now," he promised.

Her cheeks got a little pink but she left the heels on and reached back to unclasp her bra. He was watching her so intently she appeared to be getting nervous again as she hesitated to discard it.

"Not this again," he teased, hoping to make her feel less uncomfortable. "I've already seen it all, baby girl."

She tossed the bra aside and moved towards him as he crooked his finger at her.

"Such perfection," he sighed as she crawled over him. He lifted his head and wrapped his lips around one of her breasts. Her nipple instantly hardened in his mouth and he used his fingers to pinch the other one until it did the same. She sighed, her head falling back.

"Have you been able to pleasure yourself since we were together?" he whispered against her ear, his strong hands gliding over her skin.

"Yes." She nodded. "I bought a vibrator."

"Very good." He ran his tongue along her ear. "Do you enjoy making yourself come?"

"I enjoyed it more when you did it," she admitted.

He chuckled. "Yes, well, sex is definitely better with someone else. I'm just glad you've been able to find release—it's not good to hold it in."

"Dante?"

"Yeah, baby?"

"I keep thinking about last time—what you had to do to get me off—what if I can't—"

"Shh." He put a finger on her lips. "If you did it by yourself, you'll be able to do it without me having to take extreme measures. The first time is the barrier—after that, your body knows what it wants."

"Touch me," she whispered. "Please."

"Oh shit," he said suddenly, groaning as he reached for his wallet. "I know you're on the pill but I have no condoms with me. I'm sorry, *querida*, but I'm positive I can find other ways to pleasure you if you aren't comfortable without them."

She shook her head. "I trust you."

"Have you ever had sex without one?"

"No." Her eyes met his questioningly.

"Only with Larissa," he said, though she hadn't asked. "And only after she talked me into letting her get pregnant."

"Okay." Her voice was breathy, soft.

"Your eyes tell me something else," he said gently. "Are you worried about diseases or pregnancy?"

"I—" she hesitated. "Pregnancy, I guess—I know you probably have to be healthy to play baseball."

"You don't want children?" he asked carefully. "You don't want them with me? Or you don't want them now?"

"I don't want them now, since we've just gotten together, but it's more about you than me."

He cocked his head. "What do you mean?"

"Are you ready for a baby? If we're in that less than one percent that unexpectedly gets pregnant while on the pill, are you prepared to go through another pregnancy so soon? Are you over the last one? He was your son, Dante. *Louis* would be how old now?"

He briefly closed his eyes. "Ah, *querida,* you are very special to think of that—Louis would be almost three months old now."

"And five weeks from now, if we were to have a positive pregnancy test, how would that make you feel?"

Dante hesitated, looking into her eyes and seeing something he'd never seen before: pure, unadulterated honesty and sincerity. She was genuinely more concerned with how he would handle the emotions of unexpectedly fathering another child than what it would mean for her to be pregnant by a guy she barely knew. "I would like it very much," he said after a moment. "I agree that it's too soon, but that wasn't the question—you asked how I would feel a few weeks from now if we got a positive pregnancy test. The answer to that is simple: I would be happy. I didn't know how much I wanted to be a father until I had a child on the way. But you? How would you feel?"

"Terrified!" she chuckled. "We hardly know each other—"

"You just told me you trust me," he interrupted. "And we've had a deep, intense bond from the moment we met. I want you to feel safe, though. What we have goes beyond sex and we both know that—if even the slightest chance of pregnancy bothers you, we'll wait until tomorrow. I have at least a hundred and fifty ways to make you come without putting my dick in your vagina." His eyes glittered with a combination of desire and teasing.

"I'm honestly not that concerned," she said, wrapping her arms around his neck. "I'm good about taking my pill every morning, and I'm okay with us not using condoms. We're *going steady,* right?"

He grinned. "Yes, we are." He found her mouth again, nudging it open with his tongue and curling it with hers. She was still the most delightful thing he'd ever tasted, and the sweet sounds coming from her throat hardened him again in seconds. It amazed him that despite her shyness, she'd never hesitated to kiss him with everything she had. Even the very first time, when she'd been terrified and didn't know him, as soon as his lips touched hers she'd instantly kissed him back.

He caressed her skin with his fingertips, every touch resonating through both of them. She came alive as he cupped her ass and lifted her so that she wrapped her legs around his waist. He felt her arousal against him, hear her soft moans of pleasure, and was anticipating the way it would be when they finally came together. So many months of missing her, craving her, needing to be with her both physically and emotionally. Without breaking their kiss, he fell back on the bed with her astride him, her legs on either side of his hips.

He flipped them over, covering her body with his but holding himself up as he rested on his elbows. Gently stroking the side of her face, he nuzzled the curve of her neck and rubbed his jaw along her soft shoulder. "Beautiful," he whispered. "And all mine."

"Since the first time you touched me," she admitted.

"I'm very much looking forward to watching you come again," he murmured, lowering his head so his supple lips could suck one of her nipples deep into his mouth. He bit down just enough to make her yelp and then eased away, his tongue soothing the sting. He moved to the other breast and took his time, watching her get worked up, arching against him and breathing heavily.

"Dante!" she whispered his name, fingernails digging into the skin of his back.

"Patience, little one," he chuckled. "You'll be screaming my name all night."

She wrapped one leg around his waist, adjusting her hips so that his cock rested between her legs. Dante chuckled and moved away just enough to make her groan with disappointment.

"Six months!" she hissed in his ear. "Don't tease me!"

His eyes darkened with lust as he met her annoyed gaze and realized she meant it. He paused briefly, wondering how best to satisfy her aching need, and then thrust deep with one swift snap of his hips that made her breath rush out in a whoosh and her eyes practically roll back in her head.

"Dante..." Her fingers dug into the sheet beneath her as he began to move within her.

He made love to her with deliberate precision; hard, forceful pumping that was tempered by the loving strokes of one hand on her cheek and whispered endearments that made her heart flutter with happiness.

"So tight... So fucking beautiful..." he whispered against her ear, his breath hot and heavy.

"Dante!" Her legs shook as she clasped them around him tighter, her back arching up. "More! Please!"

He slid his hands under her and pressed her to him as he flipped them over so she was on top again. "Take the lead, *querida*—I can feel how much you want to."

"Oh!" She gasped.

"That's my girl," he groaned, moving with her. "Show me how much you missed me."

For Becca, six months of longing caught up to her in an orgasm so strong that her heated flesh convulsed repeatedly. He was unable to stop his own growl of pleasure, completely unprepared for the intensity of what it felt like to spill himself into her. The intimacy made them both shudder and she dropped against him, burying her face in the side of his neck.

"Okay, *querida*?" he inquired softly, his hands lingering on her bare skin.

"So intense," she whispered. "So much…everything."

"Everything?" He brushed kisses along the side of her face since the rest of it was hidden against his neck. "Look at me, beautiful. Tell me what you're feeling."

"That I never, ever want you to leave."

He smiled. "Why would I leave?"

She didn't seem to know how to respond and just burrowed deeper into his body.

"It's not like before, baby doll. I'm single, I'm here, I'm all yours."

"Promise."

"What?"

"Promise you won't disappear again." She lifted her head until she was looking into his eyes.

"Technically, you're the one who left me," he said lightly, his gaze remaining locked on hers.

"You told me you had to go home to another woman—what else was I supposed to do?"

"There is no other woman anymore," he said gently. "Nothing but you and me. You gotta trust me, baby girl."

"Then promise." She didn't even blink.

"You're something else," he chuckled, touching her face. "I promise, *querida*. I'm not going anywhere."

She moved back into the curve of his neck and he closed his eyes, savoring every second of this wonderful new intimacy between them. He'd never been in love before, but he was falling hard and fast.

8

BECCA WOKE UP SLOWLY, FEELING MORE RESTED THAN SHE HAD IN A LONG time. The shining sun told her it was late and she rolled over, disappointed to find the spot beside her empty, even though the rumpled pillows and bottle of lubricant on the nightstand reminded her that it had been real. Damn, had he left? She felt a twinge of despair before grabbing her phone to see what time it was. Almost noon. She hadn't slept this late in a long time, and she swung her legs over the side of the bed, anxious to use the bathroom before checking to see if Dante was still here.

She was sore—really sore—and she made a mental note to run a hot bath in a little while. Something caught her attention, though, and she lifted her chin, breathing deeply. *Food*. Was Dante cooking? She'd gone grocery shopping, knowing she would be home for a couple of days, but he didn't seem like the type to actually cook something.

Quickly brushing her teeth and washing her face, she pulled a brush through her tousled locks and let them hang down her back before getting dressed. It was Christmas, and she was with the sexiest man in the whole world, but she didn't have the energy to wear real clothes, so she settled on sweats and a T-shirt. Impatient to find out what he was doing, she stepped out of her room and into the hall. She was immediately assaulted by the smell of something amazing—cinnamon and bacon and something she couldn't quite identify.

"Dante?" she called out tentatively, walking into the living room.

"Merry Christmas, *querida*." He came out of the kitchen in the slacks he'd been wearing last night and what appeared to be one of her Sidewinders T-shirts—an XL that she slept in sometimes.

"Merry Christmas." She looked around the room in wonder. She didn't know how he'd done it, but there were flowers, baskets of fruit, and gifts everywhere. "Dante, what...?"

"It's Christmas," he said with a smile. "And I thought it would be more fun if we had presents and such—isn't it?" He paused. "This was supposed to be my kid's first Christmas, and even though he would've only been a few months old, I know I would have bought out the stores for him. This kind of made me feel better."

"But you didn't know you would be here," she protested. "And we didn't get to bed until late and—"

"Must you think all the time?" he laughed. "I knew I was going to see you the day before and the moment we kissed at the party I knew we were going to be together so I had my assistant take care of a few things."

"On Christmas Eve?!" Her eyes were wide with disbelief.

"I pay her a lot of money to be available to me twenty-four/seven," he said. "And frankly, placing online orders for me is something she can do in her sleep. I also let her buy herself a few trinkets. Anyway, come." He held out his hand and she couldn't help but take it.

"But I don't have anything for you," she murmured.

"You gave me my gift last night," he whispered against the side of her face. "Crying out my name while I made you come, over and over, was the best gift you could ever give me."

"That's just sex!" she protested.

"Really?" He met her eyes. "You made me promise to never leave you, but what we have is *just sex*?"

"Well, no, but it's not a gift."

"Becca. What material item could you possibly buy me that I don't already have?" He pulled her against him. "Giving me access to you—your body, your heart, your emotions—those are the things that mean something to me. Knowing that you stayed faithful to me while I was technically engaged to another woman—even if you did it unintentionally—is the kind of thing that fulfills me. Feeling you give yourself to me, after all these months apart, is more than I possibly deserve."

"It still feels like sex," she murmured.

"Deep down you're just an old-fashioned girl, aren't you?" he asked with a gentle smile.

"Probably."

"And I love that. I love the little things that make you who you are...

worrying that your house is messy or that sex isn't an actual gift." He shook his head. "I don't know what I did to deserve you, *querida*, but I plan to do everything in my power to keep you happy."

"Yeah?"

"We're going steady, right?"

"That's what you keep telling me." A tiny giggle escaped her.

"I plan to make you so happy you'll never want to leave the house."

She met his gaze suspiciously. "Why do I get the feeling you're the bare-foot-and-pregnant kind of guy?" She narrowed her eyes playfully. "'Cause you know that won't fly with me, Mr. Lamonte."

"No, Ms. Hernandez?" He cocked his head. "No days of lunching with the girls and play dates for you?"

She smiled faintly. "I want that very much—but somehow it doesn't feel like it would be enough. When you retire from baseball, will you do nothing at all? Just work out and play with your kids and make love to your wife?"

"If you were my wife, I would spend a ridiculous amount of time making love to you," he murmured, brushing his lips across hers. "But no, you're right, of course. I can't imagine doing nothing all day, and as a woman who's always worked, you probably can't imagine it either. However, with children in the house, it seems we would want to be with them."

She nodded, wondering how they were already talking about marriage and children. It was too soon, wasn't it? She looked into his handsome face and wondered about the darkness she saw flicker in his eyes. She'd noticed it the night they met, when he'd told her about Larissa, and today she could sense it —pain, grief—she wasn't sure exactly because it was gone as quickly as it appeared. She reached up to touch his face, trailing her fingers across his cheek. "It looks and smells wonderful down here. Thank you for making this a very special day."

"It's our first Christmas," he said lightly. "I want you to remember it."

"If you made coffee, I'll be on the road to remembering everything."

"I don't drink coffee—and I've never used a machine before." He grimaced. "Holy shit, how much of a dumbass am I?"

She laughed. "Come on, rich boy. You taught me how to have an orgasm —I'll teach you how to use a Keurig."

"I have one," he protested with a chuckle, letting her lead him to the kitchen. "It was Trey's, but..." His voice trailed off.

She looked back at him. "You stop every time you start talking about him. You shouldn't. He was your friend, like family, you said—so talk about him. Remember him. I'm sure it hurts, but it won't always, and from what Kate told me, he would be annoyed with you for acting like this."

"Kate talks about Trey?" He looked surprised.

"Oh, yes!" she grinned. "I know all about his boyfriend, Joe, and how much Trey loved Madonna…and you."

Dante smiled. "That's not a word we ever said aloud—too much Cuban machismo for that—but now I would give anything to be able to say it."

"What was his real name? Trey is not Cuban!"

He laughed. "No. It was Teyo—but he hated it."

"Of God," she nodded.

"You know the meaning?"

"I went to Catholic school until my dad left and we couldn't afford it—so yeah, I know a lot about the Bible."

"Is that why sex makes you blush?"

She laughed. "No, that's probably just because I'm a prude."

"You're not!" he chuckled. "Trey's mom used to make him go to church too—they were very religious. They stopped talking to him when he came out; couldn't accept he was gay. In the end, I was the only family he had. Damn, I wish I could tell him how much I loved him." He sighed.

"He knew." Sensing he was getting a little melancholy, she reached for the coffee machine and turned it on, fixing him with a look. "That," she pointed, "is the power button."

Dante scowled.

They spent most of the day eating and making love. Every time they were close to each other, passion seemed to overwhelm them and they were naked again within minutes. Dante had been going slow with her, anxious to get reacquainted with her body and her needs. Though he already knew her well when it came to sex, this time there was intimacy involved too, and he sensed that she needed more than orgasms to be fully satisfied. She needed him to guide her without making her submit—not yet anyway.

She liked and needed that kind of thing too, but the only way she would trust him like that would be to first solidify their emotional bond. It scared the hell out of him—the very thought of loving this woman and committing to her —but he knew that would be the only way he could have her. Becca was not the kind of girl who wanted a casual relationship, and even though he'd never been in a healthy one before, he realized it was time. She was all he'd thought about for months and now that he had her back, she was everything he'd imagined and much more.

Waking up the morning after Christmas, he was surprised to find her still curled into his shoulder, exactly the way she'd been when they'd fallen asleep. It was strangely familiar, as if they'd been doing this for a long time, and he watched her sleep for a while. She was beautiful, he thought, gently twirling a lock of her hair between his fingers. Though her eyes were closed, he could picture the silver-blue color that had mesmerized him the moment he first looked into them. An odd mixture of blue and gray, they were downright stunning. Her mouth was incredible too, with full lush lips that were a natural red color. Even without makeup, her skin was flawless, a golden color that looked tan all the time, much like his own. They would make beautiful babies...

The thought startled him and he had to shake his head, wondering what the hell was wrong with him. He'd been aching for her for half a year, and all he'd cared about was getting her back in bed. Yes, she was special and he had no intentions of merely using her for sex, but he hadn't planned on asking her to *go steady*. Who the hell did that anymore? Yet he had, and he didn't know who was more surprised—him or her. She'd laughed and blushed, something he loved about her, but he wasn't entirely sure what he was doing.

Their one night together had been magical, but she'd been right when she'd expressed concern that his comments afterwards had been triggered by the emotions of powerful sex and a coupling that had been more than physical. However, when it was all said and done, they didn't really know each other. She was a smart but not very worldly career woman who'd never been in a serious relationship before. He was a professional athlete who'd been married, divorced, engaged and almost a father once—all things he'd failed at miserably.

"Why are you staring at me?" she murmured, nuzzling closer to him, her hand sliding down to grip his bulging erection.

"Waiting for you to wake up so I can make you scream my name a few times," he chuckled, pressing his lips to her forehead.

"I should brush my teeth and—"

"No need." He found her lips and sucked them between his own, his tongue snaking in to seek hers forcefully. He kissed her until she moaned, her grip on his cock becoming firmer and more insistent.

When he pulled away she whimpered with distress and he pushed her onto her back. "You ready for more, baby girl?"

"More?" She tried to focus.

"Yesterday I made love to you—today I want to fuck you."

"Okay." She blushed but there was no mistaking the desire in her eyes.

"What can I use to tie you with?" he asked.

"Scarf in my closet," she murmured. "There's a bunch on a hanger."

He nodded. "Get your vibrator out." He slid out of bed and went to her closet, finding a couple of scarves made of silk that he hoped wouldn't chafe her beautiful skin.

She came out of the bathroom, a pink vibrator in her hand, the smell of toothpaste lingering on her lips.

"You brushed your teeth!" He chuckled. "Now I have to."

"I'm not going anywhere." She crawled back into bed.

He was quick about freshening up, amused that she was so concerned with something he found so trivial—yeah, it was nice to have clean breath and to wash the crud out of your eyes in the morning, but in order to have intimacy you had to be comfortable without doing those things too. She would learn, though; he would show her what it was like to share everything with someone. He'd never shared his soul before, but he'd shared everything else and Becca was the first woman he'd wanted to go that far with.

His mouth found hers the moment their bodies came together, but instead of the sweet, passionate kisses of the last twenty-four hours, he was rougher now. He claimed her body by covering it with his much larger form and gripping her wrists in one of his hands. He tied them to the headboard in seconds, making sure to keep the bindings loose—sometimes using regular clothing for this type of thing backfired because the knots got too tight and he didn't want to hurt her, especially not the first time since they were back together.

"You ready, baby girl?" His mouth hovered close to hers. He wouldn't hurt her, but he scared her when he went into what she considered his dominant role.

"Yes," her breath hitched a little and he just smiled, kissing her.

"Relax," he whispered, trailing his tongue down her neck and along her collarbone. He taunted her as he kissed her, starting at her neck and going all the way down her torso, finding every spot that made her shiver and shake, gooseflesh breaking out all over her skin.

He took the vibrator and turned it on low, pressing it to her clit and watching her jump. Grateful he'd found a pharmacy that had been open yesterday, he reached for a condom and saw her frown in confusion.

"You only use this in your pussy, right?" he asked, motioning to the vibrator.

She nodded.

He put the condom on the vibrator and then lifted her hips.

"Dante!" Her voice filled with panic and he put a finger on her lips.

"Trust me, *querida*." He put the vibrator between the cheeks of her ass, pressing lightly against the rosette of tight muscles he knew had barely been touched, and only by him. "The vibrations there will make your orgasm more intense—that's all."

Her breath was coming in little gasps but she nodded.

Using his broad shoulders to keep her thighs apart, he moved between them and pressed his tongue against her slit. He licked from top to bottom, pausing when he got to the vibrator. He moved it gently, pressing it firmly against the tight little hole in her ass. She gasped, but he kept on, making sure to tease her without actually penetrating it. She wasn't ready for that and he wanted everything about their time together to be pleasurable for now; there was plenty of time to push her limits later.

"Dante...do you hear—"

"Shh, relax."

She closed her eyes but could have sworn she heard a noise in the living room. For a moment she lost herself in his warm hands and mouth but then she heard steps in the hall that made her jerk.

"Dante!"

"Becca, if you're stalling—"

"I'm not—listen—I think my mother's home!"

9

Becca had to hand it to him, because the moment her words registered, understanding dawned. He started to move, and he moved fast for a guy with a raging hard-on and absolutely no warning. He released her hands with a few flicks of his fingers and stilled the vibrator at the same time he stuck it under the mattress. With her arms free, Becca grabbed the sheet and pulled it up over both of them just as her mother knocked on the door.

"Becca, are you awake, honey?"

"I'm not alone, Mom!"

Her mother hesitated. "Well, neither am I. Maybe you could get dressed and come out?"

"Give us a few minutes, please." Becca closed her eyes and groaned. "My boss is here. Oh my fucking God, my boss is here with my mother and I'm in bed with my new boyfriend, naked."

"Sweetheart, how old are you? Twenty-seven?"

She nodded.

"I'll be thirty-three in February. We're adults, and last I checked, you own this house—I don't think we owe anyone any explanation other than the respect of dressing appropriately and speaking respectfully in front of your mother."

"I know, but...ugh." She groaned again. "How do I act? My mother has never had a boyfriend and I've never had one that I brought home!"

"You act like you always act. This is your home and I'm your boyfriend. This is also your mother's home and Pierre is her boyfriend. We all know each other—except your mother and I—and we will make polite conversation until we decide what to do next."

Becca got up and started pulling on her clothes. "I was on the verge of an epic orgasm, too!" she pretended to pout.

"If they decide not to leave, we'll go to a hotel," he whispered. "And you will finish that orgasm—promise!"

They finished dressing quickly and Becca was grateful that he squeezed her hand tightly as they opened the door and padded into the kitchen. She heard her mother's soft laughter and a man's deeper answering rumble. She glanced at Dante and he winked, sliding his arm around her shoulders as they walked into the room.

Donna looked up and a pleased, if not slightly startled, smile crossed her pretty features. "Hello, sweetheart!" She reached out to hug her daughter. "Introduce me to your friend."

"Mom, this is Dante Lamonte. Dante, my mother Donna Hernandez."

"Very nice to meet you." Dante took Donna's hand between both of his. "I've heard so much about you from Becca."

"I didn't realize you two were spending the holidays together," Donna said as she looked over at Pierre. "But it's very nice to meet you! I think you both know Pierre."

"Merry Christmas, Becca." The tall, middle-aged man kissed Becca's cheek and shook Dante's hand. "I didn't know the two of you were dating."

"We met on a few occasions," Dante said smoothly. "But I was involved with someone else. Now that I'm single again, it was opportune that we ran into each other."

"I thought you were going to be gone a few more days," Becca said finally.

"We have an announcement," Donna said, glancing at Pierre nervously. "So we thought we should come home and tell everyone."

"Are you getting married?" Becca asked, her eyes widening.

Pierre chuckled, reaching for Donna and pulling her close. "Not yet, but I've asked her to move in with me. I want her to quit her job and enjoy life. With me."

Becca couldn't think of anything to say, her thoughts reeling as she looked at her mother's flushed, excited face. She wanted her mother to be happy; she'd had a tough time since Becca's father left, but damn, why did she have to fall in love with Becca's boss?

"You look underwhelmed," Donna said quietly when Becca was silent.

"I just—I'm happy for you," Becca said, meeting her mother's gaze. "But he's my boss. No matter what you say, every single day I'm going to worry about whether or not something going on at home is going to affect me. You guys can say that it won't, but until you've had a real fight, until you've argued about something personal and important, you don't know for sure. And that leaves me potentially in the middle."

"That won't happen, Becca!" Pierre let go of Donna and motioned for them to sit down at the kitchen table. "Please, let's talk. I know this is uncomfortable for you."

Becca sank into a chair with Dante on one side of her and Donna on the other. Pierre sat across from her and ran a hand through his thick silver hair.

"We've talked about this, at length," Donna said quickly. "He's given me his word that no matter what happens with us, it won't impact you at all."

"That's a difficult promise to make," Becca said. "Anything could happen."

"I'm a responsible businessman who runs a professional sports franchise —you really think I'd let my personal life affect someone who works for me?"

"It happens. Shall we discuss Libby Montville?" Libby had been the successful head of marketing for an NFL team. Her older sister had been dating the general manager, and when the dust settled after their very nasty, public break-up, Libby Montville had been persona non grata in the football world, even though she'd done nothing wrong.

Pierre sighed. "Yes, what happened to Libby was wrong, but you have to believe that I wouldn't do something like that. You're a grown woman who does an amazing job for the team. I would never, ever do anything to hurt your career, no matter what happens."

Becca shook her head, aware that nothing she said would change anything and that she was going to have to put on a happy face and pretend like everything was okay. "Yes, okay." She got up and started making coffee, knowing that she had to do something to keep busy or she would explode.

"Becca?" Donna was at her side, her fingers digging into her daughter's arm. "I know you're upset, but I promise—"

"It's fine," Becca said under her breath. "I love you—I want you to be happy—and even if I didn't, you've already made up your mind."

"Becca." Donna looked sad. "You'll see, everything is going to be okay."

"I know." Becca turned to the refrigerator and got out some of the leftovers from Christmas. "I'm hungry," she said. "Shall I make something?"

"I was thinking we could go out to breakfast," Pierre said. "You don't have to cook."

"I like to cook." Becca gave him a tight smile.

"Pierre, I think maybe Becca and I need some time to talk about things," Donna began.

"I have plans with Dante today." Becca got out several coffee mugs. "And I have to work tomorrow, so this is our last day to be together." She busied herself at the sink, cutting up fruit as she tried to still her shaking hands. Part of her knew she was being a bitch, but for fourteen years she'd put her mother's needs before her own, and now her mother was completely disregarding this potential for disaster.

"I'm sorry," Pierre stood up and joined Becca and Donna at the sink. "It didn't occur to me that this would be a problem for you, Becca."

"Of course it didn't," she said, shrugging. "You're the boss. Nothing that happens affects *you* professionally."

"What if we made it official?" he asked. "An addendum to your employment contract?"

She shook her head. "That just makes me look insecure and like I'm trying to take advantage of the situation. Look, it's fine." She waved a dismissive hand. "I'm making breakfast—who's hungry?"

There was an awkward silence until Dante got up and joined her at the sink. "I am. What can I do to help?"

She smiled at him. "You already are."

"I could probably eat," Pierre said after a moment, rummaging in the refrigerator.

"I see there's a ton of fruit," Donna murmured. "Let's make Belgian waffles."

"Sounds wonderful," Dante said.

Becca went through the motions, making breakfast with Donna, making small talk while they ate and nodding her head as Donna talked about packing up her things and moving.

"Becca, is this going to impact you financially?" Pierre asked as they finally began clearing the plates. "I know you're struggling with all of this, but I really don't want to make things difficult for you. Will the loss of your mother's income make it hard for you?"

"No, I'll be fine." Becca began putting dishes in the dishwasher.

"Becca, stop it." Donna put her hand on her daughter's. "I know how much you make, I know how much the bills are here, and I know how much I contribute. You'll be able to pay all the bills, but I'm not sure how much disposable income you'll have, for clothes and entertainment and such. Let's discuss it."

"When do I have time for entertainment?" Becca snorted. "I work eighteen-hour days when we have home games, which is forty-one days a year. I work twelve- to sixteen-hour days during the preseason. I work most of the summer. When was the last time I did something entertaining?" She caught the look of amusement in Dante's eyes and threw a dish towel at him. "That doesn't count—plus I didn't pay for it!"

Dante burst out laughing. "Perhaps you'd be in a better mood if you had!" he teased.

She rolled her eyes. "Look, it's fine. Everything is okay. Can we let this drop? This is my last day with Dante and I don't want to spend it arguing about this. Please?"

"Of course, honey." Donna nodded. "But we'll have to talk about it eventually."

"We'll talk when I get home from work tomorrow night," she said.

"We have dinner plans," Dante reminded her.

"It was tentative," she said. "You know dinner plans are hard, Dante. I never know what my days are going to be like or how late I'll be at work."

"Okay, we're done here." Dante pried the dish towel out of her hands and pulled her arm firmly. "It was wonderful to meet you, Donna." He smiled. "Nice to see you again, Pierre, but to be honest, I've been waiting months to spend time with Becca and this isn't how I envisioned our day."

He tugged her into her bedroom and shut the door firmly behind them. Then he leaned against it and folded his arms across his chest. "What's wrong with you, baby girl?" he demanded. "I know this could get complicated for you going forward, but Pierre is a stand-up guy and he's not going to just toss you out if he and your mom don't work out. Your mom loves you and has been alone a long time—she deserves to be happy. What's really bothering you?"

"I've done everything for her since I was fourteen!" she hissed under her breath, her fists clenched at her sides and her eyes glittering with tears. "I'm still clawing my way out of my student loans—I got scholarships but they didn't cover everything! I bought us this house, co-signed her car loan, and I paid for everything when she had her emergency gall bladder surgery three years ago—*before* she had health insurance. Fifty-two grand, in case you're interested. She's conveniently forgotten about the loans, the medical bills, the stress. Now she rides off into the sunset with her Prince Charming so I can continue to drown in the debt she created because she was so busy feeling sorry for herself when my dad left she opted to clean toilets instead of going back to school or learning a skill or something!" She swiped at her eyes angrily.

"So you're angry that she's not a strong, independent woman like you," he said after a moment. "You're angry that she chose to scrub toilets and left you to become the family breadwinner. Is that it?"

She narrowed her eyes. "Look, if you're going to take her side, I don't need that kind of boyfriend."

He approached her slowly, his eyes narrowing. "Is this going to be our first fight? Because I promise, *querida,* you won't like losing."

She turned away, defeated. "I don't want to fight, but if you can't take my side simply because I need you to—even if I'm wrong—then you should go. I'm hurt that she didn't take my feelings into account, and I'll be more hurt if you don't either."

He sighed, reaching out to pull her against him. "I'll always be on your side, but I think you're overreacting and you need to see it from someone else's perspective."

"Why? What's to see? Essentially my mother pays her car payment, her insurance and gas. She buys some of the groceries, pays the cable bill when she remembers, and gives cash to the kid who cuts the lawn for us. It's not a lot, but that allows me to pay off her medical bills and what's left of my student loan. I'll survive without her, but it makes everything harder, as always."

"Now you have me," he said softly. "I will make everything easy."

"Dante, that's not the kind of woman I am. I like presents and trips and nights out—but you're not paying my bills. You're certainly not paying my mother's bills!"

"No, your mother and her new boyfriend are going to pay her bills." He held up a finger when she started to protest. "If she chooses to leave the home you provided for her, then she needs to take responsibility for that. I'm happy to point that out, but it's probably better if it comes from you."

"I don't want to fight with her either," she sighed.

"This isn't a fight. Pierre asked what would happen financially if she moves out. This is your opportunity to tell them. Present them with the most recent statement or whatever you have, and make sure it's not in your name."

"It's in her name, but I write the check every month to the hospital. They wrote off some, but we still owe about fifteen thousand dollars."

"She owes fifteen thousand. You owe nothing."

She smiled up at him. "I'm sorry I'm being a bitch. I don't know why this bothers me so much."

"Big changes in your life, *querida.* Me, your mom, your boss...relax. It's Christmas. Let's enjoy."

"Having you in my life is a very, very good change," she said.

"I think so too." He stroked her hair as he looked into her face. "So, what would you like to do today?"

"Honestly? Nothing. It's one of the few days off I get. I want to watch movies and cuddle on the couch. Later, you owe me an orgasm."

He chuckled. "I can provide all of that. What about your mom?"

"I don't know."

"Let's find out, okay?" He touched her face and leaned forward, his lips hovering near hers. "Don't be upset. Let's enjoy the day."

"Okay."

10

DONNA AND PIERRE GOT READY TO LEAVE AFTER DINNER, SEVERAL SUITCASES, boxes and random bags in their cars. Becca stood in the doorway of her mother's bathroom, watching her throw the last of her toiletries into a small carry-on size bag. It was odd, seeing her mother moving out. She'd always imagined she would be the one who would move out someday, when she got married. Not the other way around. Nothing about this was traditional, and although it felt strange, she wanted her mother to be happy.

When her father had left, her mother had been devastated. Becca's father had been her boyfriend since seventh grade. They'd gotten married right after high school graduation and Becca came soon after. Life had been hard for two young parents who never went to college, though. From what Donna had told her, there was never enough money and eventually it wore them down.

Once he left, Donna threw herself into menial labor. Sometimes Becca wondered if it was because the physical work helped her forget the emotional pain. Her father hadn't just divorced his wife; he'd disappeared from both of their lives without a trace. Becca had no idea where he was, or even if he was still alive. Honestly, she had no desire to see him again. She'd adored her father and her heart had also been broken when he left.

"I'm sorry this happened so quickly," Donna said, closing the bag and straightening. "We've been dating since last April."

"You met during the playoffs, didn't you?" Becca remembered the way her mother had locked gazes with the attractive older man. She'd never imagined he'd asked her out, though.

"Yes." Donna smiled. "He's amazing, Becca. He's been single a long time, just like me, and we took it really slow at first. But in the last couple of months, we realized we're both getting older—what are we waiting for? I love him and want to be happy before I'm too old to enjoy it."

"I really am happy for you." Becca reached out and hugged her.

"And I'm happy for *you*!" Donna whispered back. "Holy shit, he's fucking hot!"

The two women snorted with laughter. "You have no idea," Becca murmured.

"I take it things are going well in the bedroom?"

Becca flushed. "Oh, yeah."

"Well, that's exactly how it should be." Donna smoothed her daughter's hair back from her face. "Be happy, Becca. Enjoy him—enjoy this. Love is wonderful. I went without for far too long and I'm not waiting another second."

"Please don't let him hurt you," Becca said softly. "I don't know what he's like as a man, but he's a hard, shrewd businessman that chews people up and spits them out daily. Be careful, okay?"

"He's a good man," Donna said softly. "Yes, he's hard on the outside, but that's business. He's still a human being with feelings and dreams and a family. He has two boys that he's very close to—I'm going to meet them at New Year's."

Becca nodded. "I love you."

"Love you, too!" Donna kissed her cheek, picked up her bag and headed towards the door.

Dante had promised Becca a romantic date and he intended to give her one. Though he really just wanted to spend all their time together in bed, he knew that wouldn't fly with her. Besides, he was beginning to understand that being with a nice girl was about a lot more than sex. He and Larissa hadn't done much but fight and fuck over the years. They'd both mellowed out a little after she told him she was pregnant and he proposed, but that hadn't lasted long and they'd reverted to fighting—sex went out the window after he met Kate and realized he wanted more out of life than a bitchy woman who felt he owed her something.

When he'd met Becca, he'd somehow known she was it. It had been instinctive, and even through the months of grief, in the back of his mind he'd been trying to get to a place where he could find a way to get her to give him a chance. He'd been a mess, completely out of control, drinking and hiring hookers to suck him off, but he'd been aware that Becca wasn't like any other woman he'd ever met and he might have found what he hadn't been looking for when he'd met her.

Now that he had her, with a genuine chance to win her love, he was terrified he was going to fuck it up. That had been his MO over the years, and he couldn't risk it with her. The problem was that while he knew how to please her sexually, and he had no problems being romantic, he really didn't know anything about a healthy, long-term, committed relationship. What he'd had with his ex-wife and then with Larissa had been anything but healthy.

"What are you thinking about?" Becca asked, her cool fingers on his cheek, startling him.

"How bad I am at relationships," he admitted. "How I've fucked up every other one I've had and how I don't wanna do that again."

"Your relationship with Kate is both professional and personal—and she adores you. Your relationship with Emilie seems wonderful too—and you had the very best relationship with Trey."

He smiled at her attempt to make him feel better. "I wasn't sleeping with any of them. Sex seems to be the element that changes everything—especially when I cheat."

"Do you always cheat?"

He sighed. "Not intentionally…but look at you and me. Fucked up as she was, technically I cheated on my pregnant fiancée. Do you really want to take a chance on a guy like me?"

"Are you trying to talk me out of it?" She scooted closer to him on the seat, her face close to his. "I've had six months to talk myself out of seeing you again, but the minute Kate said you would be there…I found the dress, the shoes—everything I could to make you want me again."

"Oh, baby girl, I never stopped wanting you." Their mouths were so close he felt her breath against his lips.

"But now you're pushing me away?"

He shook his head. "I'm warning you, because I don't want to hurt you. You're a light in my life that's never been there before—and I'm dark, baby. I live on the edge, always on alert, always ready to do something dramatic to fix something I fucked up. Been that way since the beginning and I don't know why; everything I touch goes to shit."

"No." She pressed her lips to the underside of his jaw, slowly licking a trail down his Adam's apple before nuzzling her cheek against the side of his neck. "You've done what you needed to do to survive; with me, you don't have to do that anymore. I don't want anything but your love, Dante."

His heart skipped a beat. Did she *love* him? Was it possible that this smart, successful, sexy little siren loved his miserable black heart? "Do you love me, Becca?"

She didn't hesitate: "I've never been in love—not as an adult—but I knew the minute you kissed me last June that I would never get over whatever it was I felt at that moment. Your touch was sexual, but it was like you wrapped your soul around mine so tightly that my heart will surely stop beating if you take it away again."

He couldn't stop himself from finding her lips, dragging them between his and using them to show her just how much her words affected him. No one had ever said things like that to him—other women talked about his money, his athleticism, his success, his looks, even his monster-sized cock—but no one had ever talked about his damn soul.

Who was this woman and why the hell had he waited six months to make her his? He might be a hot mess, but he wasn't stupid and he was cognizant of the fact that he would undoubtedly never meet another woman like her; she knew exactly how to touch him emotionally and she was willing to do anything he wanted sexually. He was never letting her get away from him again.

"I've never been in love," he whispered. "And this thing between us is new, but I know you're special, I know I need you like I need air—since you left that night, I've been empty inside. I don't have a lot of pretty words for you, baby girl, but I want you like I've never wanted anyone or anything ever."

"You've never been in love?" She looked doubtful. "Not even with Larissa?"

His face grew shuttered, almost angry. "Hell no—'specially not her! I felt I owed her, but I didn't love her. She was a difficult woman."

"Can we talk about her? Larissa?" He stiffened but she gripped his shoulders. "Dante? At some point, you have to get it all out, and let it go—at least with me."

"I just want to forget her," he admitted after a moment. "She caused me so much pain, so much…"

"But I need to know. I can't dance around it every time her name comes up, and eventually, someone is going to ask me a question that I'm going to look foolish answering."

He sighed. "I know, baby girl. It's just hard."

"Please? Will you try? For me?" She wrapped her arms around his neck.

"For you, I will do anything." He touched her face before reaching for his beer. He took a long pull and began to talk in a slow, low voice that seemed devoid of emotion, as if he was holding it all in. "Larissa went to high school with us. She was Cuban too, but had been in Miami since she was five or six. She was wild, even wilder than me back then. She ran with a tough crowd and when we started hangin' out, she dragged me with her. Everything I learned about being a bad boy, I learned from her. Me and Trey, we lost our virginity to her together, at the same time. She did him first, while I watched, and then she did me." He shook his head. "I think maybe she turned Trey gay—" He smirked since he knew that wasn't true. "One time with her and he didn't want nothin' to do with women ever again!"

Becca smiled too, understanding he was kidding.

"But seriously, she latched onto me the first time she saw me play baseball, even though I was a shy kid from Cuba who didn't speak two words of English. She got me hangin' out with other baseball players, got me speakin' English, and she was the one who sucked some scout's dick so he would come see me play."

"I didn't know that."

"No one knew but Trey." He sighed. "So even though I didn't love her—hell, I didn't even like her half the time—I owed her. Everything I have is because she got that guy to come see me. Yeah, I might have been discovered anyway, but who knows? And she threw that in my face all the time." He was quiet for a minute, lost in thought. "We dated for a while but I got rich and famous fast the first few years, and I kinda drifted away from her. I sent her money—I was never a prick about money—but I never loved her. Then I met Rose, my ex-wife. She was even wilder than Larissa. She was a model and that girl knew how to party... She's the one who turned me on to kinky sex." He shook his head. "She liked it rough, she liked pain, she liked to fuck. You name it, she did it."

"Did you?" Becca asked softly.

"Not the shit she was into, not all of it." He made a face. "I'm talking dental spreaders and—"

"Dental spreaders?" Her eyes were huge. "You mean, down there?"

"I mean in a guy's ass."

Becca's mouth fell open. "Ew!"

He laughed. "Yeah, that's what I said. So we made a deal—once a year she could go to some sex club and get her crazy on, no holds barred, and she had my blessing as long as she kept the completely whack stuff out of our bedroom. We only lasted a year, but Larissa wasn't just mad when she found out, she was fucking *pissed.* I'd married this wild Italian girl off the boat from Sicily and Rose could hold her own. Larissa would show up some place we were at and they'd go at it—like every fucking time."

"You mean, like, a fist fight?" Becca looked horrified.

"Fists flying, hair pulling, biting, kicking and scratching until somebody wound up at the hospital." He rolled his eyes. "Fucking nuts. And I was still a kid, just twenty-two, richer than anyone that age has a right to be, lovin' that these two women fought over me. It got old, though, and Rose liked to party. Jack Daniel's, cocaine, crystal meth—she did it all. I was wild, getting wilder every day, but I wasn't stupid and I knew my career was over if I started with shit like coke and meth, so I stuck to drinking on my days off. It got a little out of control toward the end of the marriage—hence the night I threw her and all her shit on the front lawn after I slapped her silly." He paused. "I'm not proud that I smacked her, but she…" He blew out a long breath. "She brought a guy home. I got home from practice and she had him tied to my fucking bed—I lost my mind." He looked at Becca, his eyes dark and hooded. "I won't lie. I'm jealous as hell. Once you're mine, you're mine. You need to know that."

She dipped her head, leaning closer to him. "If roles were reversed, and I came home and found some other woman tied to our bed, there is a very good chance I would hit you too."

He chuckled, brushing his lips on her cheek. "And you'd have every right."

"So you divorced Rose…"

"And Larissa and I had this on-again, off-again bullshit going. She was easy, convenient and we'd been together since we were kids—I trusted her. I shouldn't have, but I did. I think…" His voice faded and he cleared his throat. "I know part of the reason she did what she did was because she was desperate to keep me. I should have cut her loose a long time ago, but I kept her around because I kinda felt I owed her. She kept begging me to let her get pregnant, said I didn't have to love her, but if we had a kid together we'd always be family. I could do what I wanted, but that baby would mean we were bound together. And one weekend, she caught me in a weak moment, when she was being soft and sweet—so we agreed not to use a condom while she was there. Then she disappeared for a while. I was partying like a fucking idiot, two, three women at a time, night after night…and she called me, told me she needed to see me. She was already fourteen weeks, past the first trimester. She was afraid I would change my mind, make her get rid of it, so she hid it until it was too late."

"Were you mad?"

"I was shocked—I know it *can* happen quick, but me and Rissa, we'd been having sex for fifteen years and never had an accident, then bam! That's when I hired Kate—I knew I needed help to turn my life around. Plus the owner of the team knows the owner of the Sidewinders and he told me to hire her, said I needed to straighten up. That's when things started to change. Kate wasn't just my publicist—she was my friend. When she and Karl broke up, she was destroyed, and for the first time in my life I knew a woman who wasn't trying to trap somebody and wasn't a gold digger or anything; she was just a sweet, smart, beautiful woman who'd been humiliated by the man she loved…and I saw myself in what he did to her, even though we know now he didn't do it."

"Yeah, that was some craziness last summer," Becca shook her head. "When Karl called and asked for my help with that whole thing, he was a mess."

"All I knew at that point was that there was this great girl who'd been doing so much for me, and every fucking day on Twitter and Facebook people were calling her fat. I couldn't stand it, couldn't stand to see the hurt on her face—and I had to take care of her."

"Did you fall in love with her?" she whispered, her eyes meeting his.

"A little," he admitted. "I wasn't *in love* with her—nothing ever happened between us—but that's when I realized I wanted her, or someone like her. Someone sweet and smart, who just wanted to be in love and marry a guy who would love her back. I wanted someone like that." He sought her eyes. "And now I've found her—you."

"But when we met you were going to marry Larissa."

"Actually, I wasn't. I was planning to marry her when I proposed, which is why I did it, but instead of being happy that I'd given her what she'd always wanted, she was bitchy and mean. She was always fucking with Trey, she cut me off in the bedroom, and although no one knew, I was planning to break things off after the baby came."

"Do you have any idea why she turned on you the way she did?"

"I think she had a feeling I'd met someone—" He looked away. "Except it's more likely she thought it was Kate. She had no idea about you, but after the night we were together I couldn't even sleep next to her and even though she'd cut me off, she sensed that I couldn't stand the thought of touching her."

"I'm sorry," Becca whispered, tears pooling in her eyes.

"Don't cry, *querida*." He kissed her forehead. "It wasn't your fault—you and I did the right thing, agreeing not to see each other again. She thought Kate was the reason I was pulling away so you had nothing to do with it."

"I'm sorry I couldn't be there for you. I ache when I think about Trey… and the baby."

He nodded. "I know. Thank you."

"Did Larissa have family?"

"Her mother," he said, nodding. "Even though Rissa was a crazy bitch, she paid for it with her life, and her mother was a wreck over it. I paid for the funeral and everything… Damn, baby girl, those are some dark days you're taking me back to."

"I needed to know, and it needed to come out; we never have to talk about it again."

He stroked her hair. "What else?"

"I wish I could have been there for you."

"It wouldn't have been good. I threw myself into baseball and when that ended, I let myself fall apart. If it hadn't been for Emilie, I don't know if I would've come out the other side. I needed to grieve and it wasn't pretty."

"And now?"

"Now I have more than I deserve. My career, friends, and more than all of that, now I have you."

"What about Emilie?"

"She's a close friend that I care for a great deal, but you have nothing to worry about—what you and I have is totally different." He kissed the palm of one of her hands.

Becca looked down. "Dante?"

"Yeah, baby?"

"Are we still going to be together once the season starts?"

His eyes widened. "Why would you ask me that? Of course we are! Don't you want to be with me?"

"I do. But this will be hard…I'll be on the other side of the country and you'll be on the road. When will I see you?"

"We'll figure it out." His eyes searched hers. "As long as you want me, Becca, I'll find a way to be with you."

"I'll always want you."

11

Dante hadn't lived in a small house in a long time and staying with Becca was a new experience every day. From emptying the dishwasher in the morning to dealing with a stopped up toilet, he saw life from a completely different perspective. It was humbling to acknowledge how easy he had it. Not that being a professional athlete was easy, but that was his job, and it paid the kind of money most people could only dream about. Becca worked hard too, but her paycheck was nothing like his and when she came home at night she was tired but still had to either cook, clean, do laundry or run errands.

Even though he tried to spoil her with meals and relaxing evenings out, she still did more in a day than he'd seen anyone do since he'd lived with his parents. He wanted to take care of her, and pay people to do the things she did, but she didn't bat an eyelash and laughed when he suggested it. The honeymoon period ended quickly with all the hours she worked, and Dante was rapidly losing his patience.

Their first fight came after a month of living together. She'd worked a long day and had picked up Italian food on the way home. Instead of eating, however, she immediately threw in a load of laundry and began sorting through mail, her laptop open on the kitchen table. Dante tried several times to get her to slow down but she was distracted and unwilling to stop working.

"Becca, I understand you have to work during the day, but in the evening, I expect us to spend time together."

"We are!" she said, glancing up. "This is real life, Dante. This is what regular people do! We work and then come home and do other kinds of work!"

He made a face at her. "I thought we were using this time to get to know each other?"

She scowled. "I still have bills to pay and I need my clothes washed and—"

"I told you I would take them to the dry cleaners for you."

"I can't afford that and you know—"

"Would you stop thinking about money all the time?" he grunted. "I have more than enough, and if it means we get to spend more time together, let me pay for something as stupid as dry cleaning!"

She rolled her eyes. "You can't just sweep in and pay for everything!" she snapped. "That's not what our relationship is about."

"I know that!" he practically growled. "But I've been here a month and I see you maybe two hours a day! What the fuck, Becca?"

"I have a job!" she snapped. "I'll remind you of this during baseball season when I'm the one sitting home alone all summer!"

"I'm trying to make it so that we have time together—if you'd just let me, instead of being stubborn about shit like dry cleaning!"

"You don't understand!" She got up and huffed into the garage to put clothes in the dryer. She tossed in each piece angrily, wondering why she was so upset. He just wanted them to spend time together and she was finding excuses even though every night when they went to bed she craved his touch, his kisses, the way he made her feel. It was overwhelming how much she wanted him and it was only during the day when she was at work that she felt normal again, as if everything in her life had been turned upside down.

Going back inside she was surprised to see he wasn't in the kitchen anymore and she debated whether to go find him. Pursing her lips, she sat down and opened her email; maybe it was best to let him come to her. He was possessive and overbearing and she needed him to understand that she needed space sometimes. Things between them were intense and as much as she wanted him physically, the emotions were becoming too much. Somehow, she had to make him understand that, without driving him away.

She worked for an hour before closing her laptop and padding down the hall towards the bedroom.

"Dante?"

Dante was on the bed, hands behind his head. He looked at her without moving a muscle. "Take your clothes off," he said in a gruff voice.

She arched her eyebrows. "Sex isn't the answer to everything."

"In the bedroom, we have an agreement that you do what I say, correct?"

She nodded absently. "Yes, but I just wanted to know if you were hungry and—"

"We're in the bedroom, so take your clothes off."

She threw up her hands. "Dante—"

"If I have to ask you again, I'll punish you."

"What are you talking about?" She didn't look happy.

He was up off the bed and in front of her in a flash, his eyes darkening dangerously. "I've been patient with you, baby girl, 'cause we've been gettin' to know each other—but that ends now. You're wound up tighter than a drum and I'm not going to tell you again; take your clothes off."

"But…" She saw his eyes begin to narrow and took a step back nervously.

"I'm not going to *hurt* you," he said quietly, gentling his tone when he realized her fear was coming from somewhere outside their dominant/submissive relationship in the bedroom.

"Then what does *punish me* mean?"

"I might make you a little uncomfortable, in the context of what we do in bed and being the dominant in this relationship, but I'd never actually hurt you!" He reached out and slapped his palm against her ass, hard enough to make her gasp but certainly not hard enough to cause more than a sting or leave a mark. She met his gaze in surprise. "Did that hurt?" he asked softly, his fingers on her cheek.

"Kind of." She frowned. "Dante, I don't understand…"

He sighed at the confusion on her face. "We have so many things to talk about, I don't know what to tackle first." He looked into her eyes and saw wariness, which gave him his answer. "Come." He took her hand and led her out of the bedroom and into the living room; neutral ground when it came to sex. He also didn't want them to fight in the place where they made love and slept. He pulled her onto his lap and began stroking her hair. Thinking about what to say, he decided to be honest.

"I like to fuck," he said quietly. "I like to make love, kiss, hold hands and cuddle—all that's good, baby girl. I like it, I want it, and I'll do it as much as you want—but I also like other stuff sometimes. I know you do too, even though you don't understand it yet."

"I thought it was something we would just do once in a while, all that submissive stuff."

"Yeah, it is, but it's also a…" He hesitated. He had no interest in a full-time dominant/submissive lifestyle, but he couldn't think of another word. "It's a lifestyle," he said finally. "Not in the sense that it runs our life—you got a job, I got a job, we have friends and family and I'm not going to tell you when you're allowed to eat or what to wear. That's not what this is. But tonight? You pissed me off and I was going to—am still going to—punish you for not talking to me about whatever is bothering you and for disobeying me when I told you to take your clothes off."

Her look of fear made him put a gentle finger on her lips. "When I talk about punishing you, you gotta understand I'm not talking about *abuse*. I'm talking about sex play and a relationship that brings in some of what we do in the bedroom into the rest of our lives. Not in public—I don't live like that and I know it wouldn't fly with you either. I won't ever do this if you're genuinely sick or hurt or something happened with your family or job—but tonight? You got somethin' on your mind and you don't want to tell me. I can't have that, especially not with the trust I'm trying to build."

"I don't even know what that means!" she whispered.

"When we were at the club, you were unable to find pleasure until I tied you up and fucked you hard—you *like* it, Becca. You like me taking charge and taking all the decisions away from you. You're naturally submissive in that way, and that's part of why we had the connection we had. I gave you something you didn't even know you needed. Now that we're together, I been lettin' the sex come natural and it's been good. Makin' love to you is magical —but sometimes, like tonight, you need something more. You're wound up— whether it's about work or me or somethin' else, I don't know 'cause you won't tell me. So I'm gonna make you submit until you're relaxed enough to talk."

She frowned slightly, chewing on her lip. "Can't we just talk?"

He chuckled. "Yeah, baby girl, and we will, but right now? You're closed off and this kind of release—the kind that comes with submitting—is what you need to not just get it off your chest, but to understand what's bothering you on a more emotional level. Your anger is coming out because you're frustrated."

"What will you do to me?"

"You have to trust me," he whispered. "That's the number one thing—you can't submit until you trust. Then I'll show you the pleasure involved, like I did last June, that goes beyond tying you up. You're still a little shy and tense when we're in bed, and it's time to move beyond that."

"What if I don't want that lifestyle?" she whispered, her fingers shaking slightly.

"But you do," he said gently. "If you didn't, what happened at the club wouldn't have happened."

"You stimulated me—in ways no one ever had before—wasn't it inevitable I would have an orgasm?"

He shook his head. "No, baby girl. You didn't know me. If you didn't subconsciously want to embrace this stuff, you would have frozen up, started to cry, or used your safe word. You wanted it—you still want it—and I want to give it to you. I just didn't realize you really had no idea what it's all about."

"I read a little online," she admitted. "I don't think I like pain… When you hit me before, it didn't, uh…"

"It didn't turn you on?"

She shook her head. "No. When you boss me around and tell me to get on my knees and stuff—that makes me hot. But when you hit me? Not at all."

"Okay." He stroked her cheek. "Then we'll find other ways to punish you. It's about letting go and finding your inner strength, as well as your inner kink." He kissed her. "But you have to be willing to try, Becca, and you have to understand that once we enter into it, you can't back out."

"Ever?" Her eyes widened.

He shook his head. "If it becomes uncomfortable, or I see that you're not enjoying it, we'll stop. But I saw you embrace it the night we met—and I know you need more. Sometimes it's about what you need more than what you want, and you need this, *querida*."

"I don't know, Dante."

"Tonight, we play by my rules. If you're not turned on, if you're not okay with it when we're done, we'll discuss options."

"Promise you won't hit me?" Her eyes puddled with tears and he immediately wrapped his arms around her.

"I promise. If that's nonnegotiable—and I see by the fear in your eyes that it might be—I promise. There's a line between fear coupled with excitement, and true panic. I'll never push you to the point you panic. I know your limits and I won't go beyond them. Maybe right up to the line, but never beyond. Okay?"

"Okay."

"Now get up, go back to the bedroom, take your clothes off and wait for me on the bed."

"We didn't eat dinner," she whispered, a flush covering her cheeks.

He smiled. "After I fuck you and make you apologize for disobeying me, I'll feed you. Go."

She got up, cast one last nervous look at him and disappeared down the hall. He let out a long breath when she was gone and closed his eyes, mentally preparing himself. He liked being dominant in the bedroom, but he'd never had to explain it to anyone before.

She was wound up and he needed her to let go, but it wasn't a one-time thing anymore and she needed to understand his needs as well as her own. He didn't need kinky sex every time they were together, but in order for him to fulfill his occasional needs she needed to be submissive in the bedroom almost all the time. He would know when it was too much or when she needed romance and tenderness; the rest of the time she needed to let him have control.

12

HE GOT UP AND FOLLOWED SLOWLY, GIVING HER TIME TO UNDRESS WITHOUT too much time to work herself up. He was crazy about her and making her happy was all he cared about. The problem was that it seemed like she had no idea how to *be* happy, something he wanted to start changing. He'd never met a more tightly coiled woman and even the insane amount of sex they'd been having wasn't enough to relax her. Tonight was the first step towards making that happen.

Walking into her bedroom he almost laughed when he saw her on the bed with the sheet pulled up. Without reacting, he walked towards her and slid off his sweatpants, providing his already erect cock for her gaze. He yanked the sheet back and simply stood there, taking in her beautiful body and the nervousness on her face. She was okay, though; he didn't see fear, which was good since that wasn't his goal. There would most likely be other times when he wanted to push her limits and see how far they could go, but it was way too soon for that. Tonight, he only wanted to bring her back from wherever she'd retreated to in the last few days.

"You were a very bad girl tonight," he said in a steely tone. "I don't like when you close yourself off from me and I don't like when you raise your voice."

"We're not allowed to argue?" she asked, blinking in confusion.

"Of course. We are definitely going to argue—sometimes we'll even fight —but not like this. People fight about specific things, like who left the cap off the toothpaste, or so I've heard. But we weren't fighting tonight. I was trying to get you to relax and you were determined not to; you snapped at me continually without actually telling me what you were upset about. Now you will."

He crawled behind her, turned her over and lifted her by the hips so that her ass was in the air and she rested on her knees. He rubbed his hand over her smooth, silky cheeks, noting that she was not at all aroused. Fear had crept in and that had to end before he could show her what she needed. Lowering his head, he licked the sweet spot between her legs just the way she liked it—soft, fluttering, gentle. When the first sighs of pleasure escaped her, he pulled away, and her whimper of protest was the response he wanted.

Reaching for the items he'd bought several days ago, he contemplated the best way to teach her a lesson without frightening her. Last June he'd only had to use overstimulation and she'd gone over the edge quickly. Now she was more in tune with her body so his obstacle wasn't physical; tonight he had to break down her emotions. Whatever was causing her to pull away from him was subconscious.

"Get on your back, baby girl." He waited while she did it and then reached for the restraints he'd hidden under the mattress. He held out his hand and she slowly put her wrist in it, watching as he wrapped the Velcro cuff around it. He moved to the other side and did the same thing, tightening them until her hands were pulled as far away from her body as they would go. She would object to her legs being tied but he had her right foot secured before she could move. A tiny whimper escaped her when he did the other foot and he ran a hand down her calf, slow and tender, stroking her skin until she stopped shivering.

Taking out a small clip, he kept it hidden in his palm as he lowered his head again, pleased to see she was still wet despite her nervousness. He licked a few drops of her sweetness and let them sit on his tongue as he watched her. With soft movements he suckled her clit until it stood stiff and firm, and then grasped it between his fingers. Before she could guess what he was about to do, he slid on the clip and kept his hands on her hips as she jerked.

"What is that?!" Her breath was raspy.

"Easy…the clamp is meant to heighten your pleasure. You won't be able to come with it on, allowing me to tease you until I'm ready for you to let go."

"Dante!"

"When you're being punished, you'll call me *sir*. Do you understand?"

"I thought you didn't like that?"

"Only when you're being punished. Do you understand?"

"Y-yes."

"Yes what?"

"Yes, sir." She swallowed.

He took out the labia clamps, wondering how she would react to those, but before putting them on he gave her throbbing pussy the attention it craved. Licking and kissing her tender folds, he felt her tightening, practically begging for release; she had no idea how intense this was about to get.

Becca had almost gotten used to the clit clamp when Dante's fingers spread her lips and she felt something pinching them. "Oh!" she cried out, but Dante's tongue was instantly back between her legs, easing the uncomfortable sensation until the mixture of pleasure and pain was so intermingled she was writhing in frustration.

"What do you want, Becca?" His voice was low, sexy, taunting her.

"I, uh, you…"

"Be specific."

"I want you…inside me."

"Do you want me to fuck you?"

"Yes!"

"Say it. And don't forget what you call me."

"I want you to fuck me. Sir."

"I don't believe you."

"What?"

"Say it like you mean it!" he snapped, wrapping his hand around his cock and stroking it while she watched.

"Please! Sir! Fuck me!" Her cry was full of need this time and he lowered himself between her legs.

"This won't be like anything we've done before," he whispered. "But it won't hurt." He slid into her effortlessly, sheathing himself with a swiftness that made her grunt.

"Oh!" Her eyes nearly rolled back in her head as he took her. The clips held her open as he thrust hard and deep, and the clamp on her clit kept her on the verge of release without letting her reach it. This was a completely different feeling and she bucked, making sounds she'd never made before, going into sensory overload. She felt every inch of him, practically butting up against her cervix each time he pushed into her, the area between her legs on fire as the clamps stimulated her erogenous zones and made her strain for more.

"Apologize," he growled, his hands under her ass, lifting her so that he had maximum penetration each time he moved.

"I'm sorry!" she whimpered.

"Who?" he growled.

"Sir! I'm sorry, sir. I won't hide things from you!"

"Tell me why."

"I'm scared!"

"Of what?" He didn't let up, pounding into her tight wet channel so hard she grunted each time.

"I'm in love with you!" she cried. "And I'm scared you don't love me back!"

He pulled out abruptly and she whined with distress. "Silly girl."

"Oh! Sir, please!"

He reached between her legs and gently removed the clamps. She yelped as the blood came rushing back to the depressed areas and he eased the discomfort by swirling his tongue around them with delicate precision. His touch was the final straw and she lost control, climaxing so hard he could feel the heat shooting over her skin.

Before she'd even finished shuddering, he plunged back inside of her, this time moving slow so she felt every stroke within her sensitized inner walls. She panted, arching up to meet him, unconsciously pulling at the restraints. He reached over to free her hands and they instantly dug into his hair, dragging his head to hers. Her sweet lips sought his almost urgently and he kissed her back, letting her draw him as close as she needed.

There was no holding back for either of them, each seeking something different from the other; she wanted his love and he wanted her trust. They found what they needed as everything came together in a rush of sensations and cries that became a jumbled mass of emotions. He felt her start to grip him tighter, her whole body rising up off the mattress as pleasure burst through her again, and he couldn't stop his own thundering release. Their hearts were hammering so hard their bodies shook in the aftermath, and it wasn't until she started to shiver that he found his voice.

"How can you doubt my feelings, baby girl?" he finally rumbled against her mouth.

"You won't say it," she hiccoughed as she attempted to keep her voice from breaking. "How can I give myself to you completely if you don't love me? That's the only way I can give you what you want… Otherwise, I'm just another girl you're fucking."

"No…hell no." He brushed damp hair from her forehead and looked into her red-rimmed eyes. "If you needed the words, why didn't you ask?"

"You can't ask for that," she whispered. "Either you feel it—and give it freely—or you don't. That's a hard limit for me."

"Ah." A smile played at the edge of his mouth. "So the words are important to you."

"If they're sincere."

"You think I'd tell you I love you if I didn't mean it?" He shook his head.

"Honey, I was waiting for the right time—somewhere romantic, on a day off. I didn't want to say it the first time in the middle of a load of laundry and a trip to the grocery store."

"You still haven't said it." Her sad eyes were fixed on his.

"I love you." He nibbled her lips and used his hand to brush away a stray tear. "You are part of me, remember? Right here." His hand moved to his chest. "In my heart, always, since the first time I touched you."

Her eyes fluttered closed and in that moment he felt all her resistance melt away. Every barrier she'd put up was gone as she relaxed into his arms.

"You were angry that I hadn't told you I love you?" he asked quietly.

Her eyes opened and she sighed. "I wasn't exactly angry—I was more afraid I was going to get hurt; if you didn't love me, you were going to leave."

"I promised you I wouldn't."

"The way I feel about you is natural," she whispered. "I don't have to think about it or wonder—it's there, like another part of my body. I don't know anyone else who ever fell in love like this, after just one night, because I knew I loved you then. I thought I was being a silly girl, who finally got laid in a really big way, and because of my lack of experience, I convinced myself I was in love. Then you came back and if anything, I love you more—it's embarrassing."

"Embarrassing? Of all the shit I've done to you, *loving me* is embarrassing?"

She chuckled. "That stuff is embarrassing too, but in a different way—that's just related to sex. But love? Love is supposed to be something that comes gradually, built on experiences and some sort of solid foundation. Our foundation is solely based on sex and that's not…normal."

"Normal? Whose definition of normal?" He turned onto his side and looked at her. "*Querida*, nothing about my life since the day I signed with the league has been normal. My parents were killed three months later—did you know my parents never got to see me play pro ball?"

"I didn't," she said quietly. "I'm sorry."

"After I lost them, it was me, Trey and Larissa. I had no one else to show me anything. I was a nineteen-year-old kid making millions of dollars —and I fucked up so many times. Drugs, partying, women, hitting my ex-wife, bar fights, even some gang activity—but I got away from that quick once I saw how ugly it was. Instead, I became the world's biggest asshole, made it clear that I don't play with no one, that I'm bigger and better than anyone else, so don't fuck with me. Look where that got me, baby girl. I'm divorced, I have a record, my best friend, my ex and my baby were murdered, and I'm a kinky motherfucker in the bedroom. You're right, loving me should embarrass you—but only because I'm so far beneath you, it ain't even funny."

Her mouth fell open. "What? No! I'm embarrassed because I fell in love like a fourteen-year-old girl who thinks she's in love with the captain of the football team even though he's never looked twice at her! I'm not too good for you!"

He smiled. "On paper? I'm the one who should be embarrassed. I'm a fucking mess, Becca. But I don't want to be, and dammit, I'm trying to be a better man. For you."

"I know you are and I'm not embarrassed by you—I'm embarrassed because it doesn't seem like I should feel like this so soon…"

"But I love you, too." He held her face in his hands, brushing his thumbs along her lower lip. "So we're both kinda like fourteen-year-old girls, right?"

She snickered. "You're *so* not a fourteen-year-old girl."

"Becca, I want it all with you. The house in the suburbs, kids, maybe a dog… I never wanted any of that before you."

"Kids come up a lot," she said with a faint smile. "Does that mean you want them sooner rather than later?"

"I do." He nodded. "But if you're not ready, I can wait a little. *A little.*"

She nestled into him again and smiled. "Okay."

13

Dante had essentially moved in and after their talk he decided to stay as long as he could. He didn't have to leave for spring training until the end of February, which gave them another month or so to be together. Things would get complicated after that, but Dante was confident he could convince her to join him when he wasn't on the road and then he would work on getting her to move in with him when hockey season was over.

She'd been resistant to the idea of living together, even though they were already doing just that, and he had a feeling it was more about leaving Las Vegas and her comfort zone. Living together here wasn't really a change for her, but moving across the country to New York was a big step. They were going to have to discuss her job as well, but he opted to wait. He'd been clear that he wanted them to be together permanently, but he was letting her get used to the idea.

On the plus side, she'd begun to relax a little and even turned off her phone and email when she got home on non-game nights. In fact, today they'd been out shopping. The team was out of town and had the day off, so she'd left work at noon to meet him for an afternoon together. They'd had lunch and then hit the mall, where he had her trying on lingerie, bathing suits and sexy outfits for hours. She hated every minute of it, but seemed willing to continue because it made him happy. He wished she would embrace her sexiness and enjoy dressing up for him, but he figured it would take more than a month to get her to that mindset. In the meantime, he was having fun even if she wasn't, and he decided to up his enjoyment by taking her to an adult sex store.

"What are we doing here?" she demanded when they pulled into the parking lot.

"What do you think?" He had to laugh at the scandalized look on her face.

"Dante! What if someone sees us?"

He rolled his eyes. "We are adults, remember? It's perfectly legal to go into a store like this and buy anything from sexy lingerie to porn videos to toys. Come on, no one is staking out the sex shop to see who's stopping by!"

She hung back, a scowl on her face, but he tugged her inside, keeping a firm grip on her hand. He coaxed her into looking at everything, but her reservations were unmistakable; she wasn't particularly enamored with the idea of trying anything new.

"Come on," he whispered, his lips close to her ear. "I've shown you all kinds of things you loved—why are you reluctant to keep experimenting?"

"I don't know." She looked down. "When you bring out something new in the heat of the moment it's not too bad, but being here is…weird. I feel dirty."

He frowned. "Why? Have I ever brought you anything but pleasure in the bedroom?"

"No."

"So trust me to continue." He lifted her chin and stared into her eyes. "I love you, Becca. Stop fighting everything and learn to enjoy—me, sex, this new relationship we're exploring. Life is short—and you know I know that better than most people."

She met his gaze hesitantly but finally nodded. "Okay," she managed to whisper. "I'll try."

"Good." He kissed her gently, pleased when a smile tilted up her lips. "Now, let's go look at plugs."

"At what?!"

"I want to find an anal plug that you can wear all the time."

"All the time?" She was back to being scandalized. "Why would I do that?"

"Because someday I want to make love to your ass, and wearing one will help prepare you."

"No way," she said firmly. "I'm not interested in anal sex."

"Ah, *querida*—so many rules," he chuckled. "Didn't you just say you would trust me?"

"Yes, but that's different! That's painful!"

"I promise, when you work up to it and go slowly, with plenty of lubricant, it is not."

She shook her head. "Dante, I don't think I want to."

He sighed. "Will you wear the plug once in a while simply because I think it's sexy as hell to look at when I'm fucking you from behind? Please?"

She turned pink but finally nodded. "Okay, but promise you won't force me!"

"Force you?" He frowned. "Becca, I love you. Do you really think I would *force* you to do anything you truly don't want to do? I'm not talking about some teasing or the introduction of new things—but actual *force*? Where you say a firm no and I force myself on you anyway? That's a conversation we need to have right now because if that's what you think—"

"No." She put a finger on his lips. "I'm sorry. You're right. That was me being insecure and my prude side coming out. I know you wouldn't do that. I shouldn't have said it that way. I just meant I want you to promise that you won't be mad if I say no, because anal scares me."

"Sex has nothing to do with why I love you." He wrapped an arm around her neck and kissed her temple. "I'll never be mad about stuff like that. Now tell me—which one do you like?"

F ebruary flew by in a frenzy of activity and before they knew it, he was back on the East Coast at training camp and they were forced into a bicoastal relationship. Becca spent most of March on the road with the Sidewinders and as opening day for baseball season approached, they were already getting antsy about being apart.

It was wearing on both of them, but there wasn't a solution and they were so busy it seemed as though they barely had time to talk, much less plan a trip to get together. Dante wanted her to visit him in New York but she was busy with the Sidewinders and there just wasn't a time she could get away. Weeks slipped by and, in the midst of their schedules, Emilie had a baby girl in mid-April. Becca hated that she wasn't able to be there, but Dante was and mother and baby were doing well.

As April moved towards May, Becca got an idea she hoped was as sexy as it was romantic.

"What if we met in New York on the 28th of June?" she asked him on the phone in late May.

"Isn't that our anniversary?" he asked knowingly, smiling to himself.

"Yes. What if…" She took a deep breath. "You're off the following day, so what if we went back to Club Inferno?"

"You want to celebrate the anniversary of the night we found each other at the same place."

"Don't you?"

"Very much!" he chuckled. "But I didn't think you wanted to revisit…that type of thing."

"There's no doubt I get off on the stuff we do in private," she sighed. "So why not go back and explore more?"

"I think it's a wonderful idea," he agreed. "I'll get us on the list."

"And since the Sidewinders are going to be in Philly for a couple of the championship games, you might be able to get to one if you can work it around your schedule."

They discussed dates and times and Becca hung up feeling much lighter than she had in weeks. She couldn't wait to see him, and the idea of going back to the club both terrified and excited her. She wanted to discover more about their sexual desires and that was one place that held a lot of meaning to them. Especially since she'd been wearing that damn butt plug almost nonstop since he'd bought it for her. Hopefully, she wouldn't chicken out.

W atching the Sidewinders win the championship was the most exciting thing Becca had ever seen. Though she wasn't in the stands with her friends and Dante, she stood in the press area with tears in her eyes, watching the team fall all over each other on the ice. She'd never imagined being a part of something like this and she felt pride surge through her as she watched. Her mother was somewhere in the stands with Dante and the others and she wondered if she was as excited as Becca was. Probably not, but she had to be pretty darn excited for Pierre, if nothing else.

Walking down towards the locker room, she fielded questions from the reporters she knew as she tried to get to the team before they did. Though the team had to be available to reporters, they would probably have a couple of minutes alone before they let anyone in. The Cup was being presented to them now and they were taking turns skating around the ice with it, so she had a little time to get down to ice level to make sure she was there to keep the insanity as contained as possible. These boys were going to party hard tonight and she had to keep their interactions with the press somewhat limited.

Caught up in the excitement and general festivities, Becca lost track of time and was confused when she got a text from Dante asking her to call him immediately. Moving into the hallway, she pulled out her phone.

"Have you heard about Tiff?" he asked quickly.

"No? What's going on?"

"She's gone. She left her kids at my house, with the nanny we hired for Simone, and went with Marco!" Simone was Emilie's baby.

Becca's head was swimming. "Why would she do that?"

"I don't know—we're trying to figure it out. Looks like he blackmailed her."

"Where are you?"

"We're getting in the limo and going back to my old house—I couldn't find you and I was concerned Zakk was going to make a scene if I didn't get him out of there!"

"I'm glad you did." Becca heard the team getting louder and louder. "What are you going to do?"

"We're trying to figure that out now, so we're regrouping at the house."

"Is Emilie there with the baby?" Becca glanced around, making sure no one could hear her because although Emilie had had the baby in April, Viggo still had no idea.

"Yes, and I have to hang up—can you come?"

"Dante, it's insane here—the team just won their first championship—I can't leave!"

"Damn," he sighed. "Look, my focus right now is figuring out what happened to Tiff. You do your job and take care of the rest of the team. I'll text you any updates."

"Okay. I love you!"

"I love you, too, *querida*!" He disconnected and Becca stared at the phone for a moment before hearing her name called. A moment later she squealed as she was doused in champagne.

"Vladimir Kolnikov, I'm going to kick your ass!" she laughed, holding her phone away from her, grateful it hadn't gotten wet.

"You must catch me first, yes?" He took off running, a bottle of champagne in each hand, and she rolled her eyes.

"It's going to be a long night," she murmured, watching the guys laughing and joking. She was torn, worried about Tiff but anxious to join in the celebration. She'd been a part of this too and didn't want to miss it.

"Becca, things are getting a little wild," one of her assistants whispered. "We might want to make sure the guys aren't doing things we don't want the press to see."

"Yeah, I'd better grab a couple of guys to do the grown-up stuff while the rest of the team starts partying!" she chuckled. This was a mess, but she could only deal with one thing at a time and right now that had to be the team.

The days that followed were a flurry of activity and Becca had to fly back to Las Vegas to handle the press and media storm that was following the team after winning the championship. Dante, Zakk, Karl, Kate and a few others had moved to Dante's house in New York, trying to figure out what to do about Tiff's situation; although Becca was concerned, she already had her hands full. Marco had left without a word to anyone, and in a way, she was glad; he was an asshole and difficult to deal with under the best conditions.

Deep down she hoped he was going to retire and not come back. There were rumblings about bringing in a back-up goalie from Minnesota but she hadn't had time to pay attention to that. She'd been celebrating with the team, keeping the media informed about all things related to winning and thinking about her upcoming vacation with Dante. One night at Club Inferno reveling in the memories of the night they met sounded heavenly and she couldn't help but wonder what new things he would expose her to.

By the time she got to New York, she missed him so much she could barely stand it. So much had happened in the two weeks since the Sidewinders had won the championship she hadn't had time to breathe, but now they'd have a special twenty-four hours together and then she would be staying with him until the All-Star break, when they could get away. There was still the issue of where Tiff was, but for the next couple of days, she hoped to put that out of her mind since there was nothing she could do about it.

To add a bit of excitement to their date, they'd agreed not to see each other until they got to the club, even though her things had been delivered to his hotel room in the city. Since he lived over an hour outside of Manhattan, they'd decided to stay at a hotel tonight so they wouldn't have to commute. He'd had a game earlier but would be off tomorrow, so they could have a fun evening without worrying about him getting enough rest. Then they would head to his house whenever they got up. Although he had another week of baseball before the All-Star break, she had that to look forward to as well— four days where the two of them didn't have to do anything except be together.

She'd changed in the private club bathrooms when she arrived, slipping on a much-too-small pink halter top that gave everyone a magnificent view of her breasts and a tiny black skirt that barely covered her ass. Underneath she wore a sexy black bra and a black lace thong that didn't cover much of anything. She had a pair of peep-toe pink pumps with four-inch heels that she knew Dante would love and she assessed herself carefully. Looking at her reflection in the mirror, she wondered who the sexy woman staring back at her was. Her outfit made her a little uncomfortable but Dante had chosen it so she was going to wear it.

Leaving her things in a locker, she walked into the club and looked around. The music was loud, playing something with a heavy pop beat, and people were two-deep at the bar. Taking a breath to still her nerves, she hoped Dante would find her quickly. Though she felt comfortable here when she was with him, she didn't relish the thought of being here alone.

"So fucking sexy I'm about to throw you on the bar and do you in front of everyone." Dante's voice was a low growl in her ear and she turned with a grin.

"Hi!" She closed her eyes as he kissed her, his fingers threading into her hair.

"Hello, beautiful."

14

Dante's eyes danced with desire as he looked her up and down. He'd nearly lost his mind when she'd come through the door, and the moment he saw several men look her way he knew he had to get to her before he did something stupid. He had special plans for them tonight and there was no way in hell he was letting some random stranger anywhere near her.

"I could use a drink," she said.

"Of course." He took her hand and they moved to the bar. Despite the line, Dante motioned to the bartender, who nodded. Dante looked down at her. "Margarita?"

"Yes, please."

Dante nodded at the bartender and within minutes they had drinks in their hands.

"How did you do that?" she asked.

"Money talks, *querida*. He knows the kind of tip he'll be getting, so he skips over others to make sure he earns it."

"But everyone who comes here is rich."

"There's rich, and then there's me." He gave her his most charming grin and Becca laughed.

They found an abandoned high-top and settled on two stools, drinking and catching up on the last couple of weeks. Two drinks and a lot of kissing later, Dante had his hand under her skirt, fingers lightly skimming the outline of her thong. She was already aroused, his fluttering touch enough to make her moan with need. Closing her legs around his hand, she met his heated gaze.

"Dante, we're—"

"We're at a sex club," he said. "And I want to see you come right here in the middle of the room."

"But—"

"Do we have to make this an official dom/sub relationship or do we continue the way we've done in the past? Once I snap those leather cuffs around your wrists, everything changes."

She swallowed. "N-no, this is good."

"Then open your legs."

She did as instructed, her eyes closing when two of his fingers traveled between her slick lips. He slid inside her effortlessly and she whimpered.

"You're fighting it," he chuckled, moving one expert finger up to her clit and stroking it until it hardened. "Let go. Come for me, baby. It's been almost two months since I watched you come."

She sighed heavily, unable to stop the desire pulsing through her. "Oh..."

"That's a good girl." He sped up a little, watching her face as she began to move her hips. He pulled her against him, so her back was pressed against his front and her open legs faced the dance floor. Several couples were watching and he held her in place with his free hand when she started to squirm.

"Dante!" Her voice was a shocked whisper as she realized how he'd positioned her.

"My way or we make it official," he whispered back. His arm tightened around her waist, making it impossible for her to move and he nudged up her skirt.

She cried out softly as two fingers plunged deep inside of her again. He finger-fucked her until she was soaked, her juices covering his hand and the seat of the bar stool. Her body didn't care how many people watched, and her hips jerked against him even though he could feel her trying to fight the need building deep inside of her.

"That's it, baby girl—let it out so all these people can see how beautiful you are when you come...please?" His soft, sexy voice in her ear was the final straw and his name burst from her lips; fiery pleasure exploded through her as she rode his hand, her orgasm rocking her back against him.

There was a light smattering of applause as she stopped shuddering and she felt her face turn bright red. "Dante!" She turned, burying her face in his shoulder.

"Fuck, that was gorgeous..." He kissed her temple and smiled as she groaned.

"Why does pleasure have to come with embarrassment?"

"The embarrassment is what heightens the pleasure, *querida*." He stroked her hair as she pulled herself together enough to finally sit up.

"Did you plan that?" she asked softly, her body still molded to his.

"No. The opportunity arose and I took it—there's no doubt you were turned on knowing people were watching."

"I guess so." She was surprised to find a fresh drink waiting for her and she picked it up, glad to have something to do.

"You're all right?" he asked, linking his fingers with hers.

"Yes." She nodded. "A few more sips of this and I won't care what you make me do."

He laughed. "Don't tempt me, baby girl."

They finished their drinks and Dante stood, reaching out his hand to her.

"Where are we going?" she asked, taking his hand without hesitation.

"Now the real fun starts," was all he said. They walked through the club, around the back towards the private elevators. He pulled the special key card out of his pocket and used it to get access. This was where they'd come last time too and she felt a moment of trepidation before remembering just how good that night had been.

As they walked towards one of the private rooms, Dante stopped. He looked into her face and leaned forward to kiss her. For a moment he didn't say anything, merely enjoying looking at her.

"What?" she asked curiously.

"Do you love me, Becca?" His eyes were warm and tender, his fingers against her cheek.

"You know I do."

"And you trust that I love you too? That you became my world the first time I touched you?"

"Yes." She took a breath, her eyes full of amazement as he spoke.

"What I have planned for tonight is something I know you will enjoy—if you trust me enough to let it happen. I will never, ever, go beyond your boundaries."

"You're kind of scaring me," she whispered, leaning against him.

"That's the point, isn't it?" He smiled, brushing his lips against hers. "I know your limits. Do you trust me?"

"I do, but—"

"Then there are no buts. You know the rules: as soon as we open that door you're not allowed to say no."

She looked at the doorway and felt her heart begin to race a little.

"I would never do anything to hurt you, so when you open the door promise you will give me a chance to explain before you panic."

"Dante…"

"It was your idea to come here," he reminded her gently.

"Okay, okay!" She nudged him with her hip. "Tell me again that you love me."

"*Querida*." His mouth covered hers, taking her tongue and sucking it between his lips, fingers in her hair, pressing his body to hers. "I never knew how much I could love a woman—never knew there was someone out there who makes my life better than it's ever been. I love you more than anything in the entire world. *More than baseball*." His tone changed slightly at the end.

She pinched his thigh as he said the last part, shaking her head. "It was all beautiful and romantic and you had to throw in baseball."

His eyes narrowed playfully. "I just told you I love you more than the only other thing I've ever loved—that's pretty fucking romantic, isn't it?"

She laughed. "Yes, you big lug!"

"Are you ready?"

"Yes."

She let him unlock the door and stepped inside. Just as the last time they'd been in a room at this club, it was big, spacious and mostly empty. The bed in the center of the room was massive, obviously made for more than two people, and this time she was keenly aware of the ropes and restraints attached to the headboard, footboard and ceiling. There was a nightstand that undoubtedly had toys and accessories of all kinds, a large chair and what she knew was a well-stocked bathroom off to the side.

It wasn't what was in the room that caught her attention, but the person standing by the wall. *Jamie Teller.* One of the players for the Sidewinders. Oh God, no, she thought wildly. She turned to step back out but Dante's strong arm was holding her around the waist tightly.

"You promised to get all the information first," he reminded her.

She *had* promised him that. He'd never lied to her, never let her down, and he definitely loved her; if Jamie was here, there had to be a reason.

"Hey, Becca. Dante." Jamie moved towards them, his smile genuine as he shook Dante's hand and nodded at Becca.

"What's going on?" she asked, looking from one to the other.

"I heard you have a fantasy," Jamie said, hands in his pockets. "I'm here to help indulge you. I understand there are different rules to the game than usual, and that you're free to say no and send me on my way."

"O-okay." Becca fought the anxiety rising in her chest, and was grateful for Dante's gentle hand on her arm, lightly stroking her skin.

"You've mentioned more than once that the idea of being with two men arouses you," Dante said quietly. "I'm a jealous man, but I thought it would only be fair for you to do something that I've done many times. I don't want this to come up five years down the road."

"I don't want to sleep with another man," she protested, shaking her head. She glanced at Jamie. "No offense."

He smiled, raising his hands. "No offense taken. I'm here at the request of a friend—this is about you, not me."

"It's not black and white like that," Dante said soothingly.

"And he's a *Sidewinder*!" She wasn't nervous when she brought up the fact that Jamie played for the team; she was *angry*.

"But that's why I chose him, *querida*. First, he's a friend who knows me and whom I trust—that should be obvious since I love you more than anything else in this world and I would only let someone I trust implicitly touch you. Second, the fact that he works with you and has been through a sex scandal— that almost cost him his job—means that he has just as much to lose as you do if anyone found out. Third, he's very much like us when it comes to this life- style—he dabbles occasionally but he's not a hard-core dominant, which I believe would overwhelm you. And finally, at this stage, I thought a complete stranger would be far more stressful for you than someone you know and I believe you genuinely like."

"But, but…" Her voice trailed off and tears welled in her eyes. "How is this not *cheating*?"

"It's not cheating because I'm here and this was my idea. It's not cheating because it's a sexual fantasy, not something done behind my back."

"You said you don't do guys—ever." She looked suspicious.

"I'm not going to do him—and he's not going to do me." Dante actually chuckled. "We're both going to do you—to whatever extent you allow."

"I, I don't know…"

"Tonight we're going to have slightly different rules," he continued, as if she hadn't said anything. "Although you still can't say no, we'll have a step between yes and your safe word. If you get to a place where you think you might need your safe word, instead of red, say *yellow*. If you say *yellow*, everything pauses, instead of stopping completely. We can discuss why you don't want to continue. If it's legitimate, we may change something. If not, you can still say *red*."

"How would we look at each other every day at work after this?" Becca whispered, her eyes meeting Jamie's.

"Easy." He moved closer to them, his hands cupping her face. "We're friends. You have a fantasy and Dante wants you to experience it before…" He glanced at Dante with a look she couldn't quite decipher. "Before you talk about moving in together, or whatever you two are doing when baseball season is over. I'm not here to fall in love or get between you. Think of me as a living, breathing vibrator."

15

BECCA COULDN'T HELP BUT LAUGH. IT SEEMED LUDICROUS BECAUSE JAMIE was a feast to the eyes. He wasn't strikingly handsome like Dante, but he was the boy next door in a hot, professional athlete kind of way. His wavy brown hair was short on the sides but long in front, parted on the side with a long lock that hung down over his eye and cheek. His brown eyes were big and playful, giving a boyish look to his otherwise masculine face. Nice lips and a regular nose kept him from being overly good-looking, but everything about him was handsome. He wasn't as buff as some of the other guys on the team, but she'd seen him in the locker room without a shirt on enough times to know the chest and abs under his shirt were well-formed and hard.

"I'm here to enhance the play, but I'm not the main attraction." His eyes twinkled as he watched her looking him over.

"Yes or no, *querida*?" Dante turned her towards him. "I'm extending the opportunity to walk out because I know how important your job is—if you're truly afraid this will impact it we will find something else to do. I would never do something to hurt you, professionally or otherwise."

She looked at Dante and thought about the months of love and pleasure he'd brought her. She loved him and knew he loved her. She hadn't hidden the fact that she was turned on by the idea of being with two men, and he was giving her the chance to try it.

"Dante, I don't ever want to do this with another woman," she admitted. "If that's what this is leading up to…"

"No!" He shook his head. "Don't you see? I've been with two women—

I've been with three—but you've never truly been with anyone but me. This is the fantasy; this is why we're here. I give you my word—I don't have an ulterior motive. This is exactly what it looks like: you get to try something that's exciting to you. After tonight, we're going to bring up your favorite subject."

Her eyes narrowed. "Moving in together."

He nodded.

She rolled her eyes. "Okay, yes—anything but *that* subject!"

"*Yes?*" Jamie's eyes lit up. "We're gonna stop *talking*?" He was joking and they all chuckled.

"But—"

"You can say *yellow*," Jamie interrupted, sliding his hands around her waist. "But not yet... Right now, I'm going to kiss you. We can ease into other things if it feels okay."

Becca's eyes closed as Jamie's mouth found hers. He was gentle, his lips soft against hers, waiting for her to open them before he used his tongue. When she did, his tongue found hers with light, feathery strokes, curling and tangling almost delicately. She kissed him back, forgetting that Dante stood beside them, his fingers lightly skimming her back. Jamie tasted like bourbon and brown sugar, and she didn't protest when his arms closed around her waist and drew her against his chest. *Damn, he could kiss.* Her arms snaked up around his neck and his erection pressed into her stomach. A tiny moan escaped her and he pulled away slightly, his eyes finding hers.

"Okay?" he asked quietly.

"Y-yes." She nodded.

In her peripheral vision, she saw Dante was now sitting on the chair next to the bed, leaning back. His shirt was untucked and he was watching them, his eyes curious and assessing. Knowing him the way she did, she knew he wasn't jealous or angry. If he'd been at all upset, the look in his eyes would get dark and dangerous, but now all she saw was desire and genuine curiosity.

"Come." Jamie took her hand, pulling her towards the bed. He kicked off his shoes and climbed up, pausing to look at her. "Will you take off your top?"

"Uh..." She glanced at Dante, relieved to see his barely perceptible nod. She pulled the lightweight top over her head and dropped it on the floor.

"Leave the shoes on," Jamie said softly.

She shook her head. "What is it with you men and these shoes? They hurt!"

"Not once you're up here, they won't." He patted the spot beside him and she crawled over to him. He ran his hands down her arms, exploring her skin and looking into her eyes. When his fingers lightly grazed her full breasts, she sighed, liking the difference in the way it felt. Dante's hands were rougher, slightly bigger, and darker in color. Jamie's touch was a little softer, not what she was expecting, until he slid his hands under her bra and squeezed. Ah, that was a man's touch, the kind she liked. Her head rolled back as he lowered his mouth to one of her nipples.

"Damn, they're fabulous," he murmured.

"She doesn't like to be manhandled," Dante said quietly from where he watched.

"No…" Jamie's breath was warm on her chest. "I can tell she's a delicate flower who wants to ripen slowly." He moved to his knees, lifting Becca to hers and bringing her against him, their torsos pressed close together.

Becca was trying desperately not to think too much, not to enjoy the feel of Jamie's body more than she should, when suddenly she felt Dante's warm body behind her. He was naked—she felt his erection against her ass—and his lips moved to the curve of her neck.

"How does this work?" she whispered.

"Just enjoy," Jamie whispered. "Take my shirt off."

With slightly shaking fingers, she unbuttoned the silk shirt and pulled it off his shoulders as Dante continued to nuzzle her neck and ear.

"Now my pants," Jamie said, his hand at her waist.

Becca opened the button on the waistband and slowly slid down the zipper, watching as his cock sprung free; he hadn't been wearing anything underneath. His cock was totally different than Dante's. Aside from the fact that it wasn't pierced, it wasn't quite as long or as thick. On the other hand, it was picture-perfect, standing at attention with a nicely formed head, the entire area well-groomed.

"You can do more than look," he said softly, letting his slacks slide down to his knees.

"It's okay, *querida*." Dante's voice in her ear was soft, sexy. "I think I'd like to watch."

"Really?" She looked confused.

He paused, turning her around so she was looking into his face. "I want this for you. I want you to enjoy it—I'm not going to be jealous. I was very careful in the man I picked for this evening. Whatever you want tonight—this is your free pass. I've done it—before we move our relationship to the next level, I want you to do it too. If you truly aren't interested, we walk away right now and let Jamie go find someone to finish what you started." He brought her fingers to his lips and kissed them, just like he did when they were alone, or having pizza with friends, or sitting at the movies.

"I feel weird," she admitted. "I want to, but—"

Jamie turned her around again, finding her mouth with his, as if he knew she wanted to go all the way with this, but her love for Dante and her inexperience in this type of thing was holding her back.

Moving his hands down her waist, Jamie slid down the zipper at the side of her skirt, letting it glide down her thighs in a silky cloud of fabric. Dante tugged it the rest of the way down and Becca lifted first one leg and then the other as he pulled it free.

"God, you're gorgeous." Jamie lowered his mouth to her breasts again, bringing them together with his hands. He lightly bit down on one nipple, making her groan, and he sucked it into his mouth. One hand moved to the other breast, rolling the nipple between his fingers, increasing pressure until she cried out. He used his lips to ease the sting, licking and kissing until her fingers gripped his hair, holding him against her.

"You're wet," Dante murmured against her neck as one hand reached between her legs. "You like the way he touches you?"

She nodded slowly as Jamie continued to caress and fondle her breasts. This was exquisite torture, having one man in front of her and the other behind. She'd had no idea being with two men would awaken so many senses at once.

She was in pleasure overload now, with Dante caressing her back while Jamie kissed his way from one hip to the other, his tongue circling her navel. Her breath hitched as Dante licked a trail behind her ear, his fingers moving around front to cup her breasts. He leaned forward, bringing his head around so his lips could claim hers and take possession of her mouth. She reached up with her left hand, bringing his head closer despite the impossible angle, kissing him back like it was the first time again—passionate, needy, desperate for more.

Jamie's mouth closed around the strip of fabric at her hip, tugging it down and then moving to the other side and doing the same thing. Her mouth was still joined with Dante's as he slid her panties down to her knees.

"Dante." Jamie's voice was deep and husky. "Sit on the edge of the bed."

Dante pulled his mouth from Becca's slowly and moved to the edge of the bed, bending at the knees so his feet were on the floor.

"That's fuckin' hot," Jamie grinned, staring down at Dante's bulging erection. "Never saw one in person before."

Dante raised his eyebrows but said nothing as Jamie gave the piercing in his cock a critical once-over.

"It's very hot," Becca agreed. "Especially when it's inside me."

"Yeah?" Jamie met her eyes. "I can't wait to watch him fuck you."

"You can't?" Becca hadn't expected that.

"Come here, *querida*." Dante reached for her, pulling her onto his lap. She started to turn, but he held her in place, so that she was facing out, looking at Jamie as she straddled Dante's lap.

"That's perfect." Jamie sat on the edge of the chair that faced the bed. "Spread your legs, honey. I want you to slide down real slow… I want to see every inch of his cock disappear into that sweet pussy of yours."

Becca swallowed hard; it was strange to hear someone other than Dante talking to her this way, but it was Dante's hands on her hips, his cock pressing against her, his beautiful body against her back.

"Slower," Jamie instructed as Becca started to lower herself onto Dante's thick, hard cock. "Dante—touch her."

Dante's hands moved to her breasts, his fingers pinching harder than usual and she moaned as she slid onto him. Her head fell back as he filled her, stretching her to accommodate his girth. This position was different, and she felt every inch of him at this strange angle.

"Ride him, baby, nice and slow." Jamie was stroking his cock with one hand, watching them with a lazy, lustful gaze.

Becca lifted herself up, slowly, carefully, trying to ignore the burning in her thighs as she moved up and down. The pleasure was exquisite, intensified by the knowledge that another man watched—another strong, sexy man that was obviously aroused by her naked body. It made her want him too, but she didn't know how to make that happen.

"Damn, that's sexy." Jamie slid onto the floor, walking on his knees the three steps it took to reach them. "Eyes on me, Becca."

She did as he asked, looking into his glittering dark eyes, unable to stop herself from licking her lips.

"You want me to kiss you, Becca?" Jamie whispered, leaning forward. "You want me to touch you while he fucks you?"

She whimpered as the pressure on her breasts increased.

"Answer me, Becca."

"Y-yes." Her voice was thick with desire as Dante thrust up hard and deep.

Jamie found her mouth in one motion, his hands in her hair, stabbing his tongue against hers and demanding a response. His erection pressed against her stomach and Dante's hands moved to her hips, helping to guide her as she lost herself in Jamie's kisses. She shivered when Jamie slipped a finger between her legs, gently stroking her clit until it hardened into a taut little nub against him.

"Oh, that's what you like, isn't it?" he whispered against her mouth.

"Yes." Her breathing quickened and she moaned when he took his finger away. "Oh, please!"

"Not yet, honey." Jamie licked a trail down her stomach, pausing at the triangle of curls at the apex where her thighs met. He pushed her back so she rested against Dante's torso, and spread her legs a little further as he bent over.

"Jamie!" She cried out as his lips found her clit. He sucked softly, capturing it and tugging until she arched against him. His tongue came out and eased around it, slowly licking everything but her clit itself. He held her thighs apart with his hands, taking his time to tease her with his mouth. Dante was moving slower now, his cock gliding just a few inches in and out as Jamie used his tongue to bring her just to the edge of losing control. Then he would ease back, making her moan in distress.

"Do you want to come, Becca?" he murmured softly.

"Yes! Please." Her fingers were in his hair again, desperate to bring him back to the place that felt so good.

"When you come, Becca, you call out *my* name," he said quietly. "Do you understand?"

She nodded, her breath coming harder and faster as she arched her hips towards his face.

"Arms around my neck," Dante said softly, bringing her arms up so that she clasped her hands behind his head, leaving her breasts jutting out in front of them, round and full.

"So sexy," Jamie breathed, glancing up. Then he slid lower, his fingers opening her wider so he could put his tongue right where she wanted it. She moaned again, so close to ecstasy she was beginning to pant. He moved his tongue away, towards the lips that were stretched around Dante's cock, and Dante jerked as his tongue moved around the base of Dante's shaft, right where their bodies were joined. She felt Dante's cock stiffen even more and they began to move faster.

"Fuck!" Dante grunted.

"Jamie, please!" Dante's thrusts were getting harder and she knew he was on the verge of letting go. Finally, Jamie wrapped his tongue around her clit with just enough pressure to send her into a powerful climax that had her almost frozen with pleasure. She let out a keening scream just as Dante burst inside of her, his fingers digging into her hips as they bucked together, riding out the waves with Jamie's tongue on both of them.

"You didn't say my name when you came," Jamie said after a moment, lifting his head and meeting Becca's gaze.

"I... What?" Becca was still trying to get her breath.

"I told you what you were supposed to do." Jamie sat up, his fingers still lightly trailing along her inner thighs. "And you disobeyed me. You know the rules here, Becca."

"But I—"

"So you have a choice," he continued, still caressing her soft, silky thighs. "Either you let me fuck you, or I put you on the St. Andrew's cross down in the dungeon and you sit on display for the evening."

"What? No!" She blinked at him.

"Those are your choices, honey." He brought his hand up to her breast, a gentle touch that was a stark contrast to his harsh words.

"Dante?" She turned to him, but he didn't say anything, his eyes averted.

"Make your decision," Jamie said quietly. "Or use your safe word and we're done here." His hands were still moving lightly on her breasts, bringing her nipples alive with his thumbs as he waited for her answer.

"Dante!" She tried to turn and face Dante, but Jamie's hands moved to her arms, keeping her looking at him instead.

"He has no say—you didn't do as I instructed, Becca, and there are consequences when you don't obey. Now which is it? Me or the cross?"

"I..." Her voice trailed off and she realized what had happened. She suddenly understood that this had been a test and she'd failed one part of it, but as much as she was enjoying this, her relationship with Dante always came first. "Yellow," she finally whispered.

16

"What is it, love?" Dante's breath was instantly warm against her cheek.

"This is our *life*," she whispered. "I know you said it's okay but what happens…when we go home?"

"What happens here," he said softly, "isn't real—this is fun and games. I love you. The choice you make now is simply a different way for us to have sex—nothing that happens here is cheating. I like to watch. I *want* to watch. You're sexy as hell and he's a good-looking guy—watching him fuck you will get me hard all over again."

"Time's up!" Jamie said abruptly. "What did you decide? Me, the cross, or we call it a night?"

"You," she whispered softly.

"I'm really happy you chose me," he said, a faint smile on his lips. He leaned forward and brushed his lips against hers. "Don't think so much—just feel."

She could only nod, her heart fluttering in her chest at the thought of having sex with another man. What if she couldn't do it? What if she couldn't come for him? The thought nearly made her use the safe word, but she bit her lip to keep from doing so.

Jamie sat up abruptly and reached for her hands, pulling her away from Dante and up against his chest. "So here's the thing—I like it a little rough. I want you to give it a chance, okay? You're here to do something new—I won't do anything you don't like. If it's too much, just say *yellow* and I'll tone it down."

"Promise?" Her eyes were wary, a hint of fear in their depths.

"Promise." He kissed her, gently as if letting her warm up to him again.

He finally pulled away, pausing to push her hair behind her ears. "I'm going to get a condom," he said quietly. "I want you on your knees, face down, that sweet little ass of yours in the air."

Becca hesitated and he motioned with his head. "Now, honey."

She did as he asked and heard him rip open the foil pack. Jamie moved behind her and ran his hands over her soft, round ass. He squeezed some lubricant on his fingers and reached down to spread it between her legs. He ran his finger along her slit and back towards her ass, pressing lightly on the tight rosette between her cheeks. She tried to move, but he held her fast. "Don't," he said quietly. "I know your limits—don't defy me, Becca."

She took a deep, shuddery breath, trying not to panic, and felt Dante's gentle fingers on her cheek. His eyes met hers and he gave her a quick, private wink. She closed her eyes, trusting that he knew what he was doing when he chose Jamie to do this with them.

She felt Jamie's fingers between her cheeks and then something cool and hard sliding into her rectum. She sucked in a breath, clenching her teeth.

"Relax." Jamie's hands were gentle now, stroking her hip. "It's an anal plug—very small and short. There's a sexy red rhinestone on the end, and I like the way it looks between your cheeks when I'm fucking you—okay? Does it hurt?"

She hated anything in her ass, but she'd been wearing one for two months, so she shook her head. "N-no."

"Remember—less thinking, more feeling." His hands were moving from her waist to the small of her back, gently stroking her skin. He didn't do anything else for a little while, simply caressing her as she adjusted to the plug and the feel of his cock resting between the folds of her pussy. Her ass finally slid back, wiggling against his crotch as he continued to touch her. Dante was still stroking her face and hair, watching her intently.

Jamie didn't give her any warning, and he moved his hands to her hips, gripping them tightly before thrusting hard and deep into her. She was wet and took him easily, but surprise made her gasp.

"Jamie..." Her breath came out short and labored, her body tensing against him.

"That's right. Get used to saying my name. There's a new rule this time." He paused, digging the fingers of his right hand into her hair and tugging just enough to make her lift her head. "Are you paying attention, Becca?"

"Yes!"

"You'll call out my name at least three times—twice while I'm fucking you, and then at least once more when you come. Do you understand?"

"Y-yes."

"What's your punishment if you forget?"

"I-I don't know."

"This." He pressed against the anal plug, pushing it just a bit deeper. "Except it will be my cock. So keep that in mind, Becca. You'll call out my name—loud enough for all of us to hear it—or I'll pop your anal cherry. Understood?"

"Yes." Her voice was a breathy whisper as she buried her face in the sheet.

Jamie was thick and hard inside of her, his initial thrust sheathing him right up to his balls. She felt them slapping against her as he took her, fast and deep, his strong hands holding her in place. He wasn't kidding when he said he liked it rough; he was relentless, ramming into her with so much force she couldn't distinguish between the pain when he slammed against her and the pleasure from the way he glided through her. She was so wet she felt arousal dripping down her thigh. A moan of embarrassment escaped her and Jamie slowed slightly.

"Am I hurting you?"

"N-no." She bit her lip. "It's, it's—" her voice failed her as she started to pulse around his thickness.

"It's what?" Jamie wrapped her hair around one fist and tugged. "*What* is it, Becca?"

"It hurts but I'm so wet I feel like I'm going to come!" she cried out when he ground into her again. "Oh! Jamie, please!" She arched her back, pushing back to meet his punishing lovemaking. He was jackhammering into her now, his balls bouncing against her as they moved. He still had her by the hair, pulling harder than she was used to and tears stung her eyelids as he yanked until it burned.

"Like this, Becca?" He was grinding into her, relentless, making her cry out as he punched it in deep.

"Oh fuck!" She let out a cry of disbelief as she came so hard she felt her own juices gush down her leg. "Jamie!" She remembered too late that she'd only used his name once before she came and she whimpered with distress when he abruptly pulled out.

"You did it again," he growled, yanking her up by the waist and hauling her against his chest. "You know what this means, Becca."

She shook her head. "No, I don't think—"

"Shh." Dante was there, his body sandwiching her between them. "You made a deal, *querida*."

"But, but—" Tears filled her eyes.

"Shh." Jamie was quiet and gentle now too, his fingers moving down to press the anal plug deeper into her. "You have a choice again, honey—you can pick which one of us you want to do it; me or Dante."

Her eyes widened, meeting Dante's in confusion.

"I'm bigger," he said softly, raising her chin with his fingers. "My piercing is hard and may hurt you more than it would otherwise."

"You trust him more," Jamie whispered from behind her. "But my cock will be better for your first time. I'm not nearly as thick and it'll be smoother without the piercing."

"I don't know—"

Dante's lips found hers. "This was the deal and you must abide by it, or we leave and never come back. This has nothing to do with whether or not you disappoint me, *querida*. This is nothing but a fantasy—we go home together no matter what you decide. Even if you use your safe word."

"You're going to quit now?" Jamie whispered in her ear, gripping her waist and drawing her closer. "You let me watch you and Dante fuck. You let me eat your pussy. You let me fuck you like a damn punching bag with an anal plug in your ass—*now* you're going to throw in the towel? I promise, Becca—this will be a whole new world for you. If you don't like it, we can stop. Just give me a chance to show you, honey. You're going to come so hard, you're going to be begging Dante to take you in the ass the minute you're alone." His voice was warm and seductive, and despite her resistance to the idea, she knew she was going to let him.

"I let him lick my cock," Dante murmured against her. "I let a man lick my cock so that you could live out your fantasy—I don't do men, but I did it for you."

She sighed heavily; the two men were taunting her senses as they goaded her. Their bodies surrounded her and their rough, sexy voices made her tingle inside and out. She knew she had the final say—her safe word was law and after the last couple of hours she was positive that Jamie would not go beyond her boundaries. If she said no, he would respect it, but the kicker was that she didn't want to. She'd had three epic orgasms already tonight, and she would be lying if she said she didn't want more. She loved having both of them solely focused on pleasuring her; she wasn't ready for this to end, and if that meant allowing something she'd always staunchly refused in the past, she would do it.

"That's it," Jamie's lips were on her neck. "Let me come in your ass, baby, and I promise you will come as many times as you want tonight—any way you want."

She closed her eyes, nodding. "Yes, okay. I want to try."

"My brave girl," Dante nibbled her lips. "I'm so proud of you tonight—trying everything."

"I don't want it to hurt," she said firmly. "I mean it."

"It might hurt a little." Jamie touched her cheek. "But we'll use lots of lube and take our time. If it's too much, we'll do something else. Deal?"

"Yes."

"You're driving me wild," Dante rumbled under his breath, his arms snaking out to snatch her out of Jamie's grasp and yanking her up against him so he could kiss her. His mouth claimed hers roughly, as if demanding what was his and making sure Jamie knew that no matter what she let him do to her, Dante was the man she loved.

"Yeah, yeah, big guy," Jamie pressed himself behind her, his hands sliding around so that one gripped Becca's breast and the other squeezed Dante's ass.

"Jamie." Dante's voice was more of a growl.

"What? This is fucking hot, and don't even try to pretend you don't agree. This has been amazing—and touching you while we're both fucking her? Hell yeah."

Dante didn't say anything, but he didn't move away as Jamie's hand ran down his back. Becca barely noticed because her mouth was still practically fused to Dante's, whimpering softly as Jamie began stroking her clit with his tongue.

"You want to come first, baby?" Jamie was circling the little pearl between her legs, making her moan against Dante's mouth.

"Yes…" She spread her legs, giving Jamie access to pleasure her while Dante kept one hand digging into the hair at the back of her neck and the other fisted Jamie's hair, holding his head against Becca's crotch.

Jamie continued stroking her clit while he slid two fingers into her. She was still wet, evidence of her arousal pooling at her swollen entrance, dripping down her thigh and smearing his face. He lapped it like honey, chuckling against her pussy when she started to grind against him. He expertly fucked her with his tongue, his hands tightening on her ass and holding her still until she exploded around him, this time shrieking his name at the top of her lungs.

"This is going to be intense for you," Dante picked her up and put her on her stomach, pulling her up to her knees. "You have to relax—if you're tense, it's going to hurt. Let him take you, *querida*—give in and you will experience something like never before."

17

Becca nodded, her eyes fluttering closed.

Jamie had crawled up behind her, a fresh condom on his cock. He still hadn't gotten off tonight and she had a feeling he wouldn't last long once he was inside of her, but that was okay because she'd lost track of how many times she'd come tonight and it was only fair to give him some pleasure too.

She tensed as he slowly pulled out the plug and tossed it aside as he poured lube between her cheeks. He rubbed it in and she let out a small cry when he immediately pressed the head of his cock against the tight ring of muscles. She inadvertently clenched, so he couldn't even begin to push inside of her.

"Come on, baby, relax…it's going to hurt this way." He waited for her to let go a little, then pressed against her firmly this time. He rocked against her, pulling her back by the hips and leveraging himself so he could push in a little more.

"Don't stop yet," Dante murmured, his big hands moving over Becca's ass. "I want to see you inside her."

Jamie pressed in further, until Becca whimpered, her fingers clutching the sheet beneath her.

"Becca? You need to tell me if it hurts."

"A little, but it's okay." She was gritting her teeth, though, and she yelped when he started to move. It burned, but the discomfort battled with the intensity that was making her come alive yet again. The sensations were so new and all-encompassing; she wasn't sure she could breathe.

Jamie started to move with tentative strokes and it was more than a little uncomfortable. Becca cried out when he pushed further, sliding in with one smooth thrust that had him hilted.

"Oh, it's too much…please slow down."

"Okay. I'm not moving. Breathe."

She took shaky breaths, her body shuddering from the different sensations. Pleasure. Pain. Arousal. Warmth.

"That's it, baby. I'm all the way in—if you can relax, it'll get better from here, I promise."

"This is the hottest thing I've ever seen." Dante was watching, reclining beside them and stroking his cock erect again.

"I'm going to make this quick," Jamie said softly, holding Becca against him. "Just relax and—" He paused as Dante bent over so he could kiss her.

"I want you too," she breathed against his face.

He hesitated. "Taking both of us at once could be too much the first time. I don't want to hurt you."

"I want to try…" She was breathing hard, trying to adjust to the sensations of her ass being filled by a penis. It was uncomfortable yet her clit was throbbing incessantly, aching with need, her senses screaming for release. She'd never felt so alive—so sexy—as she did right now.

Jamie reached down and gripped Becca around the waist.

"I'm going to turn us," he said softly. He rolled to the side, using the momentum to flip them over backwards. He landed on his back with her on top of him, his cock still firmly sheathed in her ass, her legs splayed open. Dante moved over her, his fingers at her cheek.

"We'll go slow, *querida*. You have to tell me if it's okay."

"Yes." Her eyes closed and she wrapped her arms around his neck. She felt him press against her sore pussy and sighed when he effortlessly slid into her; she was so wet it shouldn't have been a surprise, but she was distracted by the pain.

It hurt like hell at first, two huge cocks inside her, rearranging her insides and making her gasp and buck against them as she tried to adjust. Dante reached down and wrapped her legs around his waist and the change in angle made the pain ease. What followed was like nothing she'd ever felt. They moved together, stroking her in tandem, slow and easy, bringing her a kind of pleasure she hadn't known was possible.

Jamie's lips were on her neck, two fingers sliding between them to softly rub her clit. Dante's lips were caressing hers, one hand in her hair, the other in Jamie's. They were a tangle of hot, sweaty sex and myriad shock waves of pleasure. Fire burned through her and she was lost, crying out for more, begging them to take her harder.

When her orgasm began she had no choice but to let it happen. It was building from deep in her belly, the sensations going from soft and fluttery to intense mindlessness, gripping her so tightly she screamed. Whether it was pain, pleasure or some combination, she didn't know anymore. All she knew was the sheer ecstasy of being fucked by two men. Her cries were raw and guttural; she thrashed against them as the endless waves rocked her into another world entirely.

Jamie came with a growl, and a moment later Dante's shout of release washed over them. It seemed like an eternity that they rode out their mutual orgasms. When they stilled, for at least three or four minutes, no one moved. Finally, Dante rolled to the side so Jamie could pull free. He got up and padded into the bathroom to clean up while Becca collapsed against Dante, her cheek pressed against his chest. His arms closed around her and he brought her up so she could nuzzle his shoulder.

"Tell me this was good," he whispered. "What you wanted."

"Yes." She closed her eyes and breathed in the scent of his aftershave mingled with the smell of sex.

"Becca." His voice was soft as he sought her eyes. "Was he gentle enough with you?"

"Yes. It was amazing." She smiled faintly, content to lie in his arms as she tried to ignore the emotions welling up inside her like a pot of boiling water about to overflow.

"What are you thinking? I can see the wheels turning… Tell me, my love."

"I loved it," she admitted reluctantly. "What does it mean that I really liked being fucked by two men at the same time?"

He smiled, his lips grazing hers. "It means that we're even more compatible than I ever dreamed…that I'm crazy in love with you and that we know exactly how to please each other sexually. It means we're going to have many, many years of pleasure together."

"So you want to do more of this kind of thing?"

"I want what you want. I think you enjoyed this evening's experiment a great deal—why would we reject the idea of doing it again?"

"But Dante—I wasn't kidding. I don't ever want to watch you with a girl. Now that I've done this with a guy, I can't even imagine watching you fuck another girl."

He was quiet for a moment, stroking her hair. "Why do you think that is?" he asked finally. "I watched you get pleasure from Jamie without any jealousy at all—it got me hard seeing how excited you were. You don't think it would turn you on seeing me with another woman, with you joining us?"

She made a face. "No."

"But you don't know because you've never done it."

"The idea of going down on another woman doesn't embarrass me or make me uncomfortable—it makes me want to gag. Totally different feeling than when you talked about anal sex—that scared me a little. This just makes me sick."

"That's how I thought I felt about another man sucking my cock," he said carefully. "Yet I let Jamie…"

"He didn't actually suck it—he just kind of touched it…"

"With his tongue!" Dante grunted. "I thought that would be repulsive to me—but I didn't feel that way when we did it tonight."

Her stomach clenched uncomfortably, dread washing over her. Despite what they'd done tonight, she didn't think she could stand watching him with another woman. Ever. "So you *want* to fuck another woman—which means you lied to me."

"No!" He gripped her jaw between his fingers and forced her to look at him. "Never. I don't want to be with another woman…but I wouldn't be opposed to having another woman with us."

She didn't say anything, looking away.

"Becca?"

"Like you said, there's no way to know for sure without doing it, but I'm not interested. For real. I'm using my safe word now—in advance."

He frowned. "You've trusted me with everything else—why not this?"

"You've told me all along that you didn't care about that," she said, pulling away slightly. "You said this was a one-time thing and we were done! Did you lie?" She felt tears threatening.

"Sweetheart, no." He reached for her, but she'd already slid to the edge of the bed. "Becca!"

"Just stop." She swiped at her face, angry at him for putting her in this position and angry at herself for letting him see how upset she was. "This was all a set-up, wasn't it? This wasn't just a one-time thing—you were testing me to see if I'd be into it."

"Dammit, Becca, no!" Dante swung his legs over the side of the bed and reached for her but she moved away, yanking her panties back on. He muttered under his breath, knowing he was going to have to fix this quickly or there would be irreparable damage to their relationship.

Jamie came out of the bathroom in his slacks, his shirt unbuttoned and his shoes in his hand. He paused, glancing from one to the other. "Oh, hell, did I do something wrong?"

"Did you know this was a set-up?" Becca snapped at him, yanking her skirt on.

"A set-up for…?" He looked at Dante.

"Becca, it's not like that!" Dante snapped back. "I just don't think you should write off anything until you try it. I didn't say I specifically wanted to do it, I only said you can't know that you don't like something you've never tried."

Tugging on her blouse she whirled and glared at him. "If you didn't want to do it, you wouldn't be pushing it on me."

"When did I push it on you?" He threw up his hands. "You brought it up and I said I wouldn't be opposed to having another woman with us! I didn't say we were going to."

"It's the same thing! That's what you always do—you plant the seeds and let me mull them over. Then you bring it up again when the time is right and I give in. Well, I'm not giving in. I told you flat out—I never, ever want to see you fuck another woman. And I don't want to have sex with a woman either!"

"I have no interest in having sex with a man!" he grunted. "But tonight I—"

"Tonight you got caught up in the moment and it was barely any contact!"

"Barely any contact?!" Dante yanked on his jeans. "He licked my fucking cock—that's barely any contact?"

"Well, maybe you're gay!" She stepped into her shoes and took a step just as one foot slid out from under her. She let out a shriek as her other ankle buckled, twisting painfully beneath her when she landed hard on the floor.

"Becca!" Dante and Jamie moved together, reaching her side and kneeling next to her. "Becca, let me see." Dante reached for her foot, straightening her leg at the knee and seeing immediately that the foot was already swelling and turning red. "Sweetheart, you've hurt yourself."

"Just leave me alone." She was trying not to cry but the pain in her ankle was excruciating and she let out an involuntary sob.

"This isn't good, Dante," Jamie said quietly. "We might want to call for the house doctor—"

"No!" Becca shook her head angrily. "I'm fine. Just give me a minute."

"Becca." Dante rested his hand on her cheek. "I'm sorry I've upset you. Honestly, I had no ulterior motives tonight. I'm not interested in a lifetime of threesomes. Yes, I've enjoyed them in the past and I wanted you to experience it because, as you discovered, it's extremely hot—but I want to be with just you forever, have a family... I'm interested in a meaningful relationship, *querida*, not a harem."

She would have smiled but her ankle was throbbing mercilessly and she closed her eyes. "I can't talk about this now, Dante. My ankle really hurts."

"We should get ice." Dante pulled on his shirt before lifting her in his arms and putting her on the bed. "Stay here with Jamie. I'll run down and get some from the bar and we're going to finish this conversation, okay?"

Becca didn't say anything and he leaned down, pressing his forehead to hers. "I love you, Becca. We have to talk about this."

"Okay." She was in too much pain to think and closed her eyes.

18

Becca saw Dante give Jamie a pointed look before slipping out and she wasn't sure why. Jamie sat next to her on the bed, gentle fingers probing her ankle.

"It doesn't look good, Bec," he said. "I think we should call the doctor."

"If I need a doctor, we'll go to an emergency room," she grunted. "There's no way in hell I'd let a doctor here look at me unless I was having a heart attack."

He cocked his head. "What changed while I was in the bathroom? You were fine—we had a good time. You were smiling, cuddling with Dante. What's got you so riled up?"

She looked away, frowning. "This was all about showing me how much fun a threesome is so he can get me to do them with other girls."

"I don't believe that, Becca."

"Why would he have told you?" she demanded. "He obviously knew you like doing this kind of thing; he hit you up to seduce me so that I would be on board for whatever he wants to do next time. And I'm *not* on board."

"Why? Didn't we have fun tonight?"

"I'm not attracted to women."

"I don't think Dante is attracted to men."

"Okay, we're talking in circles and I don't have the strength to argue. I just want to go back to the hotel and put my foot on ice."

Jamie reached out and ran a hand through her hair, stroking it for just a moment before pulling away. "You're an amazing woman, Becca. You're smart and professional, taking on the media nightmare of an entire NHL team and never breaking a sweat. You're beautiful and sexy, so passionate when you make love, it's really breathtaking. You're also a sweet, old-fashioned kind of girl who wants the white picket fence and a couple of babies—it seems to me that you could have it all if you'd just allow it."

"What does that even mean?" she demanded.

He began buttoning his shirt, a smile playing on his lips. "Honey, you protested every step of the way tonight. You didn't want to cheat. You didn't want to have intercourse with me. You absolutely didn't want to do anal. You didn't want any of it…but you didn't follow my instructions either, *knowing* there was going to be a punishment. And you were all in." He paused, meeting her eyes. "*All in*, Becca. You wanted it. You wanted *me*. You know you did. Even though you love Dante, you *wanted* me to fuck you. You really need to think about that. It doesn't mean there's something wrong with you—it just means you enjoy a little bit of kink. It's okay. It's nothing to be ashamed of. Did we do anything you didn't want to do?"

She reluctantly shook her head.

"Then what are you afraid of? We had a great time—I loved every minute of it. Touching you, touching Dante, making you come…it was amazing. What is it that's making you angry? Because that's the real reason you're fighting with Dante. You're angry at yourself and taking it out on him."

She stared at him, her eyes clouded and sad. "I don't know," she whispered.

"You should figure it out because the one thing about this lifestyle that I do like, and I do get into, is how in tune you have to be to a partner's sexual needs." He tucked his shirt into his pants and moved to stand in front of her. He lifted her chin so that she was looking at him. "The reason I can dabble in the BDSM world is because I get it. I don't like all of it, and I'm generally a really mellow guy so all the dominant/submissive stuff can be way too intense for me most of the time. But when I do come play, I'm good at it because I know instinctively what women want. I knew the minute I kissed you that you wanted me and you were going to do whatever I wanted. Dante has the same instincts, which is why he made this happen tonight. He loves you—*only you* —and this was about making your fantasies come true so that you could discover more about your sexuality. He did this for *you*, not for himself. He already knows his own desires; he wanted you to discover your own."

"It doesn't feel like it."

"Now that we're done, you're embarrassed and confused, thinking something is wrong with you, right? You think it's completely wrong you let two guys fuck you at the same time. Right? Look at me, Becca."

She looked up guiltily.

"Do you honestly think Dante is gay?"

"No." She shook her head. "We were having a fight and I said the first thing that came to mind."

"So what's going on?"

"I feel cheap," she admitted. "Like the two of you used me somehow."

"Used you?" He sat beside her and put his arm around her shoulders, pulling her against his chest. "Honey, you could have used your safe word at any time. You could have used our *yellow* code to talk about anything. You could have said no before you ever got here. Dante said coming back here was your idea."

She flushed, tears filling her eyes. "It was! And I don't understand why. Why did I want two guys to fuck me? What's *wrong* with me?!"

"Oh, honey, don't cry." He hugged her tightly. "Look, if I did something that makes you feel bad, I'm sorry. I know you enjoyed it, but I'm genuinely sorry you're feeling regret after the fact."

"I'm angry at myself, not at you." She sniffled, pulling away and looking down at her swollen ankle. "And my ankle really, really hurts."

"Shit." He looked down too, wincing at the ugly bruise that had already begun to form. "When Dante gets back—" He stopped mid-sentence as a loud whistle pierced the silence.

"What was that?" Becca asked in confusion.

"Oh, shit!" Jamie hurriedly got to his feet and slipped on his shoes. He reached for Becca and lifted her, moving her from the bed to the chair and talking as he moved. "Listen to me and don't interrupt. That's a police whistle, which means there's a raid going on. They're going room to room, blowing the whistle and taking people out—"

"Oh my God, what—"

"I said *listen!*" he hissed. "You and Dante were here having a drink and I showed up. We decided to hang out. You don't have to talk about what we did —Dante and I are rich, spoiled athletes who can afford private rooms if we want, you understand?"

Becca nodded numbly.

"You took a bad step, twisted your ankle and Dante went to get ice—that's the only reason we're alone."

She could only nod again.

"Do not tell them anything else and if they try to book you, ask for a lawyer. Don't defend yourself, don't say you weren't doing anything wrong— just ask for a lawyer. Nothing we've done here is illegal—they must be looking for underage kids—so don't play the victim. And more than anything

else, play up the ankle!" He'd barely finished talking when the door flew open
and police burst in, telling them to put their hands up.

The next hour was a blur for Becca. She, Jamie and dozens of others
were rounded up and put in a police bus of some kind. Dante was
nowhere to be found and Jamie kept a gentle arm around her shoulders as they
were taken into the police station. There were people everywhere; chaos,
noise, laughter, yelling. Jamie had carried her off the bus and into the station
and someone had been nice enough to get her an ice pack. He held it on her
foot as they waited for the police to go through all the personal items that had
been collected and check IDs.

As they waited, she ruminated over the evening, an uneasy feeling
spreading through her. Replaying everything they'd done in her mind, she felt
humiliation creeping through her gut, making her want to crawl under a bed
and die of embarrassment. Both of them at once, inside her, pulling her hair,
making her scream and beg them for more.

Who did that? What kind of woman was she that she let two men fuck her,
not just at the same time, but taking both their cocks as though that was
perfectly acceptable in polite society? She'd never imagined doing something
so kinky, so incredibly wrong. And Dante had taken her there, exposed her to
something that was so far out of her comfort level she couldn't fathom
looking at either of them ever again.

Then they got hauled away by the police like criminals. She had no doubt
this would be in the news and even if they didn't recognize her, Jamie's name
and face would be front and center. With her standing right next to him, his
arm around her. *Fuck.* She was completely screwed and she had no way to get
out of this.

There was movement at the doors and Becca felt like the world was
starting to implode around her. "Oh, no," she whispered miserably.

"What is it?" Jamie leaned over.

"That's Benton Krauss—he used to be a sports writer and then he moved
up to the news desk. Shit. He knows me."

"We didn't do anything wrong," he reminded her. "It's okay."

"Excuse me." A man in an expensive suit and a booming voice spoke.
"I'm Philip Marchand. I represent Mr. Teller and Ms. Hernandez. Are they
being charged? If not, I demand their belongings be returned immediately or
I'll have to—"

"Yeah, yeah, hold your horses." A harried desk sergeant rolled his eyes.

"Teller…Hernandez…yeah, they checked out. They just need to sign for their stuff."

Jamie got up and slid an arm around Becca's waist as she limped to the counter.

"Were you hurt by the police?" Mr. Marchand's eyes narrowed.

Becca shook her head. "I'd twisted my ankle before they busted in—who are you, exactly?"

"Mr. Lamonte called me as soon as he heard you'd been brought in."

Becca opened her mouth but before she could say anything Benton Krauss approached them. "Becca, is that you?"

She turned, pasting on a fake smile. "Hey, Benton. How are you?"

"What are you doing here?" he asked, glancing around.

"I was at a club with some friends. I guess they got raided."

"Club Inferno?" He flashed her a smarmy grin. "*You* were at Club Inferno?"

Her eyes narrowed. "I'm not sure how that's any of your business."

"You and Teller were at Club Inferno together? I thought you were dating Dante Lamonte—" He paused. "Holy shit, were you cheating on him with this guy?!" He burst out laughing.

Becca rolled her eyes. "Dante was with us, dumbass! I twisted my ankle dancing and Dante went to go get me some ice. The raid happened like two minutes after he left and Jamie stayed with me because I couldn't walk."

"Interesting." Benton gave her a smirk. "I'll be seeing you around, Becca. Hope you feel better!" He sauntered off just as the sergeant gave her back her purse and ID.

"There's a car outside," Mr. Marchand said. "Let's get out of here."

They headed for the exit and the moment they stepped outside dozens of flashbulbs went off. Becca held up her hands instinctively, turning her head at the onslaught of bright lights. Jamie slid an arm around her, pulling her closer to him as the attorney ushered them into the waiting limousine. Becca covered her face with her hands.

"Fuck!" she hissed under her breath.

"Everything will be fine," Mr. Marchand spoke quietly, typing something into his phone. "The seventeen-year-old daughter of a state senator was at the club and someone tweeted a picture of her on a St. Andrew's cross. Her father saw it and called in a bunch of favors. He wants the place closed down, but that has nothing to do with either of you. You weren't doing anything wrong and you're both of age. This is a non-issue."

"Except for the part where I was seen coming out of a police station with the man I was arrested with—a man who isn't my boyfriend, by the way!"

"Mr. Lamonte is aware of the circumstances tonight."

"Mr. Lamonte isn't my fucking boss!" Becca groaned. "And he—" she jerked a thumb at Jamie, "—works with me. I'm not allowed to date him! Fuck, fuck, fuck! My face is going to be everywhere tomorrow."

"Becca, we can tell them the truth," Jamie said quietly. "You and Dante were there, you ran into me, you twisted your ankle, and when he went to get ice, the place got raided. I was holding on to you so you wouldn't fall. We didn't do anything wrong."

"By the time the media gets through with me—it won't matter what I say," she sighed. "Don't forget—this is what I do for a living. I know how this is going to spin and I'm going to look like a fucking bimbo."

"Dante can make this go away," Jamie said softly.

"If it gets into the papers, it'll be too late," she said quietly. "When Pierre sees this, I'm going to lose my job."

"That's ridiculous!" Jamie protested. "Why would he fire you? For being out dancing with me? So what if it was a sex club—we were fully dressed when they found us and Dante was there too! And frankly, just because it's frowned upon for you to date one of the players, that doesn't mean you absolutely can't. What would they say if you and I announced we're a couple?" He made a face. "They can't say anything."

She just shook her head. "Mr. Marchand, where is Dante?"

"Waiting for you at your hotel," he replied.

"Will you drop me off, please?"

"Of course." He turned to Jamie. "Where are you staying, Mr. Teller?"

Jamie gave him the name of his hotel but kept his eyes on Becca; she was even more upset than she'd been before the raid and he didn't know if she had a right to be or not. They hadn't done anything wrong, but she was right about the media; they could spin this any way they wanted and she could wind up looking bad professionally. The timing was particularly unfortunate, after the fight she'd had with Dante and knowing how conflicted she was. He hoped Dante was going to be able to get through to her because the look on her face was one of defeat.

19

Becca was even more furious by the time she got to Dante's hotel room. She was stiff, limping, but when he walked towards her she held up her hand, stopping him. She limped to the couch and sat down, putting her swollen foot on the coffee table.

"*Querida*, what happened?" He tried to lean over for a kiss, but she turned her face.

"*What happened?*" She turned sad, lifeless eyes to him. "The club got raided and Jamie and I went to jail. Where the fuck were *you*?" Her words were angry but her voice held no emotion whatsoever.

"I went into the kitchen to get a plastic bag for the ice and when the raid started, one of the managers grabbed me and a couple of the cooks and took us out the back. I had no ID, no wallet, nothing. I tried to get back in, told them I'd been there and needed my ID, but the police wouldn't allow it. It took me nearly three hours to get my phone and wallet, and I'd already sent a lawyer for you."

"Thanks for that, at least." She struggled to her feet and made her way into the bedroom. She went to the closet and started pulling out her clothes.

"What are you doing?" he asked quietly, watching her.

"Packing. I made a reservation on the seven o'clock flight home."

"Why?"

"Because I need to start damage control."

"For what? You didn't do anything wrong."

"Did you miss the part where reporters got pictures of me and Jamie coming out of the fucking police station?!" She threw up her hands and looked down at her chest. "Look at me! I'm in a fucking halter top and a skirt so short you can see my ass. I look like a twenty-dollar hooker who got arrested with one of the players on the team I work for! What part of this doesn't seem like a problem to you?!" She threw the stack of clothes in her hand into her suitcase in a huff.

"Becca, I understand it's been a stressful evening and—"

"Stressful for whom?" she snapped, glaring at him. "You didn't get hauled out of there like a common criminal—I did! You weren't sitting at the fucking police station for three fucking hours—I was! No one took your picture for the papers—they took mine." She threw the rest of her things in the suitcase and then stomped into the bathroom.

Shaking with anger and frustration, she leaned against the sink and took a few deep, steadying breaths. She pulled her hair into a ponytail and yanked off her clothes, grateful for the robe hanging behind the door. She washed her face, brushed her teeth and finally used the bathroom. Her ankle was on fire, her stomach was churning and she felt like she was going to throw up. Coming to New York had definitely been the worst idea she'd ever had.

"Becca?" Dante's deep voice came through the door as he knocked. "Can I come in, please?"

"I'll be out in a minute." She wiped her face and reached for one of the hand towels on the counter. She needed more ice for her foot and the towel would keep her skin from getting too cold. With a deep breath, she opened the door and stepped back into the bedroom. "Would you get me some ice, please?"

He nodded. "I already got some." He took the towel from her and went into the other room. He was back a moment later, a plastic bag of ice in one hand, the towel in the other.

Becca got on the bed and he put two large pillows under her foot, elevating it, and then wrapped the towel and ice around it.

"Thanks." She leaned back, staring off into space.

"Becca, I'm sorry I wasn't with you when this happened."

"I know."

"I'm also sorry we fought," he said quietly, rubbing his hand over his head. "It's been a long night. Why don't we get some sleep and when we get up—"

"I have to leave for the airport in an hour or so," she interrupted. "I'm just icing my foot until I have to go."

"Becca, seriously, this isn't going to be a big deal. Let's get some sleep and tomorrow I'll take care of everything. You're upset and staying up all night to—"

"Dante, I need to go home. This trip has been a disaster and I'm exhausted. Can we please not fight anymore?"

"Fine. I'll come too. We can get a flight together a little later in the day."

"You have to be on the road the day after tomorrow; you can't come to Vegas."

He paused, meeting her eyes curiously. "It almost sounds as if you don't want me to go home with you."

"It doesn't really matter at this point, does it?" She leaned over to adjust the ice on her foot. She had no idea how she was going to walk through the airport with her foot like this.

"Why is that?"

"You have to think about baseball and I have to go home and deal with whatever shit storm is about to take over my life."

"We have the whole day to be together before I have to go," he said. "Why are we ending our trip early? If there's any fallout from what happened tonight, it's better for us to be together."

"No, I don't think it is." She stared down at her lap, toying with the belt of the robe. "You handle things by doing something else even more obnoxious or outrageous to make people forget about the original thing. That's not how it works for me, Dante. If this gets blown out of proportion, I have to figure out how I'm going to save my job."

"Why would you lose your job?" he asked quietly. "I'm not sure I understand exactly what the problem is. What are you worried about? Someone finding out you were with Jamie last night? Big deal. We'll tell them we were there together and—"

She held up a hand. "I already know what to say! Jamie and I went over the cover story—no one will ever know I let both of you—" She stopped abruptly, shaking her head. "Never mind." She slid her legs over the side of the bed. "I have to start getting ready."

"Becca." His voice was low, gritty, and he stood in front of her. "What the fuck is going on with you? Talk to me."

"I've never been to jail before," she said, looking up at him. "I was humiliated and terrified. My *boyfriend*, the man I love, wasn't with me. Instead, the guy he asked to have sex with us tonight was. Not only that, we got caught on camera leaving the police station with a very expensive lawyer. Innocent people don't get fancy lawyers, Dante—people who are up to something do. The press was everywhere, and people recognized me. I promise you, a few hours from now, there is going to be some torrid headline about Jamie and me and I need to get in front of it. I know that you don't care what people think of you, but I care what they think of me. Now please let me finish packing so I can get out of here."

He stared at her, his eyes hard and inscrutable. "So what you're saying is that you're embarrassed and humiliated that you allowed yourself to be used like a cheap little tramp by two men tonight, so you're going to cover those feelings by walking away from the man who loves you and weather a potential media shit storm on your own. Am I in the ballpark?"

She looked into his face and shrugged. "I don't know how those two things are related. I'm doing the responsible thing by getting in front of this. If you like, I can keep your name out of it."

"No, I don't fucking like!" he snapped, grabbing her by the shoulders. "Becca, why are you doing this, pulling away from me? Is this because we had a threesome? Is that why you're angry? You wanted it—I know you did! Jesus Christ, Becca, if you got cold feet why didn't you use your safe word?"

She shook her head back and forth, willing herself not to cry. "You wanted me to want it and I wanted to make you happy! I'm in love with you and I want you to love me too, so I was willing to go along with almost anything… but now I realize I can't! That's not who I am—and that's not the life I want. I don't want to sleep with different people! I don't want to have threesomes and, and, do that stuff and—" Tears were spilling down her face, and Dante pulled her into his arms.

"Why would you think that?" he whispered in her hair. "I *already* love you —I don't care about that other stuff."

"But you do," she whispered, pulling back slightly so she could look into his face. "I know you wanted me to sleep with him—that was the plan all along—and I did it because, in the heat of the moment, of course it felt good and was fun… but in the light of day, I can't. I can't wake up every day not knowing who I'm going to have sex with or who I'm going to watch *you* have sex with. I can't, Dante. I'm sorry. I love you—more than anything—but the humiliation I feel isn't going to be fixed by talking. You have the right to be who you are, but I have the right to be who I am too. I'm just a simple girl… too simple for a guy like you." She touched his face and then gently extracted herself from his arms.

Pulling clean clothes out of her suitcase, she went into the bathroom to get dressed. She looked terrible, but she would shower and clean up once she got home. Right now, she wanted to get as far away from New York as possible.

Dante said nothing as Becca got dressed, packed up the last of her things and prepared to leave. He sat on the edge of the bed and watched her, his heart constricting painfully in his chest as he replayed her words over and over in his head. *You wanted me to want it and I wanted to make you happy.* He didn't know what had happened to make things go so far south tonight, but he knew it had nothing to do with kinky sex and having a threesome. Somehow their big anniversary celebration had gone horribly wrong and she was leaving.

Hell, she wasn't just leaving New York; she was leaving him. She hadn't said the words, but he could see the look in her eyes and knew that dominating her into staying wouldn't work this time. She'd completely shut him out; his Becca, the woman he loved, wasn't even here right now. This woman, the version of Becca who was now wearing a huge protective suit of armor around her heart, was going to take the Becca he loved and hide her away.

"Could you call a bellman for me?" she asked.

"I'll carry your bag," he said, getting up.

"No." She put a hand on his shoulder. "It's best if we're not seen together. Please just call someone for me."

He wanted to say no, but he simply nodded and made the call. "Five minutes," he said.

"Thank you."

"Becca, please don't leave." He needed to try one more time. "Can't we try to work this out?"

"It's too easy for you to talk me into things and I really have to go."

"Why are you so distant?" He brushed his fingers across her cheek. "Despite what happened tonight, you have to know I love you."

"You told me once that you weren't capable of love," she said sadly. "And while I don't think that's completely true, it's probably more true than I realized. You have a whole different set of rules—in love, in life, in everything. When Trey and the baby died, you went through a vulnerable time, opening yourself up more, so I thought maybe it would be okay. But now I know that you're still not a guy who wants anything as simple as the basics—love, trust, marriage. That's just not you."

Her words coursed through him like ice water, spreading a kind of desolation within his soul that he hadn't felt since the night they'd told him Trey and his unborn child were dead. He'd never felt pain like that before, and though it wasn't as acute now, it was still agonizing enough to make him lose his breath. She didn't think he was capable of love; he'd wanted to believe he was, but Becca had just confirmed everything he'd thought about himself. His failings as a human being were too numerous to count, but failing to love

Becca the way she deserved would be his most significant disappointment to date.

"Thank you for taking me under your wing last year," she whispered, her voice suddenly thick with emotion. "For bringing me out of my shell and showing me I wasn't broken as a woman. I'll always love you for that—" Her voice caught and she put her fingers to her lips before gently pressing them to his. His hand came up to capture them, holding them against his mouth, his eyes meeting hers with an intensity she'd never seen before.

"It is I who should be thanking you, *querida*," he whispered back. "For months of helping me feel human—the only time I've ever felt that way."

"Take care, Dante." She pulled her hand away reluctantly as the knock came on the door.

Then she turned and walked out of his life.

20

BECCA DOZED ON THE FLIGHT, JERKING IN AND OUT OF CONSCIOUSNESS AS dark thoughts kept her from truly relaxing. The events of the previous evening weighed heavily on her heart and walking away from Dante was almost more than she could stand. If it wasn't for the sharp pain in her ankle she might have fallen apart; instead, she alternated between sleeping a little and icing her foot. By the time she landed in Las Vegas, it was swollen beyond recognition and she called her doctor before she even got to baggage claim. She took a cab home so she could get her car and then headed straight for the doctor's office. By the time they took X-rays and the doctor looked at her, they determined it was a bad sprain and recommended she stay off it for a few days.

That wasn't an option, she thought warily, limping out to her car and going home. She showered, put on clean clothes and a little makeup and headed to the arena. Her phone beeped, indicating she'd missed a call and she saw her mother's name on the screen. Crap. If the shit had hit the fan, her mother probably knew all about it and there would be no way to avoid her. Hoping for the best, she called her back.

"Becca!" Donna's voice was panicked. "Are you okay? What happened last night? Were you arrested?!"

"Everything is fine. I was at a club that got raided because apparently some senator's seventeen-year-old daughter was there, but obviously I'm not underage so there weren't any charges or anything. I'm home and on my way to work."

"You're home?" Donna was confused now. "Aren't you and Dante on vacation to celebrate your anniversary?"

Becca sighed. "Mom, Dante and I broke up."

"What?! What are you talking about? What happened?"

"It's a really long story and I can't talk about it right now. I've got to go in to the office and make sure my face isn't plastered all over the media."

"The picture of you and Jamie coming out of the police station is already out there," Donna said quietly. "How do you think I found out?"

"How bad?" Becca was almost afraid to ask, but she knew her mother would be frank.

"Well, to be honest, you look rode hard and put away wet. It's not flattering, but the story isn't bad. It mentions that you were allegedly at Club Inferno when it was raided, but that no charges were filed and that you and Jamie work together. There was speculation about Dante, hinting that you were cheating, but we know that's not true."

"No, of course not." Becca swallowed. Did letting another guy fuck her count as cheating if it was Dante's idea? That probably wasn't a question she should ask her mother.

"Honey, I know you think I'm old, but I know what kind of place Club Inferno is and you told me that's how you two met. Was Jamie there with you?"

"Mom, I'm already humiliated enough. I don't think I can talk to you about this."

"Who are you going to talk to about it? You don't have any close girlfriends except Kate, and she's going to be torn between you and Dante. Who else can you trust but me?"

"Mom, it was…" Her voice trailed off. "I can't even tell you how ashamed I am of the things we did."

"Why?"

"*Why?!*" Becca had to take a breath. "Mom, I was with Dante and Jamie. *Together.* At the same time."

"Really?" Donna's voice dropped a few octaves. "How hot was that?"

Becca nearly missed the turn into the arena. "What do you mean?! Aren't you horrified?"

"Why would I be? I can't even imagine what it would be like to be with two guys like Dante and Jamie—you must've come about a thousand times! I'm envious."

Becca groaned. "Seriously, Mom? Do you not understand the ramifications?"

"Of having a threesome? No, I don't. You're all adults. What's the big deal?"

"I can't, it's just, look, I'm at the arena. I have to talk to Pierre and make sure I don't have to do damage control for Jamie."

"You didn't do anything wrong," Donna said firmly. "I'm serious, Becca—don't do this to yourself. I don't know how a child of mine is so uptight, but we'll have to talk about this later."

Becca stared at the phone in disbelief before stuffing it in her purse. It was going to be a long day.

P ierre was in his office when she knocked on the door and he motioned for her to come in. She squared her shoulders and stepped in, hoping he wasn't going to fire her on the spot. She hadn't spent much time perusing the headlines, but while it was embarrassing, it wasn't illegal or even immoral. Being with one of the players on the team would take some explaining, but hopefully Pierre would believe the story they'd come up with.

"Hi." She spoke as bravely as she could, though her voice was subdued.

"Hi, honey." Pierre looked up and took off his glasses. "Have a seat, kiddo. How's the ankle?"

"It's sprained, but I'll be okay."

"You should be at home." He paused. "You should be in *New York*."

"After what happened?" She stared at him. "I have to make sure none of this blows back on the team."

"Why would it?" He cocked his head. "You weren't arrested and you weren't doing anything illegal. I know you're not dating Jamie, even though those pictures tell a slightly different story. I spoke to him earlier and he explained everything, so I'm not even sure why you're here. It's not illegal for Jamie to be at a club—he's an adult and he was with another adult."

She met his gaze. "You know what kind of place that is."

"It's a night club. They can speculate that it's the most exclusive sex club in the country, but that part of the club is private. The only details that were released were about the senator's daughter, and that has nothing to do with you or Jamie. Now go home and put your foot up."

She blinked. "Um, thank you, but don't you think I should make sure—"

"Becca, it's the off-season and we just won a championship. No one is going to think twice about Jamie partying, *legally*, at a night club, with a woman he works with. It could have been problematic for you and Dante, but Jamie said Dante was there with you and the only reason he wasn't taken into custody was because he was getting you ice. Wasn't that the truth?"

"Yes, of course," she spoke hurriedly. "I just thought..." she sighed.

Pierre frowned. "Becca, what's going on? You look like hell, if you'll pardon my saying so. Your foot is as big as a balloon and you look like you're ready to jump out of your skin. Did something happen?"

"Not like you think." She had to pray that her mother didn't tell him *everything*; she'd kill her if she did.

"But?"

"I was really angry with Dante. I know he went to get ice, but he left me there with Jamie and we got *hauled off* while he was outside. We didn't do anything wrong, but he left me there!" She felt tears threatening and she turned away.

"Oh, sweetheart." Pierre got up and moved around the desk, reaching out to hug her tightly. "Becca, it was bad luck, bad timing—but you can't believe he did that on purpose. How could he have known? And he left you with Jamie—someone who's a friend. Jamie took care of you, didn't he? He didn't let anyone at that place hurt you?"

"No." She shook her head, tears pouring down her face as she sobbed in his chest. It had been years since she'd had a father figure in her life, and now she just broke down, suddenly not caring about her job or her reputation or anything else. It hadn't occurred to her that she missed her father, but in that moment she realized she did. More than anything. It had been her and her mom for nearly fifteen years, neither of them ever seriously involved with a man until now.

"It's okay, honey," Pierre rubbed her back gently, stroking her hair with his other hand. "I don't know what happened in New York, but if you need to talk about it, I'm here."

"No one is ever there to take care of me," she whispered. "It's always me taking care of everyone else... Why doesn't anyone want to take care of *me*?"

"Oh, Becca." Pierre held her tightly. "I don't have a daughter, sweetie, and I'm really excited about becoming your stepdad. Maybe I could take care of you a little bit, since you don't have a father anymore. If you want me to."

"I don't even remember what it's like having a dad," she choked out. "It's like I've been an adult since the day he left."

"I know." He let her cry, without asking any questions.

"I'm sorry," she said after a while, reaching for a tissue on his desk. She wiped her eyes and sank into the nearest chair, exhausted and embarrassed.

Pierre perched on the edge of his desk and watched as she struggled to come to terms with whatever she was dealing with. "You know, in my experience, sometimes you have to have faith."

She looked up wearily. "In what?"

"That whatever it is you're dealing with will work out."

"I'm not sure this is something Dante and I can work out," she admitted softly.

"Is he the reason you went to that club? Your mom told me it was an anniversary of sorts—that's where you met?"

She sighed. "We met there a year ago yesterday. I'd gone there because it had been so long since I'd been on a date, I thought I could pay someone to sleep with me." She flushed. "I mean, I had a guest pass and thought, what the hell, it's not like I meet men at home. So I went and he was at the bar. It was just a one-night stand, obviously, but we both felt something. It was special—it was more than sex. He had all that craziness with his fiancée, though, so we went our separate ways. Then we ran into each other at Christmas and you know what happened after that."

"So you went back to the club for what? Just to be at the place where you met? Or something else…?" His blue eyes held no censure and she looked away.

"Both. A little bit of a walk on the wild side and to celebrate where we met. Then Jamie showed up and I hurt my ankle and…" She bit her lip. "Now it feels wrong, like we did something dirty."

"Did you want to do it?" he asked carefully.

"Yes!" she nodded miserably. "It wasn't until we were sitting in the police station that I felt cheap and stupid."

"Why would you feel that way? You went there with a man who loves you and I believe you love him as well. Whatever you did was consensual—even if you did it up on stage in front of the whole club. Everyone that goes there is into their own thing—you're entitled to have sex in whatever way you enjoy. Other than that, it's not Dante's fault the club was raided."

"I was just so fucking scared and it was hours before he sent the attorney for us…it was like I was abandoned. *Again.*"

"I'm sure your mother has told you this, but it's not your fault your dad left either," Pierre said quietly. "He made his decision because he was an asshole, not because of anything you or your mom did."

"I know that in my head, but my heart will always wonder."

"Dante isn't your dad. He's a good man, and he loves you."

She looked down, wishing she could tell him the rest of the story.

"Did you break up with him?"

"Kind of." She let out a breath. "And now it's like I'm empty inside—as though being without him leaves me with nothing but a remnant of who I was."

"Yet I get the feeling you're not planning to call him."

She looked down. "We broke something… I don't know if we can fix it."

"Because you went to a sex club and I'm assuming did something…kinky?"

"Yes."

"You went willingly, enjoyed yourself and neither of you were hurt?"

"Yes. It's just me second-guessing myself. And him."

"Go home, sweetheart. Get a really good night's sleep. Wake up tomorrow and do something nice for yourself—a massage or a pedicure or whatever it is you women like. Then call him. Seriously. Take twenty-four hours to come down from the insanity...a big anniversary, kinky sex, going to jail, flying across the country, thinking you might lose your job—it would be a lot for anyone. When you've taken a little time to think, call him and talk. I think you're making a mistake leaving him, Becca. He's a little rough around the edges, but he loves you."

She nodded as she grabbed her purse. "Okay. I'm going home."

"Don't come in tomorrow. Rest. Recuperate. Unwind. If someone on the team gets arrested, I'll call you. Otherwise, stay home."

"Thanks." She smiled faintly. "And thank you for listening—really."

He winked. "Any time."

21

Becca got home and stripped, running a hot bath with Epsom salts. She poured a glass of wine and then sat in the tub, her eyes closed. She just wanted to think. Her body was sore, her heart ached and her mind was a jumble of confused thoughts and painful realizations. Nothing made sense to her right now and she had no one to talk to.

She was too embarrassed to talk to her mother, Kate was too close to Dante to confide in her about him, and other than Dante there was no one else she was close to. What did that say about her? In addition to apparently being sexually deviant, she was so weird she didn't have any friends. That depressed her the most.

Her phone buzzed and she glanced at it. *Dante*. Her gut instinct was to refuse the call, but she knew that he was probably worried. If she didn't answer, chances were he would send Kate to check on her and she didn't want that either.

"Hi." She tried to sound normal when she answered.

"I wanted to make sure you were okay," he said quickly, clearing his throat. "And that you had someone look at your ankle."

"Yes, I'm home and I saw the doctor. He said it's badly sprained but not broken. I'm probably taking tomorrow off. Pierre told me not to come in."

"So everything is okay…at work?"

"Yes."

There was an uncomfortable silence and finally he spoke. "Okay, then, I guess I'll let you go, but I want you to know I'm sorry, Becca."

"I'm sorry too," she admitted. "It wasn't your fault the club was raided—I shouldn't have been angry with you about that."

"And the rest?" he asked mildly.

"I'm not mad, just sad and heartbroken."

"The last thing in the world I wanted was to hurt you, *querida*."

"I know." She took a breath. "Dante?"

"Yes?"

"Can we take a day or two to just think and be apart, but not be apart?"

"What?" He sounded startled.

"I love you," she whispered. "I'm having a really hard time with what happened last night, but I love you so much I ache when I think about never seeing you again."

"As do I." His voice was a whisper too.

"So can we? Take a few days to let me get everything that happened straight in my head?"

"Of course. Whatever you want."

"Dante?"

"Yes, love?"

"I shouldn't have said what I said, about you not being capable of love. That was wrong. I know you love me."

"Do you?"

"I do. I don't know if we can fix this—what I'm feeling is overwhelming —but it's not because you don't love me. That wasn't fair."

"We have to talk about things…many things."

"I know, but you're on the road…"

"I'll be on the road for the rest of the week, but then I'll be home before the All-Star break."

"I could come," she said carefully. "If you wanted me."

"Of course I want you," he said. "I've always wanted you to be here with me, Becca."

"So a few days apart and then I'll come to New York…okay?"

"Of course."

"Dante?"

He smiled to himself at the soft way she kept saying his name. "Yes, *querida*?"

"Do you really love me?"

"More than anything."

"Will you say it?"

He hesitated and then his words warmed her soul. "I love you, Rebecca

Hernandez. Even if I don't always know how to show you properly, my heart belongs only to you. And nothing will ever change that."

She smiled to herself.

"I love you, too. And I'll see you soon. I promise." She ended the call and leaned back in the tub. She had so much to think about.

Becca was getting a bag of ice when her phone buzzed. She saw Jamie's name and grimaced as she answered. "Hey, Jamie."

"Hey."

"What's up?"

"I wanted to make sure you're okay."

"Why?"

"Because I talked to Dante and he said you'd gone home. He also told me you two broke up and I kind of feel responsible."

"No." She sat on the couch and stretched out her foot, laying the ice pack on it. "I just needed to get away and be alone for a bit. I also needed to be here in case the story got out of control. It's easier for me to run interference from here."

"Becca, I'm not trying to meddle in your relationship, but I need you to know a few things."

"Okay."

"The three of us took a walk on the wild side, but it doesn't define us or change anything. For me it was one time, with two specific people that I like very much. I also couldn't cross the line I crossed with some random guy."

"What are you trying to tell me?" she asked in confusion.

He sighed. "We did what we did because it was the three of us, specifically, not just because what we did could potentially feel good with anyone."

"Wouldn't it?" she countered.

"I wouldn't be comfortable enough to do that with many other guys." Jamie suddenly sounded thoughtful. "I think sometimes there are specific situations, specific people, that just click. Dante asked me to join you guys because he trusts me, but we didn't know it would get as wild as it did. We didn't think you'd be down for half of that stuff, and he told me not to force anal because you'd never done it."

"He's been trying to talk me into it for months!" she protested. "That's why I'd been wearing a plug."

"He didn't tell me that, Becca. He said I could try anything I wanted except hitting you—spanking is my thing, by the way, but he said under no circumstances was I to hit you beyond a smack on the ass—and if you used your *red* safe word I had to stop. No matter what it was."

"So he didn't plan for…the stuff we did?"

"No. The only thing he planned was me being there. The plan was to let you experience as much of a threesome as you were comfortable with. Becca, when I told you last night it was about you, I was telling the truth. We went way beyond anything he and I talked about…we followed your cues, honey. He wanted you to live out a fantasy—you weren't supposed to get upset."

"Did you and Rachel ever have a threesome?" she asked, referring to his ex-girlfriend.

"No. We did a lot of other shit, though—she let me spank her and not just a few love taps—but we're both into that kind of thing. It's not for everyone, though."

"Oh, no, not me," Becca said with distaste.

"Exactly. Yet that worked for us. I like it rough—in more ways than one— but I don't want to hurt anyone. Not physically or emotionally. I knew how much Rachel could take and that's where we stayed. Threesomes were almost impossible for her because of how famous she is and the fear of a third party talking about it, so our kink was private."

"And you were completely faithful, only in love with her?"

"I was going to ask her to marry me. We broke up because of the steroid scandal and that shit going on with Marco—it had nothing to do with our sex life…so don't let what we did screw up what you have with Dante. He knows you're upset and wants to fix it but you're shutting him out."

"He can't fix what I'm feeling…the embarrassment and—"

"Why are you embarrassed? Out of everything, why that? In a way, you feeling embarrassed means that I did something wrong too, and dammit, I didn't. You wanted me. Both of us. Yes, we coaxed you, but there was no resistance, you didn't even use the *yellow* code! I wish you would explain what's really going on."

She was silent, gripping the phone tightly in her hand as she stared at the muted television. She didn't want him to feel bad because he was right; she'd been okay with it. In the heat of the moment, she'd wanted it, all of it, and she'd enjoyed every damn minute of it. Her orgasms had been the hardest, most intense she'd ever had, and the excitement of being with both of them had been erotic and sexy. She'd *felt* truly sexy, knowing that two amazing men both wanted her.

"Becca?"

"I'm here. I'm sorry. I don't want you to feel bad. I just…" she sighed. "I've never been sexy. I'm cute, pretty, smart, successful—lots of great adjectives have been used to describe me, but never sexy. And that night I felt sexy. Except it took something completely out of my comfort zone to feel that way. Why can't making love in boring old missionary position make me feel sexy? I'm sorry, I know that's too much information, but you asked."

"I did, and that's ridiculous. You are sexy—everyone's idea of sexy is different. Rachel is a movie star but there are still men who don't think she's sexy. Everyone has a type. Dante thinks you're sexy; hell, I think you're sexy too."

"But you didn't before you slept with me."

He frowned. "No, I did, but you were off-limits because you work for the team. It was an I-can-look-but-can't-touch thing, and I had a girlfriend, so I didn't give it a second thought. Look, I'm getting on a plane, but I want to know we're okay—you're okay."

"You and I are fine. I had fun and you didn't do anything wrong. This is all in my head, and I'm the only one who can sort it out."

"Be who you are, Becca. Rachel likes to be spanked. Dante has a pierced penis. I know a certain Swedish goaltender who's into bondage big-time. I like it rough. We're all regular, normal people who happen to like their sex to be something other than vanilla. It's okay. Really."

"Thanks, Jamie."

"I'll talk to you soon, honey." He disconnected.

22

BECCA STARED AT THE TV FOR A LONG TIME, UNTIL THE ICE ON HER FOOT melted and she fell into a restless sleep. She had dreams about Club Inferno, envisioning herself on the St. Andrew's cross, begging Dante to let her go. In the dream she was wearing nothing but a black leather bikini and those high, black spiked heels Dante loved.

He was laughing at her, calling her names, telling her she was perverted, deviant, fucked up. She woke with a start, realizing it was morning and the sun was shining. Her neck hurt from sleeping without a pillow and her foot was throbbing again. She sat up with a sigh, gingerly moving her foot and wincing. Time for coffee, breakfast and Tylenol.

She'd just turned on the coffee maker when she heard a key in the lock and her mother's voice. "Are you up, Becca?"

"In the kitchen, Mom!"

"Hi, honey!" Donna came in with a bright smile on her face and a bakery box in her hands. "I picked up some Danishes from the bakery that you like and thought we could have breakfast. Pierre told me you were taking today off."

"Oh, it smells great. Thanks." Becca finished making the coffee as her mother chattered about a trip she and Pierre were planning.

"Becca, you haven't heard a word I said," Donna chuckled, putting down her coffee cup. "Talk to me, sweetheart. I know something happened in New York beyond the raid."

"It's not easy to talk about, and honestly, I can't talk to you about kinky sex."

"Why not?" Donna blinked her big blue eyes and cocked her head. "You're almost thirty years old. I know you're not a virgin, and I wouldn't want you to be at this age. What are you going to tell me that would change anything? I don't care if you're a lesbian or bisexual or like to be paddled with a hockey stick! I might worry a little if you were into farm animals, but—"

Becca started laughing. "Stop it. No farm animals or hockey sticks! Geez."

"But there is something you think you can't tell me about? Like your threesome at Club Inferno."

Becca flushed. "Mom, it's really embarrassing."

"Okay, don't talk, listen." Donna got up and made another cup of coffee. "Back when your dad and I got together, we were kids. I mean, we met in middle school, and I never slept with anyone else. When he left, I was completely unprepared to date. I went out with a few guys, but they were creeps and the one I slept with was awful, just awful. Then I met someone at the hotel, very wealthy and good-looking. He asked me if I'd like to spend an evening with him. He said he would pay me for my time, no sex involved. I thought, okay, there has to be a catch."

"Oh my God. Was there?" Becca's eyes were round.

"Well, yes and no." Donna laughed and sat down. "He took me to a sex club. He said he didn't expect anything. He knew me a little because he came to town on business a lot and I always cleaned his room, so he knew I was a single mom and things were hard for me. He said he was looking for someone to be his submissive—I had no idea what he was talking about—and he only wanted me to watch and see if it was something I might be interested in. So I watched, and I was fascinated. I realized it turned me on, seeing some of the things they did. Not everything, but I kind of liked the idea of being restrained."

"You became his sub?" Becca just stared at her.

"I did. For five years. He was in town once a month or so, and he would always take me out to a wonderful dinner and dancing, or we'd go to the movies and hold hands like a real couple. He knew I didn't have much time for dating and that I worked two jobs, so he treated me like a princess when we were together. Then we would go to the club and get jiggy." She giggled. "It was so hot…the sex was like nothing I'd ever experienced with your dad, and I loved it."

"What happened to him?"

"He died," Donna said softly, her eyes growing misty. "Car accident. I got a letter from his attorney afterwards. He'd left instructions in the event anything happened to him that the lawyer contact me and give me a letter. It basically thanked me for trusting him and said that he was trying to get divorced. He wanted to be with me, marry me, take care of us, but it was complicated because his wife was a very powerful judge in New York. He said he kept me a secret because he was afraid she would try to hurt me somehow if she found out he had feelings for me—but he wanted me to know, just in case." She sighed, nibbling on another piece of pastry. "But he was gone and that was that. I didn't have sex again for a long time."

"I'm sorry, Mom."

"It was a long time ago but I still think of him occasionally. Luckily, he was a very successful businessman so there are pictures of him online that I can look at to remember him."

"I'd like you to show me sometime."

"Sure." Donna nodded. "I guess the moral of the story is, I like to be tied up and spanked. Pierre and I enjoy a healthy sex life that includes some of that, but we do it at home—we're too old to go to clubs and such. But we also make love…gentle, romantic, missionary style sex where he whispers that he loves me and can't wait to marry me, and we just lie there and move and stare into each other's eyes. No restraints, no paddles, no nothing but our hearts. It's lame and sometimes I can't even have an orgasm, but it's so romantic, I crave that type of sex as much as the kind where I can't stop getting off. I'm so happy, I never knew there were men like him. That's what I want for you, Becca, and I think Dante can give that to you. Whatever it is that happened at the club, there are only two questions you have to answer: Did you enjoy yourself and does he treat you the way you want to be treated the rest of the time?"

"He's wonderful all the time," Becca murmured.

"Then what is the issue?" Donna met her gaze squarely. "You had a three-some and the club got raided. So what?"

Becca groaned. "I'm afraid he's going to want to have another one but with a girl and I don't think I could stand it and it's so humiliating that I loved having both of them inside of me at the same time and—" Her face was bright red and she didn't take a breath the entire time she was talking.

"Okay, hang on." Donna held up a hand. "So you had a threesome with another guy and loved it, but you're not interested in doing it with another girl. Did he say he expected that?"

"No, he said the opposite, but that's what he does. He plants the seeds—like with anal sex. I wouldn't let him, but I wore the plug, and then Jamie—Ahhh!" Becca put her head down on the table. "You don't understand!"

"You're totally worked up about this." Donna was thoughtful. "I don't know what your relationship with Dante is like, but I think this is a conversation you need to have with him. Is it an open relationship?"

"I don't think so, but I couldn't live that way. I know he's pretty jealous and possessive, so that's partly why I'm so confused. How can he be possessive but then get a hard-on watching another guy fuck me?"

"Because it's sexy, sweetheart. That's why people watch porn."

Becca groaned. "The problem is that I love him so much, I'm afraid if we get married I'll just do what he wants because I don't want him to leave—but I know that kind of thing would destroy me."

"You're overthinking it," Donna said gently. "I don't see Dante as the kind of man who wants to share you. I think he senses that a little bit of kink works for you, and he's trying to expose you to those things. I don't believe your relationship is going to be based on that, but you have to sort that out with him, not in your own head. All you're doing now is making yourself crazy. Go to him. Talk to him."

"I'm afraid that I won't be able to think straight because when we're together I just want to be with him."

"You have to trust your gut," Donna said softly, reaching out to tuck her daughter's hair behind her ear. "You spent so many years taking care of me that you never took the time to blossom sexually—maybe that's my fault—but it's never too late. You're a beautiful, smart woman in love with a strong, successful man. The two of you can work through this, Becca."

"I'm going to see him next week, after he gets back from his road trip."

"Good." Donna grinned. "So, what's it like having two dicks inside you at the same time?"

Becca buried her face in her hands.

In true Dante fashion, he managed to take the focus off of Becca and Jamie by hitting a grand slam at the next game. He celebrated until late in the night afterwards, somehow allowing the press to get pictures of his unconscious body being carried out of a bar by two of his teammates. As Becca looked at the pictures the following day, she couldn't help but smile to herself. She knew damn well he hadn't drunk himself into a stupor the night before, and she texted him before she could stop herself.

BECCA: I don't believe for a second you were drunk last night!

DANTE: Why not?

BECCA: Because you care too much about your game to do something that stupid. And you'd never allow yourself to be carried out of a bar.

DANTE: Does this mean we're talking again?
BECCA: No. Yes. Maybe.

Her phone rang.

"I said maybe!" she said softly when she answered.

"Becca, I'm going crazy without you." His deep voice rumbled through her with so much force it felt like he'd physically touched her.

"A few more days," she whispered.

"Are you going to still love me when you're done thinking?"

"I will always love you," she admitted. "I just don't know if I can be with you."

He sighed. "I know I'm a difficult man, Becca, but I'll do anything to make you happy…anything. Just tell me what it is."

"I want you to be you," she said. "Anything else would be unfair—to both of us."

"*Querida*, I need to see you."

"I'll be in New York soon—as soon as I get myself together."

"Good night, my love."

23

Becca hadn't slept well since getting back from New York and the night before she left to go back was the worst of all. She barely slept, staring at the ceiling for hours and then tossing and turning until she finally got up and took a shower so she could go in to work for a few hours. It was still too early to go to the airport but she couldn't lie in bed anymore. She ached for Dante—his voice, his touch, everything about him.

She'd spent so much time immersed in him in the last six months, she didn't do well without him. The last few days had been exceptionally bad, but she knew if she could curl up with him right now she would sleep for two days. No matter how much she tried to tell herself she would be okay without him, she knew that wasn't true. She just wasn't sure what that meant.

There was so much more to them than just sex when they were together; he made her feel alive. With Dante she felt sexy, beautiful, successful—everything that had eluded her before they met. Though she knew intellectually that she *was* those things and many more, she'd never believed them about herself until she was with Dante.

It wasn't because he did anything either; it was simply that he showed her how much he believed in her and somehow it made her believe in herself. The look in his eyes when he watched her doing something as mundane as cooking was so potent it was impossible not to miss it now that she'd had it.

Sighing, she rested her head in her hands, staring at the phone. She knew she only had to call him and she would hear his voice, be consumed by him, enveloped in his love. God, she missed him. She still hadn't come to terms with what had happened in New York, but it had been a nonevent as far as the media was concerned. All they cared about was the senator's daughter, and she was grateful for that, but part of her still worried that by going to places like that she and Dante were taking a huge risk. Not to mention her discomfort with the things they'd done.

She groaned out loud and was surprised to hear a light voice behind her.

"That was a hell of a groan—must be a shit day!"

She jumped, but turned to smile at Kate. "Hey! What are you doing here?"

"I stopped by to say hi." Kate perched on the edge of the desk and stared into her friend's eyes. "And I'm wondering why I haven't heard from you this week. I know you and Dante broke up—don't you want to talk?"

Becca gave a little shrug. "That wouldn't be fair—you're friends with both of us."

"That doesn't mean I can't be there for you." Her dark eyes were warm. "And he won't tell me what really happened. He said you were pissed about being taken to jail—I don't believe that, so why don't you tell me the truth?"

Becca shook her head. "It's hard, Kate. And honestly, Dante doesn't have a lot of friends. I don't want to put you in this position."

"The position I'm in is caring about both of you and wanting to help. Won't you let me?"

"It's personal...and embarrassing."

"You were at Club Inferno, and I know what kind of place that is. Did he make you do something you were uncomfortable with?"

She shook her head. "No, it's not like that."

Kate sighed. "I guess we're not as close as I thought we were."

Becca's head snapped up. "No! That's not it. I just...I'm not good at talking about this kind of thing. I've never had this kind of friendship—I don't know how to open up about things that are embarrassing."

"You know that Karl and I are into bondage, right?" Kate cocked her head. "And we can get pretty kinky sometimes even though we've never done anything at a club like that."

Becca met her gaze. "Have you ever had a threesome?"

Kate shook her head and opened her mouth it became abundantly clear that the mental light bulb had gone off. "Oh. You, Dante and Jamie. *That's* what this is about."

Becca flushed and hung her head. "And I liked it," she whispered.

"Isn't that the reason you do it?" Kate whispered back, leaning over. "I mean, how hot was *that*?! I don't think Karl could stand it, though—he's *super* jealous."

"That's the thing—so are we!" Becca looked up in frustration. "That's why I left. How do you go on after that? How do you have a normal relation-ship when you look for sex elsewhere? I don't know how to come to terms with this, Kate! Everyone keeps telling me it's okay, there's nothing wrong with a little kink—but letting Karl tie you up is totally different than fucking two guys at once. How do you bring a third party into your relationship without ruining it?" Her eyes filled with tears and Kate quickly reached over to hug her friend tightly.

"Okay, shh." She stroked her friend's hair. "It's going to be okay. The first thing—completely separate from everything else—is that there's nothing wrong with you. It's okay to be kinky. It's okay to be different. It's even okay to think you're weird. It boils down to respect and safety—do you respect the people you do this stuff with and do they respect you? Are you safe when you do it?"

"Yes, of course. I've never done anything like that except with Dante and everything was great when we were together. It wasn't until after that I freaked out."

"Okay." Kate sat back and used a tissue to wipe Becca's face. "So the next thing is communication. Karl and I were together for a couple of months before he started to suggest new things when we were in bed, telling me he wanted to tie me up and do naughty things to me. He never tried anything, he simply mentioned it and let me think about it. One night I told him I wanted to try, and we started slow. He just handcuffed my hands to the headboard. As I got more comfortable, we did more stuff. I tied him up, he did me spread eagle, we added a few toys… And like I told you before, we don't do it every time. During hockey season? He's so busy—he's barely home and we're lucky to have time for a quickie before practice! So it's not all kink all the time."

"That's just it," Becca whispered. "We'd done a bit with bondage and sex toys but then…the threesome happened and we went way over the line. My line anyway. And now I don't know what to do."

"Tell him what you're thinking and what's in your heart."

"Kate, I'm head over heels in love with him—it feels like I'll do anything he wants. I'm afraid he's going to make me want things I don't want just so I can keep him. That's not how it's supposed to work."

"No," Kate agreed gently. "But that's not who Dante is. He loves you too—I know he does. You just have to talk to him. I'm sure you'll straighten this out."

"Are you going to tell him we talked?"

"Yes." Kate smiled. "But I'm not going to tell him what you've told me. I know how to keep a secret and honestly, as close as we are, he didn't feel comfortable telling me what happened, so obviously there's a limit to how much he'll divulge about your relationship. You must mean a lot to him."

"God, I hope so."

Becca smiled when she saw the chauffeur holding a sign with her name on it. She approached him shyly and he grinned back at her.

"You must be Becca," he said. "I'm Randy. Mr. Lamonte has told me a lot about you."

"I hope that's good." She laughed.

"Absolutely." He took her bag as they walked towards the exit. "How long are you here?"

"I'm not sure yet," she said.

"Mr. Lamonte talked about you nonstop yesterday—I've never heard him talk about a woman like that."

She smiled, lowering her eyes. "I'm glad. I can't wait to see him."

"It won't be long now."

Becca laughed in delight when she climbed into the limo and found Dante waiting with a huge bouquet of white roses.

"Hi!" she breathed, taking the flowers and letting him kiss her. The moment their lips touched she lost all pretense of taking things slow and attacked his mouth with fervor. His hands cupped her ass and brought her onto his lap. Their tongues swirled together in a rush of heated breath and muffled sighs until finally he broke away.

"One second, sweetheart." He pressed a button. "Randy, please drive until you hear from me again. I don't care where."

"Yes, Mr. Lamonte." There was humor in Randy's voice but neither of them were paying attention as the divider closed, giving them privacy.

"Dante…"

"Tell me you haven't missed me," he growled, pulling his T-shirt over his head.

"I can't," she gasped as he pushed her onto her back and lifted her skirt. He made short work of the thong she wore, and before she even realized what was happening, his face was between her legs. She clasped her hands over her mouth to drown out her cries of delight as he stabbed his tongue deep into her pussy.

"Mine," he whispered against her, licking her slit from top to bottom. "Mine, Becca. You hear me? This? It's all mine."

She moaned, the feel of his mouth on her keeping her from cognizant thought.

"Say it," he whispered. "Say you're mine."

"Dante!" she was already so close to losing control she couldn't make her mouth work.

"Say you're mine!" He pulled away, meeting her gaze intently.

"Of course I'm yours!" she cried.

His mouth moved back to her aching core and she went off like a rocket, a scream escaping her lungs despite her determination to stay quiet.

"Damn straight you are." He yanked off his jeans and pulled her on top of him. Before she could react his cock was deep inside of her and he was taking off her blouse and bra. "I don't know what this separating bullshit was all about, but you are never, ever leaving me again! You understand me?" His voice was harsh, but his fingers were gentle on her face. "Look at me, Becca."

She blinked in confusion but couldn't break his heady stare.

"You and me, we're in this forever. I don't care about any sex clubs or threesomes or other women—all I need is you. You just came all over my face, and that right there is all I need. Us. You." He thrust up into her and she whimpered. "So don't you ever leave me like that again, you understand? Unless you truly don't love me." This time he hesitated, waiting for an answer.

"You know I love you." Her voice shook a little as he ground into her.

"Then you don't play games with me."

"Dante, we can't—"

"I'm going to make you come over and over, until your pussy is so sore you can't walk, and then I'm going to fuck you again. After that, when you think you can't possibly do it anymore, you're gonna suck my cock until I tell you to stop! You understand?"

"Dante!" She couldn't control her traitorous body as she began to convulse around him. She didn't know what the hell was wrong with her, but his anger and possessiveness made her so wet she felt herself dripping all over them.

"That's right, baby—you're gonna come and then you're gonna come a few more times." He snapped his hips up, angling his cock right against the spongy spot he knew would bring her over the edge. Without warning she shrieked, her head falling back as she milked his throbbing cock, taking him with her.

Heart pounding, she tried to move away, but he held her fast. "You're not done," he grunted. He leaned over and pulled something out of the pocket of his jeans. "This?" He held it out. "It belongs to you, so put it on."

24

Becca gaped, staring at the biggest diamond she'd ever seen. "D-dante? What—"

"I said put it on," he snapped, pulling her against him so her breasts were crushed against his chest. "Apparently, romance doesn't work with you—so we're doing things my way from now on. Put the damn ring on and say yes."

"Y-you didn't ask me a question," she whispered, taking the ring and staring at it. Tears puddled in her eyes and for a moment she saw his face change, his mouth softening as his eyes met hers.

"Marry me, *querida?*"

"But, but—"

"This is why I didn't ask," he said in frustration.

"But we have to talk—oh!" She yelped when she felt the anal plug slide into her ass.

"No more talking," he ground out, his cock stiffening again even though it had been just minutes since he'd emptied himself inside her. "Do you love me?"

"Dante—"

He produced a blindfold from somewhere and dangled it from his fingers in warning. "Answer the question—or else."

"Yes! But I can't share you!" She managed to gasp out the last part before he clamped his lips around one of her nipples and bit down just hard enough to make her cry out.

"You will never share me," he said in a deep rumble that no longer held anger. "No matter who we fuck, where we fuck, or how we fuck—I belong to you, heart and soul. As you belong to me. Later we'll talk about all that, but right now, you will submit to anything and everything I want to do to you. Do you understand?"

A tear slid down her cheek and he paused again, wiping it with his thumb. "Please tell me you're not afraid of me."

"I'm not *afraid*!" she cried urgently. "I just, I want, please, ask me to marry you the right way…like you mean it. Everything else is okay, but that… it has to be special, not like this. *Please*."

He leaned forward and kissed her lightly, his mouth caressing hers so softly it was like the brush of a feather against her lips. He nuzzled his nose against hers and slowly ran one hand down her spine. He looked at the ring she held in her shaky fingers and gently took it back from her. Holding it up, his gorgeous eyes softened into a look she'd never seen before; nervousness mingled with pure love. "Will you marry me, Rebecca? Will you let me love you and take care of you and stand at your side for eternity?"

More tears slid down her cheeks but she nodded. "Y-yes." She held out her hand and he slowly slid the ring on.

"Then why are you crying?" he whispered, leaning his face closer to hers.

"Because I love you so much."

"And I you." He wrapped his arms around her as he brought her knees up, planting her feet on the seat on either side of him. He was still buried inside of her and he looked down at where they were joined. "See that?" he asked softly. "That's where I plan to be forever—deep in your pussy, in your heart, in your ass, in your life. Tonight you're going to get very, very used to me being in you because I'm going to fuck you until you beg me to stop."

"Oh!" Her voice cracked when he drew her down by the hips, sheathing himself all the way.

"I bought all kinds of new toys for us," he said, thrusting in and out slowly and watching her eyes get glassy. "But mostly it's going to be my cock, in every part of you, making sure you know you're mine."

"Dante!" She dug her fingers into his shoulders as waves of pleasure rocked through her. She didn't know what was wrong with her, but the more he told her what he was going to do to her, the wetter she got and the harder she came. "Shit!" Her orgasm was so intense she bucked backwards and would have fallen off of him if he hadn't held her tightly.

He chuckled. "That was unexpected, but incredibly beautiful. I'd like to see you come that hard every time."

She was panting, trying to catch her breath. "Dante, I can't, it's too much, please, let me—"

"Rest? That's a big no." He grabbed a towel that had been on the seat beside them and opened it, covering the leather next to them. Then he pulled her off his cock and set her on it, watching his seed spill out of her. "Lie back," he instructed.

"Dante!"

"Shush." He got a bottle of water and took a long drink before handing it to her. "Here—you'll need this because you're going to be doing a lot of screaming."

"We have to talk!" she protested mildly, though she was already finding it hard to concentrate because he had one finger sliding in and out of her.

"Tomorrow," he said. "Tonight, I tell you what to do and you do it."

"In the car?"

"In the car, on my couch, in my bed, up against a few walls…" He raised his eyebrows. "Any other questions?"

"No."

"Then shut up."

Becca closed her mouth.

He made love to her three more times, bringing on orgasms so strong she couldn't even cry out the last time, and she was begging him to stop the car so she could go to the bathroom. Finally, when she collapsed and was dozing against his shoulder, they pulled up to his massive estate.

"We're here, *querida*," he whispered against her temple.

"Oh." Her eyes opened sleepily and he brushed his lips against hers.

"Here." He slid a robe around her shoulders and she frowned.

"Where did that come from?"

"I knew you would be embarrassed to be naked in front of Randy but I also was intent on you not being dressed when we arrived."

She felt her cheeks get warm and he smiled.

"Honey, you're gonna need to stop blushing, because after tonight, there will be very little left for you to blush about."

"Dante!" She quickly tied the belt around her waist since he was already getting out of the car, oblivious to his own naked body.

"Randy, bring her things up to my room, please." He padded into his house, dragging Becca by the hand.

"Are you going to be a Neanderthal the whole time I'm here?" she demanded.

"Until you stop overthinking everything and learn to relax, yes." He paused in the doorway, smiling into her eyes. "But it's only because I love you and I know here—" he drew her hand to his chest, "—that you love me too."

"Have a good evening!" Randy smiled at them and disappeared.

"Do I even get to see your house?" she huffed, scowling at him.

"You'll see some of it tonight—the rest tomorrow." He linked his fingers through hers. "Are you hungry?"

"Not really."

"Then take off the robe."

"I need to go to the bathroom," she protested.

"Okay, but you're not allowed to wear any clothes until tomorrow." He held out his hand.

With a scowl, she took off the robe and handed it to him.

"Come." He tugged her up the stairs and into a massive bedroom that made her mouth fall open.

"Dante, it's gorgeous." She stopped walking and he indulged her because the look on her face was priceless.

"Not too masculine?" he asked. "Emilie thinks you'll want to change it."

"Change it?" She frowned. "Putting aside the assumption that I'll be living here, why would I change it? It's beautiful."

"Dark wood, simple decorations, lack of color…"

"I'd add something light," she admitted. "Maybe a touch of pale green or blue—but I love it. Gold is so elegant and wood is timeless."

"Enough. Come." He was pleased that she liked his room, but he had no intention of letting up on her tonight. She would submit to him fully, both physically and emotionally, and then they would talk. There was no way in hell he was letting her get away a second time and she was still skittish.

Somehow, he had to convince her that who she was—and who they were with regard to their sexual desires—was okay. He also had to make her understand that the sex was secondary. He was fully aware of the irony that it would take her perception of sexual deviation to make her understand that what they did in bed was separate from the rest of their life—the one he wanted them to have. Marriage—God help him, he wanted to impregnate her so bad he could taste it—and every traditional thing he'd never imagined wanting.

The bathroom was just as magnificent as the bedroom, and once again Becca was in awe, staring at a shower that was bigger than her whole bedroom. He turned on the water and held out his hand to her, pulling her under the spray, his body against hers.

"I promise, tomorrow you'll have the full tour," he whispered against her mouth.

"Dante, you don't have to worry about me leaving," she protested. "I said I would marry you! We just have to—"

"Tomorrow," he said softly. "Tonight is about us."

"Tonight is about making me submit!" She chuckled.

"Tonight is about giving in with more than your body and learning to stop thinking."

"Oh Dante…" She pressed her cheek against his chest, nuzzling into him as his fingers stroked her back and the water sluiced over them.

He looked down at her nestled against him and felt calm settle over him for the first time since the club had been raided in New York. It felt like she was close to him again, both physically and emotionally, and though this sex marathon was exhausting, he wasn't ready to stop. If he did, she would be thinking again by morning, and that wasn't acceptable. With his ring on her finger, she would give up everything tonight, and then he would listen to anything and everything she had to say.

After a long, luxurious shower where they washed each other from head to toe and he whispered sweet endearments to her while forbidding her to speak, he wrapped her in a big, fluffy towel and pulled her into his room. He'd drawn the curtains and lit candles, but she could see the restraints on the headboard and a pile of sex toys that made her heart skip a beat.

"Tonight you'll learn to trust me," he whispered. "Completely."

Her eyes met his warily. "Don't I already?"

"If you trusted me, you wouldn't have left."

"Dante, there are a lot of other things going on, not related to you or our sex life at all."

He was momentarily surprised. "Are you okay, *querida*?"

"About my father," she whispered.

"Ignorant prick," he muttered. "Yes, we will definitely discuss that, but right now, are you hungry?"

"No." She shook her head. "I'm too nervous to eat."

He ran his knuckles along her cheek. "You have nothing to fear. I know your limits, remember?"

"You push my limits."

"And you beg me for more. Now, go, up on the bed."

She crossed the room, her stomach clenching tightly. Something told her he wouldn't hesitate to push all her limits tonight. Instinctively she understood his need to possess her, show her he was in charge and how much he loved her, but after what had happened at the club she wasn't sure she could handle the aftermath.

She ran her hand along the soft sheets—softer than any she'd ever touched and wondered how much money you had to have to have sheets like this.

"They cost a lot," he said, watching her face. "But you just agreed to become my wife, so you should stop thinking about things like that because you'll never have to think about how much anything costs ever again."

His words sunk in slowly, and as they did, she started to tremble. The idea of someone actually taking care of her was so foreign it was as if something inside of her began to crack. She felt her resolve, her strength—everything she'd relied on for so many years—slowly coming apart. Big, fat tears started rolling down her cheeks as she looked from the massive diamond on her finger to his handsome face. "Dante, I need you to hold me," she sniffed just before the tears turned into deep, wrenching sobs.

"*Querida*." He had her in his arms as she began to shake against him.

"I can't...I don't..." She was crying so hard she couldn't finish her sentence.

"Whatever it is, it's going to be okay. I'm sorry I wasn't there when the club was raided. I was furious, terrified—I called my lawyer even before I got my phone back. He warned me that my losing control or making a scene wouldn't help you and that I needed to let him handle it. Unfortunately, it took hours to find out where they'd taken you. You don't really believe I left you there all that time on purpose?"

"But you did!" she sobbed, fingers digging into his skin as her tears ran down his chest. "Just like my father! Just like every other man that's ever been in my life! No one takes care of me—no one! Not even my mom. It's always me taking care of everyone else!"

"Oh, baby." He closed his arms around her even more tightly, lips against her forehead. "It wasn't intentional. I did what my lawyer suggested—he's very good at what he does. I trust him and—"

"I don't care about him—I wanted *you* to take care of me! I don't care about your money, I just need you! Don't you understand?"

25

Dante had never seen a woman cry like this and he began to understand the depth of the scars left from her father's abandonment. "Never again, my love. You have my word—I swear it on the memory of the child I lost—I will always be there for you. Always. Marry me tomorrow and I'll spend the rest of my life proving it to you."

She cried for a long time, until her nose was running and her eyes were red and puffy. He never let go, his strong arms holding her against him until her sobs turned to sniffles and finally hiccups.

"There's snot on you," she whispered, mortified.

He burst out laughing. "I don't care—snot, vomit, shit; if it makes you feel better, it can be washed off."

"I'm sorry."

"For what?"

"Falling apart."

"You've obviously been holding that in a very long time." He stroked her hair. "Now I understand. This is what you're afraid of, isn't it? You're not truly embarrassed about our sex life—you're afraid that it will somehow make me leave you, that perhaps bringing in another woman will make me want her instead of you…" He shook his head. "Not in a million years." He lifted her chin and looked into her tear-streaked face. "There's only you. From this day forward, you're all I want, all I need. If you don't ever want to go back to a place like that, we won't. No more threesomes, no more clubs, no more of any

of it, period. I'm perfectly happy tying you to my bed and fucking you sense-
less every night—just you and me, forever."

She shivered in the cool room, her naked body breaking out in gooseflesh
as the air conditioning washed over them.

"Come." He moved to the edge of the bed and, with her still in his arms,
stood up. "Let's get you cleaned up." He carried her to the bathroom, putting
her on the edge of the counter. He handed her a tissue so she could blow her
nose as he wet a washcloth and began to wipe her face. He worked methodi-
cally, caressing her skin as he wiped away tears and the remnants of makeup
that hadn't come off in the shower. She shivered against his warm hands and
he reached for the robe hanging on the back of the door. He slid her to her feet
and wrapped it around her, pulling her close again.

She rested her cheek on his chest, listening to the sound of his heart
beating steadily. She closed her eyes, completely spent, unable to find the
strength to say a single word. It was as if every feeling she'd been holding
back for nearly fifteen years had been ruthlessly yanked from her body,
leaving her raw and exposed. Dante's strength and rumbling voice were the
only things keeping her from retreating deep into herself.

"Are you hungry?" he whispered.

She shook her head, no.

"Baby girl, I need you to say something. You're scaring me."

"I can't," she whispered. "I'm so cold and sleepy."

"Okay." He lifted her again, carrying her to the bed. He laid her down and
pulled up the sheet and comforter, sliding in beside her. He pressed his front
up against her back, nudging her onto her side so that he could spoon up
behind her. He completely engulfed her as one arm slid over her waist and up
to cup one breast, though his touch was comforting now instead of sexual. His
legs tangled between hers and he made sure his face was just inches from her
cheek.

For an eternity they didn't move or speak, and eventually he felt her relax,
her breathing grew slow and steady and her fingers threaded into his, still up
against her breast. She began to snore softly and he shifted, turning onto his
back and drawing her up against him, her head in his shoulder, body molded
to his. He stroked her hair until daylight faded to dusk and the sun sank lower
and lower over the horizon.

Though his arm fell asleep, he refused to move, watching her sleep and
wondering if he could help her heal enough to trust him. Her admission that
no one had ever taken care of her nearly broke his heart; though he'd been on
his own a long time, he'd had wonderful parents and a happy childhood.
Losing both of his parents not long after getting signed to a major league

contract had been difficult, but he'd had Trey and more money than he knew what to do with. Becca had been both poor and alone, despite her close relationship with her mother.

The feeling of being abandoned had to be completely different than losing a parent to death. His parents had died in a freak car accident and though he'd been heartbroken, he knew it hadn't been their intention to leave him. That obviously made a big difference.

She finally stirred, rousing him from his reverie, and he brought his hand down to her cheek. "Welcome back," he said in his soft rumble.

"How long did I sleep?" she whispered, stretching.

"A couple hours."

"Oh! I'm sorry…"

"Shh." He kissed the top of her head. "I was happy to let you—you seemed exhausted."

"I haven't slept very well since the club," she admitted. "I can't seem to sleep without you."

"I'm here now," he said gently. "Any time you need to sleep in my arms, they're available."

She smiled in the semidarkness. "I love you, Dante."

"And I you." He sat up, looking down at her. "I've asked you several times today if you're hungry, and you haven't been, but I'm starving. I have to get something to eat, love. Do you want to come downstairs with me or wait here?"

"I'm kind of hungry now," she admitted sheepishly.

"Okay." He got up and padded over to the dresser, pulling on a pair of shorts. He pulled out a T-shirt and tossed it to her. "Throw that on and we can go see what Matilda left in the fridge."

Becca quickly pulled on the shirt and took his outstretched hand as they moved downstairs. He dug around in a massive stainless steel refrigerator, producing chicken salad, fresh fruit and bottled water. He reached into a drawer and pulled out several fresh croissants. As Becca opened everything and set it out, he got plates and utensils. They ate in relative silence, sitting on stools by the large rectangular island in the center of the room. After a while, the silence felt strange and she looked over at him.

"Dante?"

"Yes, love?"

"Can you make love to me?" Her voice faltered a little. "I mean, can you not…" She broke off, trying to articulate what she wanted. "I don't want to be tied up or fucked—can you *make love* to me without all the other stuff?"

He slid off the bar stool and moved against her, one hand against her cheek, the other around her waist. He looked deep into her eyes. "Always. Even when I fuck you I'm making love to you, baby girl. But if you need something different tonight—any time you need that—you only have to ask."

"I don't want to have to ask," she whispered. "I want you to sense when I need that the same way you sense when I need the other…stuff."

"Say it," he whispered. "Say the words—free yourself of the shame and the fear. My love for you doesn't change whether we fuck, make love or simply sleep. I plan to spend the rest of my life with you and each day will bring something new for us to explore, whether it's a sexual position or a child or a new house. Embrace everything we have by saying it out loud."

"I love the way you make me feel," she said, her eyes never leaving his. "I love when you tie me up and make me beg…I love when you order me to drop to my knees and suck your dick…I love it all."

"What else?" he pressed gently. "Tell me. I want to know everything you like, everything you don't like, every little thing."

"I really liked when you and Jamie…fucked me together." Her voice dropped to a breathy whisper, even as her cheeks flamed. "But I don't like worrying that by doing that someone might come between us."

"Then somehow I must find a way to convince you to trust me with your soul the way you do with your body…if something goes wrong between us, my love, it won't be because I found someone I like better in bed." He gripped her chin gently with his fingers and lifted her face so he could nuzzle her lips, keeping it just shy of actual kissing. "Tell me more."

She shook her head. "I can't."

"You can. Did you like having Jamie buried in your ass?"

She pressed her palms flat against his chest and swallowed hard. "Y-yes."

"Why can't you say it?" He brought her fingers to his lips. "I enjoyed his tongue on my cock while I was inside you. There—I said it. I liked having a man's tongue on my cock. Does that make you love me less?"

"No!" Her head snapped up. "I liked it too. I liked having him with us. I liked the feeling of being filled by both of you—I liked all of it. I just don't want that to define us."

"Define us? Never, baby girl." He took her hand. "Come on. We're going to try something completely new tonight."

"But I thought—"

"For once can you just trust me?" There was frustration in his eyes and she nodded slowly.

They made their way up to his room and he stripped off his shorts. "Come to me, *querida*."

She moved towards him and he looked down at her, his face gentle. "I can't speak for other men, love, but I can promise you that I will never abandon you. I may have to work or be in another city when something happens—like that night at the club—but I will always be here—" he touched her chest. "And here…" He touched her temple. "And this—" he lifted her left hand and ran his thumb over the diamond, "—will be there to remind you not just of our legal union, but the emotional one as well." He sat on the edge of the bed. "I don't want to take you tonight, Becca—I want you to take me."

"What?" She cocked her head.

"I can and will make love to you, but now I want you to tell me what to do." She looked uncomfortable and he held out his hand. "Not like that—not the way I do—but whatever kind of romance you want? You lead the way. You want me to kiss you, tell me. You want me to stroke your hair? Say it. You guide our lovemaking."

"Oh. Okay." A shy smile crossed her face. "Take my shirt off…"

He stood and slowly pulled the shirt over her head, letting it drop to the floor. He'd wanted to let her take her time getting him worked up, but just seeing her naked body brought his cock to life and he looked down, pretending to be annoyed. "I told you to wait!" he admonished his erection.

Becca giggled. "That's okay—I like that I do that to you." She reached out and closed her hand around him, her thumb working the tip until she felt little drops of his arousal against her skin. "Kiss me," she whispered. "One hand in my hair, the other anywhere you want except between my legs or in my ass."

"Mmm." He did as she asked, his lips nudging hers apart and seeking out her tongue. He flicked it with his, drawing it into his mouth with gusto. His left hand went right to the back of her head—he knew exactly how she liked her hair pulled when they weren't being rough—and his right thumb stroked her nipple. It pebbled beneath him, and he rolled it between his fingers until she moaned against his mouth.

"More," she whispered. "The other breast."

He smiled, taking her other nipple between his fingers and letting it harden. He fingered the tiny pebbles that had all come to life under his ministrations and watched her eyes flutter closed.

"I like when you run your fingers down my spine," she whispered. "That thing you do where you tease the crack of my ass."

He pulled her close, his mouth on hers again as he trailed one hand down her back. He caressed each bump of her spine, the indentation of her waist and the lines of her tailbone. He splayed his fingers right in the center, just above her ass, letting his middle finger slide into the crack between her cheeks. He rubbed gently, slowly, keeping a safe distance from her asshole, merely teasing her with the lightest of touches. His middle finger moved up and down, over and over, sliding a little lower each time, but stopping short of the tight ring of muscles that normally made her tense.

"Further," she whispered against his mouth. "Touch me there, Dante."

"Where?" he whispered back.

"You know where."

Because this was her game, her rules, he did as she asked, pressing one finger against the tight puckered hole. He moved lightly and had to suppress a groan when she welcomed his finger and it slid in effortlessly.

"Can you do that while you make love to me?" she breathed.

"Yes."

"Please," was all she said. Her eyes met his with a silent plea for him to take over and he pulled her close, backing them to the bed. He lay back and pulled her astride him. She hovered over his cock and guided it into her. She was soaked, absolutely dripping, and he moaned as she sank down hard.

"Ride me, baby," he whispered. "Nice and slow, so we can enjoy every second of this."

"Yes…" She swayed on him, her hips gyrating as she moved up and down.

He slid his finger into her ass again and watched her eyes close. Her breasts began to bounce as she moved faster and he felt her squeezing him. He slowly withdrew his finger and brought his hands to her hips.

"Why did you—" Her eyes opened in confusion.

"Shh." He thrust up deep, and held her in place. She instinctively tightened around him and they both groaned with sheer gratification—it was so good when they were in sync like this.

"Dante…" Her voice was reedy and she dug her fingers into his scalp.

"You feel so good, baby girl…" He released her hips, letting her start to move again. Without warning he sat up and held her torso against his. "Put your legs behind me."

She did as he asked, moaning as she sat down with all her weight on his cock. With her legs out in front of her, she couldn't move and he was in control again. Using his hips, he ground into her. Bringing his knees up, he used them to hold her up against him and he found her mouth hungrily.

"So deep," she whimpered, her breathing shallow.

"All ten inches are in you, baby girl—your sweet pussy is clamping around me and I can feel every spasm when we're like this. This is making love, baby—every inch of me surrounded by every bit of you—our chests, our mouths, everything moving together." He nipped at her lips. "I feel you starting to let go…tell me what you need."

"You," she panted. "Just you—I love you so much."

"There are no words for how much I love you," he growled. "And this? This kind of lovemaking is just for us—we'll never do this with anyone else. This is mine." He'd never lost control before when he made love to her, but his orgasm came on before he could stop it and he shot off inside her just as she cried out his name.

Her head fell back, eyes rolling back as the ripples overcame them at the same time.

"Mine!" he repeated as he watched her shudder.

"Always," she agreed breathlessly, falling against him.

They rolled onto their backs, side by side, and after a few minutes he glanced at her. She met his gaze with a soft smile.

"I love you," was all she said.

"I love you too."

"I'm sorry I didn't trust you."

"You're forgiven. And tomorrow we will talk about all those things you wanted to talk about."

"And tonight?"

"Give me ten minutes and then I'm going to put my cock right in that tight, sweet ass of yours, just like you want me to."

"Yes," she sighed happily. "Yes, I do."

26

"What would you like to do while I have a few days off?" Dante asked her the following morning at breakfast. He had games tonight and tomorrow night, and then he was off for five days. He'd never thought he would be grateful that he wasn't invited to the All-Star Game, but this year he was relieved. Last year, of course, his life had been hell and he'd bowed out, and this year he'd been playing like shit. Becca was a distraction, and he hoped that now that they'd sorted some things out, she would stop driving him crazy.

He loved her, but he didn't want to keep having to convince her of it. For once in his life, he wanted a relationship with a woman to be easy. Of course, it wasn't entirely her fault; he understood he'd brought her into multiple worlds she knew nothing about. First and foremost was their sex life, and adding his baseball celebrity to the mix only made things harder. Hopefully, they'd made progress.

She seemed more at ease this morning and she looked over at him from under her eyelashes. They hadn't gotten a whole lot of sleep last night and he she looked tired, despite her sweet smile. "I don't care what we do," she said, wrapping her hands around her cup of coffee. "As long as we're together."

"You look tired," he said softly. "Why don't you go take a nap while I do a light workout?"

She shook her head. "I'm okay—I get by on very little sleep on game nights during hockey season."

"Yes, but you're on vacation."

"I'm not actually on vacation," she chuckled. "I'm just working remotely. I'll log in and do some work while you're working out."

He leaned over the counter and kissed her, his lips rubbing against hers softly. "Tonight, we'll have to take it easy, yeah? I've got back-to-back games so I can't pull another all-nighter."

She gave him a lazy grin. "You do what you need to do. I'm good."

He stroked her cheek with his thumb and her eyes fluttered closed. He watched her for a moment and then kissed the top of her head before jogged up the stairs, already thinking about baseball and the game tonight.

This would be the first time she went to a game with him and she was a little nervous, but everything had been so stressful lately, she just didn't have the energy to worry about anything else. Instead, she texted Kate.

BECCA: What does the girlfriend of a super-hot bad-boy baseball player wear to one of his games?

KATE: You're back together?! Squeee!!!!

BECCA: That's not helpful about what to wear!

KATE: Shorts and a T-shirt? I wear jeans to Karl's games but it's not freakin' July during hockey season—what else are you going to wear but shorts? You'll die in jeans or capris... A dress would be pretty if you have something light and summery?

BECCA: Not with me. Crap!

KATE: It's only 9:00 on the East Coast—game's what? 7:00? 7:30? Go shopping!

BECCA: I don't know where anything is and Dante doesn't have time.

KATE: Quit making excuses—borrow one of his cars and go shopping! He has a GPS, and I'm sure there's a mall nearby.

BECCA: I could get cute sandals too, huh?

KATE: Yes...and lingerie.

Becca grinned to herself.

BECCA: He doesn't really let me wear any lingerie—he kind of prefers naked.

KATW: Buy something that's super sexy on top but no bottom...

BECCA: That's an idea... Okay, I need to shower and get out of here if I'm going to go shopping.

KATE: Text me pictures and I'll help you choose.

BECCA: Okay!

. . .

Becca hurried upstairs and found Dante in the bathroom brushing his teeth. He glanced at her in the mirror when she came in and spit out the toothpaste.

"Everything okay?" he asked curiously, noting the excitement in her eyes.

"Can I borrow one of your cars?" she asked, biting her lip. "I want to go shopping."

He raised his eyebrows. "Of course you can borrow one of my cars—but do you know where you're going?"

"No, but I figured I could put the address in the GPS on my phone."

"How about if Randy drives you?"

She blinked. "Don't you trust me with your car?"

He chuckled. "Honey, there is nothing I own that's more important than you, but it's more about convenience. You don't know where you're going and I kind of have a tight schedule today. If this trip is anything like when I took you shopping last time, you'll need every spare second."

She laughed. "Okay, Randy can drive me." She made a face. "Even though he listened to us screw in the car yesterday!"

"I pay Randy a lot of money to make sure he doesn't listen to anything," Dante said, pressing his lips to the nape of her neck and lightly sucking her skin.

"Mm," she sighed. "Okay, you need to stop or you won't work out and I won't find anything cute to wear tonight."

"You're going to a baseball game," he said. "Why do you need something cute?"

She rolled her eyes. "Because I'm your girlfriend and I want to look cute for you?"

He quickly kissed her and made his way into the bedroom. "Here." He pulled some money out of his wallet. "Buy whatever you want."

"No." She shook her head. "I don't want—"

"Stop." He pulled her up against him and tugged on her left hand. "See that? It means we share everything from now on, okay? I know we didn't talk about everything yet, but we will, and in the meantime, let me take care of you. Please. You complain that no one ever takes care of you but now that someone wants to, you don't want to let me."

"This is different."

"It's not. I understand that you don't want me paying your mortgage— although that's something we'll talk about as well—but this? Shopping while you're here with me, trips we take, everything we do—that's all on me. Please, *querida*. Don't fight with me about this."

She lowered her eyes. "I'm sorry. You're right. Thank you." She stood on her toes so she could kiss him and he palmed her ass with one hand.

"God, I can't wait to make love to you later..."

"I thought we were just going to sleep tonight?"

"I said we couldn't pull another all-nighter—I didn't say anything about just sleeping!"

Sitting in the stands, Becca felt a tingle of excitement as she watched the game. She'd drawn some curious glances from some of the wives and girlfriends, but they didn't appear to recognize her and she kept her eyes on the field. She was sure they would figure out who she was soon enough and was happy to remain in anonymity for as long as possible.

Kate had told her no one had really liked Larissa so hopefully they would be more accepting of someone new. Of course, looking at the perfectly coiffed and fully made-up women sitting nearby, she knew she didn't exactly fit in either. They were all dressed to the nines, showing off a ton of cleavage and even more jewelry.

Glancing down at her hand, Becca had to admit she had no problems competing in the jewelry department. Dante had insisted she wear the ring tonight and said he would announce their engagement to the press if the opportunity arose so she was in a bit of a holding pattern as far as an announcement went.

Dante struck out his first at bat and Becca inwardly cringed, although he looked up in her direction on his way back to the dugout and smiled. She could almost feel the eyes of the other women on her and she pulled out her phone to text Kate.

BECCA: I am totally freaking out—sitting here by myself is hard!

KATE: Just be calm, focus on the game and don't worry about anything. I'm sure it'll be okay.

Because she hadn't told her anything, she took a picture of the ring on her finger and texted it to her. A moment later she got a response:

KATE: Holy fucking shit! Is that for real?!

BECCA: Yup. Happened last night but I didn't know if we were telling people... I guess we are. He's going to announce it tonight if he gets interviewed.

KATE: Girlfriend, you have to warn me about this kind of thing! I'm his publicist—I need a heads-up!

BECCA: Sorry?

KATE: I'm so happy for you... are you happy?

BECCA: Yes! We still have some things to talk about, but we'll work out the details.

KATE: Did you fuck like bunnies???

BECCA: Oh. My. God. Yes! In fact, we made love a lot too.

KATE: Oooohhh...you'll have to tell me all about that when you get back.

BECCA: I will!

KATE: Talk later!

Becca put her phone away and tried to focus on the game. She wasn't a big fan of baseball but something told her she was going to have to try harder now that she was with Dante. Watching him on the field, she was impressed with his strength and agility, the way he ran and moved, and the speed and accuracy with which he could throw the ball when he got it. He was pure masculine athleticism and it reminded her of how he made love; strong, feral, focused. When he touched her, he wasn't thinking about anything else, and she could sense he was the same way now.

"Hi." A tall, lanky blonde sank down next to her. She had long hair and big blue eyes with way too much makeup, but her smile seemed genuine and Becca smiled back.

"Hi."

"I'm Cyndi Marshall, Jax's wife." She held out her hand and Becca shook it.

"Becca Hernandez." She tried to look casual. "I'm Dante Lamonte's fiancée."

"He's engaged again?" Cyndi's eyes rounded as she stared at the ring. "That's wonderful! And damn, that's bigger than Larissa's!"

Becca stomach started to churn but she just shrugged. "Dante and I have been friends for a long time...things changed gradually."

"Congratulations."

"Thank you." Becca looked back out to the field and realized Dante was up at bat again. There was something different about him this time. His whole body was rigid, and he used his bat to point into the stands on the opposite side of the field. Cyndi groaned and Becca glanced at her.

"Haven't you watched him play?" Cyndi recognized Becca's confusion. "He's letting everyone know he's going to hit a home run."

"Oh." Becca shielded her eyes with her hand and watched in sheer adoration as he swung the bat and sent the ball sailing over the back wall, out of sight. She was on her feet with the rest of the crowd, just in time to see him turn and wink at her. "Shit," she said softly.

"You're gonna be sucking his dick before every game now, huh?" Cyndi grinned knowingly.

Becca's mouth fell open. "How did you know that?"

"They always try that with someone new. Usually works great for a few weeks until inevitably it stops working, but I got a ring out of it too!"

They giggled together and Becca wondered if this woman might actually be someone she could become friends with.

I n addition to his home run, on his next at bat he hit a grand slam, sending the crowd into a frenzy and the women in Becca's section looking at her with some combination of curiosity and annoyance.

"Don't mind them," Cyndi said as the game ended. "The bulk of them don't like anybody. There's a few you'll want to get to know—Tasha and Berry—"

"Berry?"

Cyndi rolled her eyes. "Her father used to call her his little strawberry and apparently if you're from Mississippi, the nickname Berry is cute."

"Okay." Becca nodded, getting up and following Cyndi towards the exit.

"Where are you meeting him?" Cyndi asked her.

"At home," Becca smiled. "I don't have any desire to get involved in any of this craziness."

"Smart girl." Cyndi winked. "Hope I'll see you around."

"Likewise." Becca smiled and hurried outside to text Randy. He would take her home and then come back for Dante. Since Dante didn't live too far away, it wouldn't take long and it was easier than trying to sit at the stadium until Dante was ready to go. Besides, she planned to be waiting in bed for him.

"Did you have a good night, Miss Becca?" Randy asked as she slid into the back of the limo.

"It was fun," she smiled. "Do you come to the games?"

"Oh yeah. When it's just Mr. Lamonte and me, he gets me a seat so I can enjoy the game. He's good that way."

"I'm glad." She leaned back, thinking about what was going to happen next. There was another game tomorrow night and then they were going on vacation, for real this time, even though it wouldn't be for very long. He wanted to go to Puerto Rico and lie on a beach; she wanted to go somewhere a little cooler where they could maybe go wine tasting and get pampered in a spa somewhere. She had a feeling he was going to get his way, but she didn't mind. It felt like all semblance of normalcy had left them once baseball season started and she didn't want anything else to go wrong so that was a small compromise.

She hurried upstairs the moment Randy dropped her off and took a quick shower since it had been sticky out. She'd shaved earlier, so now she focused on the basics—deodorant, a dash of perfume, mascara, lip gloss, and her new lingerie. The sheer hot pink fabric brought her breasts together with a black satin bow between them and the rest of the material hung down around her hips. It opened in a reverse V, with the point starting between her breasts and flowing down from there. Without any panties on, he could do whatever he wanted. It occurred to her that she was not only getting used to the things they did together, she looked forward to and initiated them.

Staring at the ring on her finger, she felt the first real jolt of excitement. Last night's proposal had been too emotional to really focus on what it meant that he'd asked her to marry him. Though it also brought a slew of problems, it meant the beginning of many wonderful things too. She couldn't even begin to think about the wedding they would have; she wanted a big one and he'd hinted that he did too. She was a little giddy thinking about it and she grabbed her phone to text Kate, something she'd been doing a lot more of lately.

BECCA: Do you know anything about planning weddings???

KATE: Me? The girl who watched her best friend elope and then went and did the same thing? Not a damn thing except that you can hire a wedding planner when you're marrying a millionaire!

BECCA: I forgot about that... Crap, his money is going to be a problem.

KATE: Would you stop being a twit?! If he was worried about money, he wouldn't have asked you to marry him.

BECCA: You think he'll ask me to sign a prenup?

KATE: I have no idea, but his ex-wife got nothing, so you should make sure you're protected—one of those clauses for a certain amount of money for every year you're married, plus unlimited for any kids you have.

BECCA: You really know how to suck the fun out of getting married.

KATE: I love Dante, but his lawyers are going to protect him so you need someone looking out for you too!

BECCA: Thanks, Kate. I'm gonna go—I think he's home!

27

BECCA MADE SURE TO TURN DOWN THE LIGHTS AND PROP HERSELF UP AGAINST a bunch of pillows in what she hoped was a sexy position. She heard his heavy steps on the stairs and then he was calling out to her.

"In here!" she called back.

"Hey, do you want to…" His voice trailed off as he took in her sexy nightgown and the fact that she wore nothing beneath it.

"Do I want to what?" she asked, sitting up on one elbow, her hair falling over her shoulders.

"No, you definitely don't want to go out with Jax and Cyndi," he murmured, dropping his bag on the floor and kicking off his shoes. He was on the bed in a handful of long steps, his mouth on hers before she even realized what he'd done.

"We can go out…" she breathed against his lips.

"Fuck that!" he snorted. "They'll figure out we had better things to do." He pulled off his shirt, letting it drop to the floor.

"I guess you like my new nightie," she murmured as his hands slid beneath the fabric and splayed across her back.

"I love it," he growled, bringing her against him.

"But you're basically just going to rip it off me and fuck the hell out of me," she laughed.

"You got a problem with that?" he eyed her.

"None at all."

Much later, after they'd had sex multiple times and the hot pink nightgown lay in tatters on the floor, Becca was curled against his chest when his stomach growled.

"Are you hungry?" she asked softly. "You want me to bring you something?"

He smiled down at her. "Nah, that's okay. I'd rather be here with you."

"It'll only take me a minute," she said, looking up at him.

"I'm tired," he admitted. "I'd rather sleep than eat."

"I'm sorry—I shouldn't have been waiting to seduce you!"

"Shh." He wrapped his arms around her. "I loved seeing you waiting for me like that. I really do need some sleep now, though."

"I loved watching you play tonight," she whispered against his chest. "You're just brilliant out there—so focused and in tune with what everyone else is doing. Baseball is a part of you."

He smiled in the darkness. Not only did she understand his needs in and out of the bedroom, but she got his devotion to baseball too. He'd never imagined a woman like her existed and he felt a moment of sheer joy. No wonder people fell in love; he'd waited a long time for someone like Becca to come into his life and his only regret was that she and Trey had never known each other.

"I do love to play," he admitted quietly. "When I'm out there, nothing else exists for those couple of hours."

"Bet you thought of me sucking your dick when you hit that homer," she teased, running her hand down his chest, pausing at his crotch.

He chuckled. "Yeah, baby girl, I thought of you—and obviously you thought about it too."

"I think about it a lot," she said. "And if you go to sleep like a good boy, you might wake up that way."

"No way!" he said in alarm. "We do it the exact same way we did it tonight—a few hours before the game. Don't mess with my mojo."

"Really?" She knew athletes were often fanatical about their rituals and superstitions; the Sidewinders had lots of them, so she nodded obediently. "Yes, sir. No morning head."

"Oh, there will be plenty of morning head—just not on game days."

She rolled her eyes.

"I saw that," he smiled as she curled deeper into him, indicating she was dozing off.

"I know." She closed her eyes.

After a fabulous, though short, vacation, and time spent truly bonding as a couple, Becca had to return to work and Dante was back on the road. Baseball season was in full swing and they both had things to do. She'd promised to commute to New York between now and when hockey training camp started in September, but when he was on the road it was easier for her to be at work in Las Vegas. It was hard on them, but they'd spent a lot of time talking through all their issues and it felt like they were on the right track now. With a wedding planned for sometime next year and Dante agreeing to spend the winter in Las Vegas, it felt like they were in a good place.

Dante was lost in thought, lying on the bed in a hotel room in Milwaukee, when his phone rang. He was surprised to see Jamie's name pop up on the screen and he answered absently, his mind on the game tonight and when he would see Becca next.

"Hello, my friend."

"Dude." Jamie's voice was low, almost a growl, and there was no doubt he was restraining his temper.

"What's wrong?" Dante read people well, and he knew Jamie better than most.

"Who did you tell?!"

"Who did I tell what?"

"You know, if you're gonna talk about who sucks whose dick, it's gonna come out that you were part of that party."

Dante felt a moment of alarm; not because he was afraid people would find out about his sex life, but because any news about their threesome would inevitably include Becca. "Okay, you know damn well I wouldn't tell a fucking soul about what we did—and neither would Becca. The only people that know are her mother and Kate, and I'm willing to bet neither one of them told anybody."

"Well, someone talked."

"Tell me what happened."

"I'm home, in Toronto, and hung out with some of the guys I grew up with. We had a few drinks and one of them asked me what it was like to suck a cock, said he always wondered."

"Did you ask him how he knew?"

"Of course not! I asked him what the fuck he was talking about and he said it was okay, we all like to take a walk on the wild side at clubs like that."

"And?" Dante was losing his patience.

"He said he saw pictures."

"*Pictures?!* Of us..." Dante couldn't even say the words as he imagined Becca's horror.

"Yeah. I asked him where and he said online, but he couldn't remember specifics. I told him it was Photoshopped, but dammit, Dante, this is bad. What the fuck?!"

"I don't like it either, and Becca..." He cursed under his breath.

"Becca's going to lose her mind," Jamie said quietly. "We have to find out how this happened. I thought he was bullshitting about the pictures, but if there could actually be pictures...that means someone in that club took them."

"If someone in that club took pictures, I'm going to own it," Dante hissed under his breath. "I'm making a few calls. Hang tight." He disconnected. The first call would be to Kate; damage control was essential for Becca. Then he was calling his lawyer. If there were pictures out there, someone was going to pay.

Club Inferno had a strict no photograph policy unless they were personal photos in one of the private rooms. No group photos, ever. No photos during public scening. Phones and cameras were usually checked into lockers when you arrived, and though some people kept phones with them, everyone had to sign a confidentiality agreement; if any photos got out without permission, you were banned from the club and those in the pictures were free to sue. And Dante was definitely going to sue.

Fuck, he thought with irritation. As much as it pained him to think people would see pictures of Jamie going down on him and Becca together, it didn't bother him that much; he'd survived worse scandals. A few grand slams during pivotal games and people would forget all about it. Besides, all he had to do was threaten to retire and then everyone would be talking about that instead.

On the other hand, he knew it would be completely humiliating for Becca and the embarrassment would be overwhelming for her. He was already in panic mode, thinking about what he needed to do to protect her. He could hear her voice in his head, sobbing, asking why no one ever took care of her, and he was damned if he was going to let her down now. It just didn't look like there would be a way to stop this if these pictures existed, so his job would be to protect her from the fallout. He made a mental note to call Pierre Bouchard next.

Becca was in a meeting with the sales and marketing departments discussing the upcoming season when she saw the notification on her phone that she was trending on social media. At first she ignored it, thinking it probably had something to do with Dante and not really interested in what gossip was going around the internet. After the fourth or fifth notification, she absently clicked on the link and saw the picture for the first time.

Her chest tightened painfully and she blinked a few times, trying to focus on what she was looking at. *Was that…?* She felt her stomach clench and a wave of dizziness washed over her. It was a picture of her, Dante and Jamie having sex. She was riding Dante's lap and Jamie's face was between her legs.

With shaking fingers she hit the accompanying link and was taken to a page showing more pictures, some of them close-ups of…everything. Her heart was hammering so hard she was sure everyone in the room could hear it, and she hurriedly stood up.

"I'm sorry," she whispered, her voice barely audible. "I have to make a phone call—I'll be back!" She rushed out of the room and back to her desk, landing on her chair just in time to beat the wave of nausea that went through her. She took a few deep breaths and had to put her head down.

"Becca?" Pierre's voice was gentle, and she felt his hand on her shoulder.

"I, uh, need a minute," she whispered, unable to raise her head.

"I know about the pictures," he said quietly. "What can I do?"

"Nothing," she choked, tears pooling in her eyes. "I'm going to die."

"No, you're not." He squeezed her shoulder. "I've got your back—we all do."

"You have to fire me," she said in a tiny voice. "You have to protect the team from this."

"Have you talked to Dante?"

"N-no."

"You should."

"I will. I just, I can't breathe…" She felt like she was hyperventilating and Pierre moved quickly, pulling out her chair and pushing her head down between her knees.

"Breathe, in and out, nice and slow…come on." He held her hair back. "You got this."

"My whole life…oh my God." Becca couldn't breathe, couldn't see, couldn't even think; she was drowning in an ocean of embarrassment and hopelessness. Nothing had ever felt this humiliating, and she knew she was going to lose her lunch any minute now.

"It's okay." Pierre dropped to his knees. "Come on, Becca, you're tougher than this. Kate's already on the job—"

"Oh my God! The whole team is going to see those pictures!" Her face flamed and she grabbed the wastebasket under her desk just before her stomach revolted.

"Okay, hang on." Pierre got up and rushed to get some paper towels from the nearest bathroom.

28

Someone was going to pay for this, Dante thought as he scrolled through the pictures. If he could find the person responsible, he was positive he was capable of murder at this moment. Seeing his beautiful Becca in such a compromising position broke his heart, but he was too angry to feel bad right now. He'd been on the phone with half a dozen lawyers, Kate, Pierre and now he had to make a call that would cost him—but Becca was worth it.

"Hello?" Jamie sounded distant, tired.

"It's me." Dante was exhausted, and he had a game in a few hours. He couldn't think about that now, though; Becca was his priority.

"What did you find out?"

"Definitely a leak at the club," he said in a tight voice. "We've narrowed it down to a couple of people and I hired a hacker to find out where those pictures originated. I should know in a few hours."

"Great."

"Listen. I need something from you."

"From me?"

"What I'm going to ask isn't a small thing—it's huge. I know that and I understand that I will owe you—big. Probably forever."

"Uh, okay."

"I need you to fall on your sword."

"What?"

"I need you to ask for a trade. Leave the Sidewinders."

"What?!" Jamie couldn't have sounded more shocked.

"I know you don't want to, and I know it will suck, but I have things to offer you beyond money. I can make sure you never, ever have to worry about no-notice drug tests. I can get you on almost any team of your choosing—there are three or four that simply can't make moves because of the salary cap, but out of thirty teams in the league, you have your pick of about twenty-five. I will also make all of this go away—you have my word."

"You want me to ask for a trade?" Jamie was still dumbfounded.

"One of you will probably have to go—and it cannot be Becca. She would never get over it. I know it's asking a lot, but I'm willing to do whatever it takes. I will even supplement your income if they don't give you what you're making with the Sidewinders. Jamie, I need this. Whatever it takes. What do you want? I have to do this for her. She can't, she won't…" He sighed. "She's not like us. She won't survive this if I don't fix it."

Jamie was silent for so long Dante thought he might have hung up.

"Jamie?"

"Yeah, I'm here." Jamie took a breath. "I want to play for Ottawa. It's closer to my family, but I don't want to play in Toronto; too much of a media circus. I'd never live this down in Toronto. It's more mellow in Ottawa, I think. I hope."

"What else?"

"I'm not going to blackmail you," Jamie grunted. "We wound up in this mess together. You didn't do this to me, and you're right—Becca is going to be hit the hardest. I'll help you protect her. You're definitely going to owe me, though. I don't know when or for what, but you're going to owe me."

"Whatever you want."

Jamie chuckled even though it wasn't funny. "One favor, Dante. Then we'll be square. That's what friendship is about. I, uh, what do you want me to do?"

"I've already spoken to Pierre. He said he would make sure the trade was quiet with a positive spin—you wanting to be closer to your family works out well."

"Okay. So…"

"Call your agent. You just won a championship—teams will be looking for guys like you to bring some energy and excitement to their team. Don't just pitch to Ottawa. Let me throw out some feelers to multiple teams and you'll get a better offer. Trust me. Are you sure Ottawa is where you want to end up?"

"Yeah. If I can't play for the Sidewinders, I want to be closer to my family."

"This is going to go away," Dante said with steely resolve. "Thank you for helping me with this. I won't forget it."

"No," Jamie agreed. "You definitely won't—'cause I won't let you."

"But you never, ever say a negative word to Becca. *Me entiendes?" You understand me?*

"Dude. This is about protecting her—and she's my friend too! Of course not."

"Okay, good. Now, get on the phone and get the wheels turning. I've got a game and then I have to get to Becca."

"Have you talked to her?"

"No. I had to make sure things were under control first. Pierre told me she was in quite a state, and I know when she gets like that nothing I say will matter. I have to make things right first."

"Anything else I can do?"

"No, my friend. You're about to make the ultimate sacrifice."

"It's going to take a few weeks to make this happen if we start talking to multiple teams."

"That's okay. It will give me time to fix things."

"Dante, are you sure you know what you're doing?"

Dante chuckled. "You don't know me very well, do you?"

They talked for another minute before Dante hung up. He stared at the phone for a long time and decided against calling Becca. She would either be hysterical, completely incommunicative or angry; he couldn't do anything with any of those emotions. Instead, he sent her a text.

DANTE: I love you, querida. I'm sorry about all of this, but understand that I will fix it. Trust me. If you love me as much as you say you do, put your faith in me this time. Don't run away; just trust me. Know that I will move heaven and earth to make everything okay. I'll see you very soon. Xoxo D

He put his phone in his pocket and started to get ready for the game.

Becca read Dante's text a hundred times but couldn't bring herself to call him. He had a game starting in a little while and she didn't want to distract him. This wasn't his fault and there was no reason to upset him too. It was the only thing that had made her smile all afternoon, though she was grateful to get a text from Jamie as well.

JAMIE: It's going to be okay. Dante and I have your back; whatever it takes to make this go away, we'll do it. We didn't do anything wrong—remember that.

Maybe not, but it sure felt like it. The looks she'd gotten from the guys in the sales department had been a combination of awe and pity, and she probably would have collapsed if Pierre hadn't intervened. She was home now, her mother and Pierre in the kitchen making dinner while she hid in her room. The pictures of the threesome had gone viral in less than an hour. They were everywhere; the internet, radio, TV news stations—it would have been amusing if she wasn't so completely humiliated. This kind of public scrutiny was totally unfamiliar to her and she wondered how Dante did it day in, day out.

Dante was going to be on TV tonight, she realized with a start. God, it was going to be a nightmare for him, which was something she hadn't even considered. She grabbed her phone and immediately texted him, suddenly feeling terrible that she hadn't answered him earlier.

BECCA: I love you too. I'm sorry I didn't respond sooner but I was kind of overwhelmed. I'll be watching the game, though, and I'm giving you a virtual BJ right now.

"Becca?" Her mother's voice startled her. "Are you hungry? Dinner's ready."

"I'm not hungry," Becca called back.

"Come sit with us. Brooding all by yourself isn't going to help anything."

"All right." Becca padded into the kitchen and sank into a chair, resting her chin on her palm.

"It's going to be okay," Donna said gently.

"Are you going to have to fire me?" Becca asked Pierre in a tired voice, her eyes meeting his sadly.

He shook his head. "Jamie's asked to be traded."

"What?!" Her eyes widened and she sat up straight. "Why? No! You can't do that."

"It has nothing to do with me," he said. "He said he wants to be closer to his family so his agent is looking for a deal and we're looking to see who we might get in exchange. This happens all the time in sports. You know that, Becca."

"But he doesn't want to leave! He loves it here."

"Shit happens." Pierre shrugged. "He took the choice out of our hands."

"So you were going to have to make a choice?"

"I don't know," he admitted. "But we were going to have to deal with this. Although there's nothing wrong with what you did, that's not the image the team wants to portray."

"How mad is Mr. Finch?" Becca asked, referring to the team's owner.

"Not mad—disappointed. Jamie's been in one scandal after another—

twice with steroids, the sex tape with Rachel and now this...he's a bit of a liability even though he's a great player."

"And what about me?"

"You work hard for us, Becca. What you do in your private life is your own business, and no one wants to see you go. Unfortunately, because you work with the press, you're undoubtedly going to have to take a lot of shit over this, and the media is going to be relentless because it involves Dante Lamonte. There's no way around that. I will completely understand if you want to leave the job and—"

"I'm not leaving my job!" Becca snapped, her eyes narrowing. "If you fire me, that's different, but I'm not leaving. I worked hard to get where I am."

"What about Dante?" Donna asked carefully. "You're going to continue to live on the other side of the country? How is that going to work?"

"We don't know yet," Becca admitted. "But I'm not ready to stop working. I'm going to work until we have a baby or...something."

Donna's eyes twinkled. "Are we having a baby?"

Becca sighed. "Not right now, Mom. We're in the middle of a sex scandal, we're not married, and frankly, I don't even know if I can keep doing this."

"Doing what?" Donna frowned at her. "Please don't tell me you're breaking up with Dante again."

"No...I just, well, I don't want to do this all the time. It's one thing after another and it's starting to bother me."

"Wow." Donna made a face at her. "That man adores you—would do anything for you—and you're not sure you want to put up with a little bit of drama? Really? I don't know what your definition of love is, but that's certainly not mine."

Pierre didn't say anything, focusing on the food in front of him as Becca just stared at her mother angrily. "Why do you always take his side?" she asked quietly.

"Because you've done nothing but push him away," Donna said. "And it's ridiculous. Do you have any idea how lucky you are? How wonderful he is? Why do you always do this?"

"I'm not doing anything!" Becca snapped. "This wasn't my fault. Oh, but I guess it was, right? Because I went there and let them—"

"Stop!" Pierre finally looked up and scowled at her. "You need to stop this, Becca! It's hurtful—it doesn't affect me, but it certainly affects you. You're making yourself crazy with these moral limitations you put on yourself and the man you supposedly love. If you didn't want to do those things, you wouldn't do them. But you do, so instead of constantly trying to pretend you're something you're not, why don't you just embrace who you are?"

Becca stared at them, her mouth drawn in a tight line. Without a word, she got up and left the room, slamming her bedroom door behind her. She leaned against it and closed her eyes. They were right, and she hated them for it. She was ashamed of her sexual desires, which meant that she was ashamed of Dante's as well. How could she love a man she was ashamed of?

Hell, how could she love herself? She couldn't, she realized sadly, and that was the hardest thing of all. The irony of it wasn't lost on her; he'd once told her he wasn't capable of love and she'd told him he was wrong. Instead, she was the one who wasn't capable of love. Obviously there was something wrong with her because she knew she would never find someone who loved her more than Dante did.

With a heavy heart, she logged in to the computer and booked a flight to New York for the day after tomorrow. Dante had games tonight and tomorrow night and then a day off, so she would see him then; it wouldn't be fair to break things off right before he had to play.

She wouldn't tell him she was coming either, because he would undoubtedly make all kinds of romantic plans for them, and that would make things harder. He deserved to find someone who didn't have the hang-ups she did, and would love him unconditionally. She owed it to him to end things in person, though, and return his ring. It was the right thing to do. Even though nothing had ever felt more wrong.

29

THE ROOM WAS EERILY SILENT AS DANTE SAT AT THE MASSIVE CONFERENCE room table, his lawyers on either side of him. One of the owners of Club Inferno, Eamon MacCaffrey, wasn't having a good day, and Dante kept his face stony as his lawyers talked about lawsuits, financial restitution, slander, bad press, and so much legalese his head had begun to spin. They'd been in this meeting for over an hour and as the lawyers went at it, Dante remained stoic while Eamon looked increasingly nervous.

"I just want out!" the man exclaimed. "It's too much—the security breaches, the health inspectors, confidentiality agreements…"

"Then you should give it to me," Dante said impulsively. "Let's not make the lawyers richer. We can avoid lawsuits and a lot of time in court. Sign it over and be done."

Everyone in the room fell silent.

"Dante," Philip Marchand spoke under his breath. "We need to research this before—"

Eamon made an impatient gesture with his hand. "No! I want out of the damn place! My business partner bought it and said it would be great—but it's been nothing but a pain in the ass. We might have to exchange some money for insurance purposes but we can draw up papers to reflect us coming to an agreement."

"Fair enough." Dante nodded at Philip.

"But I have something else." Eamon drummed his fingers on the table. "If you give me your word that you won't sue me after the fact, I'll give you a name."

"I already have the name," Dante raised his eyebrows.

"You have the name of the person who released the pictures. You don't have the name of the person who told him you'd be there and when."

Dante felt his pulse quicken, though his face remained impassive. He shrugged, as though he was only faintly interested. "Really? What does that mean? I was targeted? By someone I know?"

"You were." Eamon nodded. "I didn't know until this morning. I found some old surveillance video and he was with Russ." Russ was the club employee who'd sold the pictures to the tabloids.

"And you want me to promise not to sue you in exchange for that video?"

Eamon nodded. "Up to you, mate."

Dante inclined his head. "Do you want this in writing?"

"Nah. Gentleman's agreement—a handshake in front of these lawyers —will do."

Dante held out his hand and they shook. Eamon did something on his phone and his lawyer nodded. Picking up his own phone, the attorney glanced at Philip. "I'll just email this to you and you can get it to Mr. Lamonte."

Philip nodded.

The others were busy talking numbers, contracts and other details that Dante systematically tuned out. He waited impatiently for Philip to receive the email and then forward it to Dante's phone. When he felt the vibration alerting him to a new email, he slowly opened the file and hit play. What he saw made his jaw clench. The hand not holding the phone closed into a fist at his side and he abruptly stood up.

"Sonofabitch," he hissed under his breath.

"Sorry, mate." Eamon looked genuinely unhappy. "Didn't realize who he was at first."

"I have to go." Dante waved him off when Philip started to get up. "I'll get a cab. Get me the contract for the club within twenty-four hours. Right now, there's something else I have to do."

He strode out of the offices and into the elevator. He couldn't remember ever being this angry—or feeling so betrayed. He needed to do something, but he didn't have a plan yet, and he wasn't stupid enough to do something impulsive. Becca was his priority, and he had to focus on that. They still hadn't spoken other than last night's brief texts and he knew she was either upset with him or retreating from the world. Or some combination of both. He'd needed to have this meeting first, though, to make sure everything was being handled. Now he could talk to her, explain what was happening.

He pulled out his phone when he got to the ground floor and called her, waiting impatiently as it rang. It finally went to voice mail and he frowned, wondering why she wouldn't be picking up early in the day. "It's me," he spoke into the phone. "I've been thinking about you, baby girl, and I have some news. Will you call me, *querida*? I know you must be feeling very alone right now, but I promise you're not. I'm taking care of this, okay? Trust me. I love you." He hung up and hailed a cab.

B ecca listened to Dante's message a while later and sighed. She knew if she talked to him before she got on the plane tomorrow she would lose her resolve, but she had to be strong. He'd suffered too much—lost too much —to be stuck with a woman who was embarrassed by their sex life and too weak to withstand the media scrutiny of being involved with a man like him.

He needed someone tougher, someone who would stand by his side with her head held high. Maybe someone like Emilie, who despite her shyness, was the strongest woman she'd ever met. After everything she'd been through, she'd started over, had a baby on her own and was moving on from her own scandal. Becca wished she could be more like her.

EMILIE: Can you talk? I need to talk to you!

Emilie's text startled her and Becca grimaced. They'd become close over the last couple of months and she hated the idea of losing her friendship, but Emilie and Viggo were together now; she would be okay. Still, it wasn't fair to completely ignore her.

BECCA: Kind of busy right now—everything okay?

EMILIE: Viggo wants to get married! When can you talk???

Shit. Becca sighed again and dialed Emilie's phone.

"Hi!" Emilie sounded breathless.

"What's wrong? Isn't it a good thing that he wants to get married?"

"Yes, but nothing's changed!" Emilie replied. "He's still bisexual and I'm still…me."

"Maybe he loves you," Becca suggested.

"He loves his daughter," Emilie said sadly. "I don't want to get married because of her."

"Why do you think that?"

"Between the porn video that was released and then having a baby behind his back..." Emilie let out a long breath of air. "I don't know how we'll make this work, Becca. What shall I do?"

"You have to talk to him—and be honest."

"Like you're doing with Dante?"

Becca froze. "What does that mean?"

"You think I don't know what you're up to? Hiding out, not here by his side like you should be. He handled a shit storm last night at the game—it was terrible. Didn't you see it on the sports channels?"

"I, um, I didn't watch anything." Becca felt a twinge of guilt. Damn, after she'd texted him she hadn't really thought about how much Dante might need *her*; she'd been too busy thinking about herself.

"He's not even playing," Emilie said quietly. "Last night was bad and this morning he left—I don't know where he went, but he's not playing tonight. I think the team told him to straighten this stuff out before he came back."

"Oh, no!" Becca felt even worse now. He'd truly needed her and she hadn't given it a second thought. Of course, she'd already figured out that she wasn't good enough for him; that's why she was going to end things.

She cleared her throat. "I feel bad about all that, but I'm going to talk to him in person. In the meantime, we're supposed to be talking about you."

Emilie hesitated. "Look, I know how you feel—you know I've been there —but it wasn't Viggo's fault that our sex tape was put on the internet, and these pictures are not Dante's fault. Whatever it is you're thinking, you have to stop. Dante hasn't thought about himself at all since this happened—all he's thought about is you. You really should get online and watch the news reports of the game last night. He loves you, Becca."

Becca closed her eyes, willing herself to be strong. "He deserves better, Em," she finally whispered. "He deserves someone strong enough to be at his side—not someone so caught up in her own shit that she can't be there for him."

"He doesn't need you to stand up for him, Becca—he just needs you to let him take care of you."

"I don't know what to do either, Em. Can you live with Viggo being bisexual? I don't know if I can live with…threesomes and sex clubs and all that."

"It's hard," Emilie agreed. "But I have Simone to think about."

"Yeah." Becca reached for a tissue and blew her nose.

"We both have to try."

"I'm coming to New York," Becca said reluctantly. "Don't tell him—I want it to be a surprise."

"And what will you do when you get here?"

"I'll make sure he's okay, and then I have to at least consider giving back the ring. I don't know if I can be what he needs."

"Oh, Becca."

"What are you going to do?"

"I'm going to close my eyes and jump."

"What does that mean?"

"It means—bisexual or not—he's my daughter's father. I have to try. If it doesn't work out, it can't be worse than not trying."

"I'm proud of you, Em." Becca felt a sharp pain sweeping though her and she took a deep breath. "You're doing the right thing. Anyway, I have to go."

"Becca, are you sure—"

"I'll see you soon," Becca whispered as she disconnected. This, she thought to herself, was surely what hell must be like.

B ecca breathed a sigh of relief when she saw Randy waiting for her just outside the security gates. She waved, glad he was there so she didn't have to worry about renting a car. She'd called him and explained that she was coming in to surprise Dante, making sure that he didn't tell him he was picking her up.

"How are you, Miss Becca?" Randy looked genuinely concerned. "Mr. Lamonte has had a rough few days."

She nodded. "It's been hard all around."

"Well, I'm sure you being here will be good for him. With Miss Emilie gone—"

"Emilie and Viggo already left?"

Randy nodded. "Took them to the airport a few hours ago—they went to Sweden. I guess they're getting married."

"She said yes." Becca smiled to herself. "That's good."

"He's gonna break her heart," Randy shook his head. "That boy's a wild one."

Becca glanced at him. "Why do you think that? He adores her."

He shrugged. "Seen him with women—seen him with men. It's not right. You gotta pick one or the other, you know? It's not natural to go both ways."

Becca felt a moment of discomfiture as she climbed into the limo.

"Don't you agree?" Randy glanced back at her after he climbed into the driver's seat.

Becca frowned. She didn't think Dante would want her talking to one of his employees about something like this, but Randy had obviously seen the pictures and knew the story. "I think it's more complicated than that," she said after a moment.

"Do you swing both ways, Miss Becca?" Randy pulled into traffic.

"No," she said slowly, "but sometimes I think you get caught up in a moment that's exciting and passionate—is that wrong?"

"Two men, two women—that's wrong. That's not what God intended."

She wanted to ask him if he'd managed to ask God that question person-ally, but decided against it. She would have to warn Dante that Randy had said some very judgmental things.

"Now Miss Larissa," Randy continued. "She knew what was right and what was wrong."

Becca's head shot up, startled. "Wh-what do you mean?" she managed to ask in a calm voice, even though she was getting a little nervous about the direction this conversation was going.

"She knew Mr. Lamonte pushed the envelope, but she was strong—she kept him in line. You, Miss Becca, you're not strong like Miss Larissa."

Becca narrowed her eyes. "I don't think you have any idea how strong I am."

"Someone has to take him down a few pegs—Miss Larissa was doing that. Then she died and he found you. I don't think you're strong enough to make him the man he needs to be."

30

off. And Randy had no right to talk to her this way.

"I'm stronger than you think!" she snapped angrily, her eyes blazing. She gently eased her hand into her purse and wrapped it around her phone, wondering how to get out of the car and away from him.

"If you were strong, you wouldn't have let him make you do those vile things." Randy's eyes met hers in the rearview mirror. "I think you're a nice girl, Miss Becca, but the things you let him do to you—that's wrong. If you don't repent, God will punish you."

For the first time she could remember, Becca didn't hesitate to defend herself, Dante and even their lifestyle. "The god I believe in isn't judgmental like that! He gave us free will so that we could use it for things that make us happy. Otherwise, why would he have given us the ability to think?"

"A murderer has the ability to think—but he thinks bad things. Some people are evil. Like Mr. Lamonte."

"He's not evil!" Becca hit the speed dial for Dante's number and set the phone on her lap, hidden by her purse. "He's kind and generous, talented and smart. He's been especially generous with you."

"Money is the devil's tool—godly men don't need money."

"So why do you work for him then?"

"I'm doing God's work—and I will bring him to his knees until he sees the error of his ways."

"Just how are you going to do that?"

"With you, of course."

Dante was so happy to see Becca's name pop up on his phone, he answered with a grin. "Bon jour, *querida*." He waited for her response but all he heard was muffled voices and static. "Becca?" He heard voices in the background and suddenly he recognized them. Hers. Randy's. Frozen in place, he listened intently.

...I'm doing God's work—and I will bring him to his knees until he sees the error of his ways.

Just how are you going to do that?

With you, of course...

Dante's blood ran cold. What the fuck?! Why was Becca with Randy and what the hell was he talking about? Becca had obviously called him so that he could hear their conversation, but he had no idea where they were or what was going on.

...If you hurt me, Dante will kill you.

Mr. Lamonte will have to answer for his sins when he meets his maker. No harm will come to you—you're just the bait.

I'm not going to let you hurt him! You'll have to kill me too.

Sometimes the innocent pay to spread His word. Just as Jesus sacrificed himself, I will sacrifice you...

Holy fuck, the guy was bat shit crazy, and he had Becca. Dante was on his feet, pacing, unsure who to call. He didn't have many friends, and the few he had were mostly in Las Vegas. He had one friend in New York, but what the hell could Jax do? Emilie and Viggo had left for Sweden, which meant that Becca was on her own. *Again.* Well, not this time. He grabbed his phone and dialed Randy's number.

"Good afternoon, Mr. Lamonte." Randy sounded just like he always did.

"Did Becca's flight arrive on time?" Dante spoke casually, hoping his guess that Randy had picked her up at the airport was correct.

There was a slight hesitation and then a chuckle. "It sure did. You want to talk to her?"

"If I wanted to talk to her, I would have called her," he said. "I'm in Manhattan and need you to come pick me up."

"That's kinda gonna be a problem, Mr. Lamonte. I don't think I'll be able to today."

"If you hurt her, you slimy little fuck," Dante didn't even try to pretend anymore. "I'll rip you to shreds with my bare hands."

Randy chuckled. "You should call her and say good-bye, Mr. L. I really don't think you'll find us in time to do it in person." He disconnected.

Dante immediately called Becca, his heart pounding in his chest.

"Hi." Becca sounded quiet.

"I'll find you," Dante said quietly. "He hasn't hurt you, has he?"

"Not yet," Becca murmured.

"Can you tell what direction you're going?" he asked quickly. "Are you heading north towards my house?"

"Yup."

"I have to go," he said regretfully. "I have to figure out where you are so I can get to you. Keep reminding him it's me he wants—and remember I love you, baby."

"I love you too."

S ince Randy had driven him into Manhattan this morning for his meeting, Dante had no way to get back. Public transportation would be a nightmare at this time of day, so he rented a car. Within thirty minutes he was on the road, praying traffic would cooperate. If he didn't get held up and he could find an open stretch of highway, he could be in Westchester County in less than an hour in this car.

He didn't know what he would do when he got home, but he was sure Randy would contact him. Obviously, he had something on his mind and he'd taken Becca to lure Dante to wherever they were; he just didn't understand what Becca was doing here. He'd guessed that Randy had picked her up at the airport, but he didn't know why or when she'd made this plan. Shit, he had a lot of questions and no way to get any answers.

His phone rang and he put it on speakerphone. "Yes?"

"Dante, it's Em! Listen—"

"Aren't you on the way to Sweden?" he interrupted.

"We're in a limo heading back to your house. I just wanted—"

"No! Under no circumstances are you to go back to the house!"

"What? Dante, what's going on?"

"Is Viggo with you?"

"Yes, of course. Our flight was cancelled and—"

"Let me talk to him."

"Um, okay." Emilie handed the phone to Viggo, who took it curiously. "Dante?"

"Listen to me—Randy has kidnapped Becca. I'm on my way home, but you need to take Emilie and the baby to a hotel! He's lost his fucking mind and I don't think you're safe at the house."

"What the hell is going on?" Viggo grunted. "Do you have any friends who aren't crazy?!"

"He wasn't a friend!" Dante snapped. "He's my fucking employee!"

"Yeah, sorry." Viggo paused. "What can I do to help?"

"Take care of your girls. I can't do anything except wait to hear from him and then trade myself for Becca."

"You can't do this alone," Viggo said after a moment.

"Your responsibility is to Emilie."

"You took care of her for me for almost a year—it's only right I return the favor."

"You didn't know she needed you—that wasn't your fault."

"Nonetheless." Viggo said something to Emilie in Swedish. "Look, I'll find somewhere safe to leave the two of them and then meet you at your house —little bastard doesn't scare me."

They briefly discussed logistics and Dante hung up.

"Trey? You payin' attention up there?" He couldn't believe he was talking to a dead man. "If you are, I could use a little help right now. You got me, homeboy?"

Then he took a leap of faith. Somewhere in his fucked-up life there had to be some good other than Becca; he dialed Jax's number.

Becca watched the city limits disappear and the highway become a two-lane road. Soon there were no buildings or houses at all, just a few random mailboxes on the side of the street. She wondered where they were and the GPS on her phone was no help because she'd lost the signal about twenty miles ago. She'd texted Kate several times, so she would know what was going on, but Randy didn't seem to care that she was on her phone. That was a bad sign so Becca tried to keep track of landmarks and anything else that might help her if she managed to get away. Something told her that wasn't likely, though.

"We're almost there, Miss Becca," Randy seemed like his usual cheerful self.

"Why are you calling me Miss Becca?" she asked. "It's not like you're working for Dante anymore."

"What else would I call you? You're not married, so you wouldn't be missus, and we're not friends, so Becca is too familiar."

She frowned. "We're not friends now because Dante and I have sex you don't approve of?"

"You shouldn't let him talk you into those things…it makes you look cheap. Now the whole world has seen the pictures and you're both going to have to pay."

"You said you weren't going to hurt me."

"Well…not much. Depends on how much Mr. Lamonte is willing to do to prove he's repentant."

Becca felt a little sick to her stomach, wondering what he expected Dante to do and what he would do to her to manipulate him. She wouldn't allow it, though. No matter what, even if he raped and tortured her, she wouldn't let him use her to hurt Dante; somehow, she had to be strong enough to get through this without either of them dying. Dante had suffered so much emotional pain last year she couldn't stand the thought of him being hurt anymore.

I love him more than I love myself, she realized miserably. She'd always loved him, probably a little bit even before she'd met him, but now that they'd been together as a couple she realized just how much he meant to her. Even if they weren't meant to be together, she would die before letting a creep like Randy hurt him.

<hr>

Becca thought she was going to die in the heat. Sitting in the old barn behind the main house, there wasn't even the slightest breeze. Randy had left her there, a tight leather cuff on her left wrist that attached to a rope tied to a slat in the wall. She couldn't budge it, so she had about six feet she could move in any direction. She'd been sitting on a smelly bale of hay for the last three hours and was going out of her mind.

She was hot, sweaty and desperately had to go to the bathroom. For a while she'd been scared, then she'd moved into nervous, and now she'd reached the pissed off stage. She was really hot, really uncomfortable and really, really mad. If Randy got close enough she was going to kick him right in the nuts.

She stood up and stretched, hoping to find some relief, but there was none. She yearned to take off her T-shirt but that probably would only invite trouble, and she was in enough. This really sucked.

She heard footsteps outside and promptly sat back down on the hay. Randy came in with a bottle of water and an apple. She knew there was a chance the water was drugged, but she didn't think getting dehydrated would help either. Though she was reluctant, she took the water and drank deeply, ignoring him.

"I'm sorry it had to be this way, Miss Becca." He sat a few feet away, looking at her.

"You're not sorry!" she snapped.

"I really am," he said. "You're a nice girl, but once I saw those pictures, I realized that you're like the rest of them. I don't want to hurt you, but that's the only way to get Dante to stop what he's doing."

"What, exactly, is he doing?"

"Going against the word of God."

Becca resisted the urge to roll her eyes and just looked at him. "Not everyone believes in the same gods, Randy. Jews don't believe the same things about Jesus as Christians. Buddhists honor a real man, who once walked the earth and whose ideology is now represented by the Dalai Lama. Muslims—"

"It doesn't matter!" he interrupted with a hiss, his face tightening angrily. "The word of God is clear! Corinthians 7:2 says, 'Nevertheless, to avoid fornication, let every man have his own wife, and let every woman have her own husband.' There is no room for the things you do!"

"In John it says, 'If we confess our sins, he is faithful and just and will forgive us our sins and purify us from all unrighteousness,'" she shot back, scowling.

"You think you know your bible, girl?" He took a step forward. "Galatians: 'Now the works of the flesh are manifest, which are these; adultery, fornication, uncleanness, lasciviousness, idolatry, witchcraft, hatred, variance, emulations, wrath, strife, seditions, heresies, envyings, murders, drunkenness, revellings, and such like: of the which I tell you before, as I have also told you in time past, that they which do such things shall not inherit the kingdom of God.'"

She folded her arms across her chest and glared. "Luke: 'Judge not, and ye shall not be judged: condemn not, and ye shall not be condemned: forgive, and ye shall be forgiven.' What else ya got for me?" All those years of Catholic school were obviously paying off.

"Don't play with me, little girl. I've been patient with you because I sense the good girl buried within you, but you aren't godly enough to use those scriptures!"

"John: 'There is no fear in love; but perfect love casteth out fear: because fear hath torment. He that feareth is not made perfect in love.'"

He walked up to her and slapped her, the sound almost deafening in the otherwise silent barn. "You will not take the Lord's name in vain!"

"I didn't!" she hissed, rubbing her hand over her burning cheek. "I quoted him to remind you that God forgives—he's not full of righteousness and hatred like you!"

He slapped her again and this time Becca had to fight the tears burning behind her eyes.

"Go ahead—lecture me some more!" he growled.

"Daniel: 'The Lord our God is merciful and forgiving, even though we have rebelled against him,'" she whispered, refusing to break eye contact.

This time his hand was in a fist and she tasted blood when it connected with her mouth. She gritted her teeth and refused to back away, though she felt a slight wave of dizziness and realized he had, indeed, drugged her. She knew it was only a matter of time before she lost consciousness and she swiped at the blood on her lip angrily.

"Learned your lesson yet, girl?" he taunted.

"All I've learned is that you're a hypocrite." She closed her eyes when the next blow came, and then there was blissful darkness.

IT WAS NEARLY MIDNIGHT BEFORE THE PHONE RANG AND DANTE WAS ABOUT to crawl out of his skin when he saw it was a video feed from Randy using FaceTime. He growled into the phone when he answered, "She'd better be alive and unharmed!"

"She's taking a little nap," Randy said pleasantly. "She has quite a mouth on her—is that what you like? Or is it the way she lets you defile her?"

"What do you want?!" Dante yelled, the veins in his neck beginning to pulse.

"You."

"When and where?"

"Come by yourself—the appearance of police or anyone else means I hurt her more."

The camera moved to where Becca seemed to be asleep on a bale of hay, in her bra and underwear. There was a rope around her neck, and though it was slack right now, Dante saw where it was tied to some sort of beam in the ceiling. The picture zoomed in and he hissed deep in his chest when he saw what appeared to be cigarette burns up and down the inside of her thigh. He felt Jax's hand on his shoulder, squeezing, and heard Viggo's sharp intake of breath.

"You'll get a text with the address—leave the redheaded stud and your blond friend behind. I allowed her to sleep through it for now, but I can always wake her up for what I have planned next. If you bring police, she'll asphyxiate before they can get to me. I have cameras all over the grounds."

The screen went dead and Dante whirled, his chest rising and falling with the need to contain a kind of rage he'd never before experienced.

"What do you want to do? You can't go alone. You know this." Viggo was at his side, his voice quiet.

"I have to!" Dante grunted, feeling in his pockets for his keys.

"What if we wait fifteen minutes and then send help?" Cyndi suggested quietly.

"I don't—" Dante's phone buzzed and yanked it out, staring at the address. "Where the fuck is this?!"

"That's the middle of nowhere," Jax said, looking over his shoulder. "It'll take you close to an hour to get there. Probably no cell service, so you'll be hard-pressed to call for help once you're there."

"Maybe not." Cyndi smiled as she began walking out of the room. "Don't go anywhere, Dante—I have something that will help."

Dante was too riled up to stay still but he was anxious to see what Cyndi had. When she reappeared a moment later he frowned. "What is that?"

"It's a satellite phone," she grinned. "Grizzly Adams here likes to go on extreme survival trips, but I made him get this because last time he did it, our son broke his leg and I couldn't reach him for three days!"

"Thank you." Dante's face softened slightly. "I appreciate it."

"Look, we're coming too," Jax said. "No way in hell you're doing this alone. I know that area out there because that's where we do our survivalist training." He glanced at Viggo. "Can you hike, do some minor climbing?"

Viggo nodded. "I can do whatever is necessary."

"Text me the address," Jax said. "And don't worry—he'll never see us coming. We'll be about fifteen minutes behind you 'cause I need to get some gear."

"Thank you. All of you." Dante nodded before turning to jog out to the car. When he got his hands on Randy, he was going to kill him, slowly and painfully.

D ante's grip on the steering wheel was so hard he felt the sweat pooling between his skin and the leather, but he couldn't let up. He was seething, the sight of Becca's raw, bleeding skin burned into his mind. The fact that this motherfucker had actually touched her left him reeling; he didn't even know what he would do when he got there. He had no doubt Becca would be in a vulnerable position, so instantly attacking him wouldn't be prudent.

No, he would have to use his brains and his street instincts to guide him;

luckily he had plenty of those thanks to Larissa. He shook his head, amazed he was thinking of her at a time like this, but she'd been the one to take a shy kid from Cuba and show him how to protect himself on the rough streets of Miami.

As he drove out of the city limits, he focused on clearing his mind of anything but driving and remaining calm. Randy had been the one who gave information to Russ so obviously he'd been unhappy with Dante for quite a while. Taking it to this extreme was surprising, though, and Dante intended to find out what the hell his problem was. Being embarrassed was par for the course for Dante; he didn't even think twice about it anymore.

He knew it was hard for Becca and poor Jamie couldn't seem to stay out of trouble, but Dante let that stuff roll off his back. He hit a few grand slams and everyone forgot everything except what a great athlete he was. It was kind of funny, the way he could target his game when he needed to, but that's what made him a superstar in the baseball world. A lesser player probably would have been gone by now.

The GPS told him he was getting close and he slowed down, turning on his bright lights and scanning the area. The turn was onto a rough, unpaved road and he bounced along slowly. He didn't see anything at first, but then a house with lights on came into view. He stopped the car and turned off the lights, opting to get out and walk. He could be heading into a trap, but there was no help for that. Becca was in trouble and he would sacrifice himself to keep her safe; it was his fault she was in this mess in the first place.

"You made good time." Randy came out from behind the house and walked towards him.

"You hurt her," Dante said in a steely voice. "I told you I would do whatever you wanted—why would you hurt her?"

"Because she's obviously a whore, like the others. I thought this one was different, but after I saw those pictures I realized she isn't worthy either."

"Worthy of what? Me?" Dante narrowed his eyes. "She's too good for me!"

"Larissa was the woman you should have been faithful to."

"I *was* faithful to her!" he snapped. "She's the one who betrayed me!"

"You cheated on her." Randy folded his arms. "At least once."

Dante wondered how the hell he knew that, but if he was friends with Russ, he'd obviously been watching him for a while, and that pissed him off even more. "So you been watching me all this time?" Dante moved forward, his gait slow but purposeful, his accent heavier as the fury surging through him kept him from focusing on any kind of intonation. "You been keeping track of what I do, and who I do it with?"

"I thought for sure you and Kate were going to get it on, but she's a lady with morals who made you do the right thing. Initially I thought Becca was going to be a nice girl but she ruined it by going to that club with you. Now she has to pay for your sins, because I'm sure you made her do those things."

"I did," Dante said, stopping just a few feet in front of Randy. "That's why you shouldn't do this to her. She only did those things because she was afraid I would leave her if she didn't, so you need to let her go."

Randy chuckled. "Oh, but it's so much fun watching you get upset. You want to see her? I don't know if she's awake yet, but I'm sure she'll be relieved to see you're here."

Dante took a breath. "Tell me what you want, Randy."

"You have to repent for your evil ways—and join your soulmate in the afterlife."

Dante grunted. "You talkin' about Larissa? You want me dead so I can be with her?" He laughed derisively. "She didn't love me…she only got knocked up so she could get a paycheck."

"She was the woman for you!" Randy yelled, raising one fist and shaking it. "She made you who you are and you owed her! A baby, a life—everything!"

"I didn't kill her," he said calmly. "She teamed up with that crazy bitch Therese and that's what got her killed. Otherwise, we'd be married now." That wasn't true, but Randy had no way of knowing that.

"Does Becca even know she's a homewrecker?"

Dante pressed his lips together, trying to keep from exploding since he didn't know what condition Becca was in right now. "I used her—it was a one-night stand and if you've been watching me so closely, you know I didn't have nothin' to do with her until months later."

Randy snorted. "Only because you were grieving—mourning a baby that wasn't even yours, you know."

Dante glanced at the man sharply. "Really? And you know this how?"

"Larissa told me." Randy smirked at him. "She knew her days with you were limited but she felt like you owed her since she's the reason you even play baseball! The only way she would get money from you would be to have a kid, and that's the only reason she did it. She told me everything! We were friends; she could have loved me if I'd had more time with her."

Dante arched an eyebrow. "You realize she was suckin' my dick every night from the day she moved in?"

Randy snarled. "She did what she had to do to get what was rightfully hers!"

"So she was basically a whore."

"Fuck you!" Randy lunged at him but Dante sidestepped him and shook his head.

"You don't want to do that," Dante said evenly. "You know you can't take me, old man."

"When I'm done with your girl back there, you're going to let me do whatever I want to you."

"You still haven't let me see her."

"Then by all means, let's go do that."

Randy turned and strode behind the house and Dante followed. This was escalating and he didn't have a plan unless Viggo and Jax showed up. Even then, he didn't know what they could do. If Randy had a gun, it was highly unlikely no one would get hurt and he really didn't want anyone else to get hurt because of him; he would always blame himself for Trey's death. Whatever was going on now was his fault, once again, and he had to force the images of the burns on Becca's thighs out of his mind as he strode towards the big, dark barn. Damn, she was probably terrified in there. Just the thought made his heart start pumping double time.

He quickened his pace and walked through the door that Randy had left open. His breath caught in his throat as he took in the scene before him. Becca was standing, hands tied behind her back, the rope tied around her neck hanging loosely from a beam in the ceiling. The other end of the rope was in Randy's hand and he was pulling it taut.

Oh, fuck no.

32

"YOU NEED TO LET HER GO," DANTE GROWLED THROUGH CLENCHED TEETH. "She's not the one you want."

"She's the reason you broke my Larissa's heart," he snarled back. "After you were with this one, Larissa told me you wouldn't touch her anymore."

"If she didn't love me," Dante ground out, glaring at him, "why would she care who I was with?"

"Because she wanted to hurt you the way you hurt her!"

"She got my best friend killed—she definitely hurt me way worse than I ever hurt her!"

"Not good enough!" Randy yanked the rope until it pulled tight, making Becca gasp, her eyes wide with fear.

"I should be in Becca's place," Dante said. "I'm the one you want to punish."

"But I *am* punishing you," Randy smiled. "Watching the woman you love die will be exactly the type of pain Larissa wanted you to feel."

"I won't let you kill her," Dante advanced on him slowly. "You're going to have to kill me too, and then nothing will hurt either of us."

"But I'll have the satisfaction of knowing you're going to burn in the bowels of hell!"

Dante snorted. "For real? That's what you got?" He chuckled. "All the shit I done? The devil is afraid of *me, pendejo.*" *Dumbass.*

"You'll burn! And your whore with you!" He yanked on the rope so that Becca was standing on her tiptoes, her breath coming in gasps. Dante snarled but before he could move Randy pulled a gun from behind him. "Don't even think about it. She'll be dead before you can get this away from me—I'll yank hard enough to break her neck." He walked backward, holding the rope taut and tying it around an exposed slat on the far wall.

Dante pointed a finger at him. "You have a death wish, *maricon*?" *Faggot.*

"The only one dying tonight is her. And maybe you."

"Dante, no." Becca's voice came in huffs as she struggled to breathe. "He's going to kill me anyway—don't sacrifice yourself for nothing!"

He met her terrified gaze with a tender look. "If he kills you, I have nothing left to live for, *querida*." He saw a shadow in the doorway and knew it was now or never; either Jax and Viggo were here or he was fucked anyway. Hearing Becca gasping for breath was more than he could stand. He dove like he was trying to reach home plate in the bottom of the ninth of the World Series, throwing his body as low and as far as he could. He hit his target, taking out Randy's feet and they went down in a heap. Dante watched the gun fly off to the side and tried to position his body in a way that inhibited Randy from seeing it.

"Get Becca!" Dante yelled when he spied Viggo and Jax bursting through the doors. He brought his knee up between Randy's legs and the man howled in pain, pulling his body into the fetal position. "You fucking burned her—you burned my beautiful Becca? Motherfucker, you're a dead man!" He drove his fist into the side of Randy's face, his expression indifferent as blood burst from the older man's nose.

"Dante!" Becca was sobbing now, coughing and sputtering as Viggo pulled off his shirt and tried to cover her.

"I got him, man." Jax put his knee in the middle of Randy's back, pinning him to the ground with his weight. "Go take care of Becca."

Dante got up slowly, breathing hard and glaring at the man on the floor.

"'But as for the cowardly, the faithless, the detestable, as for murderers, the sexually immoral, sorcerers, idolaters, and all liars, their portion will be in the lake that burns with fire and sulfur, which is the second death!'" Randy was yelling at the top of his lungs.

"Fuck you." Dante leaned over and spit in the man's face. "You think hurting an innocent woman makes you godly? I think it makes you the devil incarnate." He turned and in two long steps had Becca in his arms. "I'm so sorry, baby girl…I'd kill him if I could get away with it."

"No." Her voice was raspy against his chest.

"Dante." Viggo handed him his T-shirt and Dante took it gratefully.

"Come on, put this on so my friends stop staring at your tits."

Her eyes widened but then she smiled wanly as she realized he was joking.

"Yeah, okay." She pulled the T-shirt over her head and rested against Dante's broad chest. "I was so scared."

"I know, baby." He gently ran his fingers along her bruised throat.

"What do we do with him?" Jax asked, still holding Randy down.

"I say we tie his ass up and leave him here," Dante grunted.

"I don't want to start our life with blood on our hands," Becca whispered. "Just leave him where he is and let's go."

"Is that what you want, baby?" Dante looked deep into her eyes and she nodded. "He deserves to go to prison, at the very least."

"But at what cost to our privacy?" She turned to look down at Randy. "'And above all things have fervent charity among yourselves: for charity shall cover the multitude of sins.'"

"Amen," Viggo muttered.

"No more scandals," Becca whispered. "No more drama. We walk away from here and forget this ever happened."

"Becca…" Dante was scowling, looking down at Randy with pure hatred.

"Please?" she whispered. "For me. Can we just go? Think about it—cops, a trial, lawyers, interviews—it will never end, Dante. *Please.*"

He took a long, deep breath and met Jax's eyes. Jax nodded just slightly and Dante's glance moved to Viggo, who also nodded, albeit reluctantly. "All right," he said after a moment. "Let's get out of here."

"Can you find my purse?" Becca whispered.

"I see it," Viggo said, walking towards the brown leather he saw peeking out through some hay.

"My suitcase is in the limo," she said.

"I'll get it," Viggo headed outside.

"Whore!" Randy yelled out.

Jax put his booted foot on Randy's throat. "Go 'head," he drawled. "Say it again."

Randy gurgled something before Jax kicked him in the nuts. His howls of agony were the last thing they heard before they got into Dante's car.

"Let's get out of here," Jax said. "Cyndi can take me to get my truck later —we left it in the woods and I just want to get home."

"We should go to a hospital," Dante said quietly.

"No." Becca shook her head. "After the pictures in the media this week, if we're not pressing charges, they might think *you* did this. I just want to go home."

"You want to go back to Vegas?" he asked softly, pausing to look at her before putting the car in gear.

"Your home," she said. "*Our* home."

Dante nodded as he pulled onto the street. "Are you in pain, honey?"

"My thigh burns…" Her voice faded as she glanced down and saw what he'd done; she hadn't noticed it before. "What the fuck did he do to me?!"

"Looks like cigarette burns," he said gently. "I've got some cream at home, should help with the pain."

"Oh my God. Did he…" Her voice trailed off.

"I don't know," Dante admitted. "Do you…feel anything?"

She shook her head as she noted that there was no discomfort in her genital area. "No. I don't think so."

"You sure you don't want to go to the hospital? Have yourself checked?"

"No." She made a face. "If I thought he'd raped me, I would, but I'm pretty sure he didn't and I just want to go home."

"Can I call Em?" Viggo asked after a moment. "I'm sure she's frantic, waiting for news."

"Of course," Dante nodded. "You can go get them once we get home."

Viggo grumbled when he realized he couldn't get a signal on his phone.

"I appreciate your help," Dante said to his friends. "I don't know how things would have gone…"

"It's all good," Jax shrugged. "That's what friends are for."

"If he'd hurt her—"

"It's over," Becca reached for his hand and squeezed it. "Let's not think about the what ifs."

She fell asleep on the drive home and Dante gently picked her up when they arrived. Viggo took Emilie's car to go get her and the baby while Jax called Cyndi. Dante thanked them once more before carrying Becca up the stairs and into the bathroom.

"I'm filthy," she whispered.

"I know. We'll take a nice, cool shower so the burns don't hurt."

"Okay." She rested against him as he undressed them and stepped under the water. She didn't move as he ran a washcloth down her back, her arms and legs, before turning her and doing the front. He quickly washed her hair, noting that her eyes were barely staying open and her legs buckled a few times.

Rinsing them both off, he stepped out and lifted her into his arms, wrapping a large towel around her. He laid her on the bed and slowly dried her off before quickly rubbing down his own body and pulling on a pair of boxers. He pulled a T-shirt out of his drawer and eased it over her head, watching as she rolled against him, burying her face in his shoulder.

"Hold me," she whispered.

"I'm here, baby girl." He kissed the top of her head. "Do you want me to brush your hair so it's not full of knots in the morning?"

"Okay." She forced herself to sit up when he came back with a comb and he worked the knots out of her tangled hair. Finally, when it was soft and knot-free, he wrapped his arms around her and pulled up the sheet.

"I'm sorry," he said, lips against her face. "All these bad things keep happening to people I love. I'm fucking jinxed. I don't want you to live your life wondering what's going to happen next, so if you need to stay away from me..."

Despite her exhaustion, she opened her eyes and met his regretful gaze. "I love you," she whispered. "Staying away from you would be like ripping out my heart and putting it in a meat grinder. I came to New York because I didn't think I was good enough for you—every time the going gets tough I want to walk away—and you deserve better. I don't want to be ashamed of who we are because our love is beautiful, even though I couldn't shake the feeling that what we did at the club is wrong—"

"Baby—"

She put two fingers over his lips. "But as I sat there and listened to Randy tell me you were a sinner and that we were going to hell, I realized that while I'm still kind of embarrassed and coming to terms with all of that—I don't believe we're bad people. I think you're the sweetest, gentlest, kindest man I've ever known. I love you with everything that I am. When he started talking about using me to get to you, I wanted to die before I let him hurt you. Through all the pain and embarrassment, there is nothing I want more than to be your wife, give you a son...and be with you forever."

The emotion in his chest was overwhelming as he pulled her close, holding her so tightly he was afraid he might hurt her. "I don't want you to wake up every day ashamed," he whispered softly. "I want you to be happy, light, free from the pain of the past—I'll do anything to give you that."

"You already have," she murmured, pressing her lips to his throat. "You give me everything. I just didn't realize it until that stupid fuck sat there talking about how evil you were."

"I feel evil sometimes," he admitted. "It's my fault Trey is dead, my fault you've been embarrassed so many times...I'm tired of being in the middle of a different shit storm every other day."

"No more," she said, scooting up so she could look in his eyes. "It ends now. I don't care what anyone thinks and if the Sidewinders want to fire me, fine. I can work for Kate part-time and wait tables for all I care!"

"You're never going to wait tables, baby," he chuckled. "If you want to work for Kate, I got no problem with that, but I plan to put a baby in you the minute you say you're ready, so there's no waiting tables in your future."

"No baby yet," she said quietly. "I need a little time for it to be just us, okay? For me to get used to everything we've been through. Can you wait a year?"

"Yeah, baby girl. I can wait as long as you need me to." He kissed her, his lips parting hers softly, a gentle co-mingling that told her how much he loved her.

"I'm so tired, Dante." She closed her eyes, utterly exhausted now that she'd told him how she felt.

"I love you, *querida*."

"I love you too."

33

Becca woke alone, as usual, and she chuckled to herself as she accepted that Dante would always be an early riser who got up before she did. Unless she asked him not to once in a while, when they could wake up together and make love. How long had it been? Too long, she thought with a grimace. She grabbed her phone and texted him.

BECCA: Where are you? I'm naked. My thigh really hurts…I might need someone to rub it…

She smiled to herself when she heard his steps on the stairs not twenty seconds later.

"I thought you said you were naked," he chuckled as he stepped into the room.

"I am." She yanked off the T-shirt and grinned.

"You missed me?" he asked, putting aside the papers he had in his hand as he crawled across the bed, his eyes glittering dangerously.

"Every second of every day," she breathed, sliding up against him. She winced as the hair on his legs rubbed up against her thigh.

"That hurts?" He paused, leaning back and running gentle fingers over the welts. He'd rubbed antibiotic cream over them last night after she'd fallen asleep and they were much better this morning, but she'd jumped when the hair on his legs brushed against them.

"I'll be okay," she said. "I just need you to touch me…I need you inside me, Dante. I need…you."

"Oh, baby girl, you've got me—always." He kissed her but pulled away again. "I can't make love to you knowing you're in pain—two seconds, baby." He got off the bed and went into the bathroom, coming out again with things she couldn't quite see.

"What's that?" she asked.

"Most of the burns are here," he ran his hand along the affected area. "I'm going to put ointment on them and cover them with bandages. After we make love, we'll take them off, but I can't concentrate if I think you're in pain—not the kind of pain that *bastardo* caused you."

Her insides turned to mush as she watched him tending to the wounds on her thigh, his fingers as gentle as a summer breeze as he covered her skin. How she'd ever doubted that they belonged together she would never know, but seeing him take care of her was like nothing she'd ever experienced. The raw tenderness, completely unaffected by his erection or her naked body, moved her in ways nothing else had. Despite their unmistakable desire for each other, he put her comfort—and the pain from these wounds—first. So many things made sense now, so when he put his supplies aside and reached for her, she melted into him, burying her face in his chest.

"You okay?" He lifted her chin.

"Your touch—the way you love me—is something I can feel both inside and out. It literally penetrates right into my soul, and I actually feel it, like the very essence of how you love me fills something that I never realized was empty. I can't quite explain how it feels knowing your love is part of me."

"Fuck." His fingers dug into her ass as he pulled her astride him. "What you just said is so damn beautiful, and instead of thinking of something romantic to say, my dick went into overdrive instead."

"That's okay," she smiled, running her fingers along the line of his jaw. "That's part of who we are together—romantic, sexy, horny as hell! I'm not ashamed of what we have when we're together...not anymore."

"God, baby girl, I love you so much."

His mouth took hers aggressively, with a hunger she hadn't felt from him before. This transcended sex; this was pure human need. His desire to possess her not just physically, but emotionally as well, was heady. It was the sexiest, most romantic thing she'd ever experienced and she kissed him back with passion she didn't realize she was capable of. The sex they had at the club, or when he tied her up and made her beg him to let her come, didn't require the kind of passion she was feeling now. This was different, so intensely focused on the bond they shared, so much more than the act itself, so all-encompassing she didn't think she could stand it when he slid inside of her.

His cock pried her open one mesmerizing inch at a time, spreading her legs, her folds, her pulsing lips. She shook around him, every inch of her body quivering with a basal need to have more. He took her to new heights with every stroke, the connection moving from the apex between her legs straight to her soul, as though it resided in a specific place within her body.

"Dante!" His name slipped out between kisses, all but disappearing into his mouth. "I love you!"

"Yeah, baby…you do." He couldn't stop moving now if his life depended on it, totally immersed in everything that was Becca; her lips, her soft, round curves, the way her pussy clutched at his cock. It was all Becca today, giving him something no one had ever given him before. This was pure, genuine, 100% love. There could never be another word for it; the woman he was buried inside of had turned her entire being inside out and given it to him as their bodies moved together. Loving her, making love to her, and being in love with her were one and the same; there would never be anything, or anyone, else.

He plunged deep and forced himself to pause, waiting until her eyes fluttered open and met his. "First time I touched you," he rasped, "you took my heart with you when you left. Never been anybody before you like this and there will never be anyone else…say it, Becca. Say you're mine, baby girl."

"Completely," she panted.

He reached down to bring her legs up around his waist. He slid his hands under her ass and lifted her against him so he could move deeper, thrust harder and make her lose control. Watching her come was still the sexiest thing he'd ever seen. Back when he'd given her that very first orgasm, he'd thought it was because the chemistry between them was special. More than a year and many orgasms later, he knew it was because *she* was special.

"Dante!" Her breathing quickened and her legs tightened instinctively. "Oh, baby, please, please…"

"Come for me, *querida*—just like the first time, just for me."

His sweet words undid her and she unraveled around him, her shriek piercing the air as she lost herself in pulsing flesh and ecstasy that left her mindless and numb, oblivious to the growl that built with his release. Neither of them moved, immersed in each other and the exquisite aftershocks of their simultaneous orgasms.

"I guess you forgot that Emilie and Viggo are home," he said after a while, a cheeky grin on his face.

"Aw, shit," she groaned. "I howled like a fucking banshee too."

"It was really loud," he agreed, chuckling.

"Shut up!" She winced as she lowered her legs. "Oh, ow! Dante, take the bandages off please—it burns!"

"Of course." He quickly removed the bandages he'd put on and saw that they'd rubbed a couple of the welts raw again in their lust. "We'll need to clean and dress these again, *querida*. I don't want them to become infected."

"Okay." She lay back as he applied more ointment, his deft fingers gently cleaning each wound, making sure there were no signs of infection, and covering them with the medicine that would help them heal.

When he was done, he went into the bathroom to wash his hands and she followed him, needing to use the facilities. He glanced at her as she sat on the toilet and he smiled. "Do you know how long it's been since a woman was comfortable enough to pee in front of me?"

She smiled. "I've never peed in front of anyone other than my mother."

He leaned over and kissed her. "I'm very flattered."

"Dante?"

"Yes, love?"

"We have to talk."

"I know, baby. Matilda is here so—"

"Matilda is here too?!" Her eyes widened and she turned pink. "Dammit, Dante! There are going to be rules in this house when I move in!"

"You're moving in?" He cocked his head. "Soon?"

She rolled her eyes. "Stop changing the subject—when I move in, I have to be made aware when there are people in the house. I'm not embarrassed that we make love, but it's private sometimes. Sometimes I don't want anyone, not even Emilie and Viggo, to hear us. When we're at the club, it's different, but in our home, I need to be able to make a *choice*."

He froze, trying to assimilate all the information she'd just thrown at him.

"Are you mad?" She asked when he didn't say anything for a while.

"What?" he started. "No, of course not! I'm just...well, you said a lot of things. When we go back to the club? When you're living here? Are those things happening?"

"Yes, of course they are! Not right this minute, but soon."

"What I started to say," he said, trying to wrap his head around everything, "is that I'll ask Matilda to bring up coffee and croissants, if that's okay. Then we can talk—in *private*."

"That would be lovely. Thank you." She leaned over the sink to wash her face and he left her to it.

Ten minutes later they were dressed and lounging in the small sitting area by a large bay of windows. Becca grinned when Dante poured her coffee for her and he arched an eyebrow. "What? You don't like when I'm a gentleman?"

"I love it!" she giggled. "It's just not very…Dante Lamonte-ish?"

He made a face. "Perhaps that's the old Dante Lamonte—this one wants to do nothing but make you happy."

"I like the old Dante," she said softly. "So don't change him."

"Okay." He sank into the chair with a grin. "Then pour my damn hot water, woman."

She chuckled, but got up and poured the water for his tea, earning a soft pat on her behind.

"So, I have something for you," he said after she was sitting down again. He handed her an envelope. "I know at first glance this is a very odd gift, but I'd like to explain before you open it."

"Okay." She held it in her lap, watching his face.

"You said not that long ago that no one ever took care of you…" He stared out the window. "I hated that. Hated that you felt that way, but also hated that it was something out of my control. When this opportunity fell into my lap, I realized it was a solution for more than one thing. First, we take control of what was an embarrassing situation and make it our bitch. Second, it will give you financial security—no one will ever have to take care of you in that way. As long as you, or we, keep an eye on the business, you will always be a very wealthy woman."

"Dante…" Her eyes widened as she stared at the large envelope in her lap. "What—"

He held up a finger. "But it's also a way of exorcising your demons. Club Inferno is yours, Becca. Run it, lease it out to an independent club promoter, sell it—I don't care. But that's your security—so you never have to worry about your job or your mother or anything else related to money."

"Dante!" Tears began spilling down her cheeks as she stared at him. "It's too much! I can't—"

"You can." He got out of his chair and dropped to his knees in front of her. "Club Inferno is where we met, where I fell in love with you—where you gave yourself to me. I never, ever want you to feel shame when you think of it. I want you to own it—take it and make it whatever you want it to be—and fuck the rest of the world. You are my everything, Becca, and it's because of Club Inferno that I have you."

34

BECCA TOSSED THE ENVELOPE ASIDE AND WRAPPED HER ARMS AROUND HIM. "I don't know the first thing about, I mean—"

"We'll find the best people to run it for us." He was thoughtful. "Trey's boyfriend, the man he loved here in New York, Joe—runs a bodyguard and security firm. I'm sure we can get excellent people to work security for us. We'll get an accountant to go over the books with a fine-tooth comb and we'll hire a business consultant to help us structure the fees so that it's profitable. You can be as involved as you want, or completely hands-off—as long as you're happy."

"I don't even know what to say," she whispered.

He leaned forward and rested his head against her chest. "Say that you love me."

"I love you."

"Say that this makes you happy."

"It makes me overwhelmed, but happy too."

He lifted a hand to caress her cheek. "Although Randy was responsible for telling people where I was going and when, a man named Russ was the one who secretly set up cameras to take those pictures. I'm suing him for more than he'll ever be able to pay, so hopefully he'll never be able to fuck with people again. I've also made it a stipulation of the lawsuit that he has to formally and publicly apologize to all three of us—you, me and Jamie."

"Oh." Her eyes rounded.

"You don't have to leave the Sidewinders, Becca, but I'd like you to." He put a finger on her lips when she started to protest. "I'm not demanding this—it has to be your choice—but I don't want you living in Las Vegas while I live here. Even if I got traded to another team, I would be closer to you, but not with you because there's no baseball in Vegas. You asked me to take care of you and that's what I want to do. I know you can take care of yourself. I know you can wait tables or scrub toilets or deliver newspapers so that you have a roof over your head, but that's ridiculous. I'm rich—very, very rich. I want us to have a baby—several of them—and I want to see you sitting on the floor playing with them when I get home." He toyed with a lock of her hair. "I am also aware that all of those sentences began with what I want, so I need you to tell me what *you* want. There are no wrong answers, *querida*."

"I want you," she said automatically. "I want to have your babies—as many as my body will carry without making me miserable—and I want to be with you all the time. If you really want me to leave the Sidewinders, I will."

"No, my love—I want you to leave the Sidewinders only if that will make you happy. If you're leaving grudgingly, if your heart is still with the team, if you're not ready to go, please don't."

"A month ago I wasn't ready," she admitted. "But now, after everything that's happened, I might be. I just..." She sighed. "It's going to look like the reason I'm leaving is because of those pictures and I don't want *that* to be the reason."

"Then I'm going to have to knock you up," he said with an exaggerated sigh. "Today, maybe. Is that a good reason?"

She snorted. "I'm still on the pill—it'll be at least a month before you can knock me up."

He just smiled. "So maybe not today." He ran his calloused thumb over her cheek. "Perhaps then you stay another season...so you can leave on your own terms. We'll aim for being pregnant this time next year?"

She nodded and smiled before leaning forward and resting her forehead against his. "Dante?"

"Yes?"

"What did Randy mean about Louis not being your baby?" Her eyes were soft and filled with concern.

Dante snorted. "He was talkin' out his ass—you think I didn't consider that? She was desperate to keep me, so I always worried that the kid wasn't mine and planned to do a DNA test when he was born."

"And?"

"I asked for it to be done at the autopsy," he admitted. "I needed to know if he was mine."

"Was he?"

"Yes." Dante sighed. "That was one thing she was honest about, I guess."

"I'm sorry, babe."

"It's okay. Randy was trying to get under my skin, but obviously, it didn't work."

She stroked his hair and let it all sink in before narrowing her eyes and giving him a cheeky grin. "Since babies come up a lot, you should know that before you get me pregnant, you're going to have to marry me. When, exactly, are you going to do that?"

"New Year's Eve?" He cocked his head. "Is the Sidewinders' schedule out for next season?"

"Of course." She reached for her phone and found the calendar.

"Is there a game on New Year's Eve?"

She scrolled through the dates. "No."

"Are they in the middle of a road trip?"

"No."

"Then we could get married in Las Vegas—with all the people we care about. I'm sure Pierre will give you a week to go on a honeymoon. I'll start training camp in February, your season will end in April or May—"

"Bite your tongue!" she laughed. "You want me to tell you your season will end in September?!"

He laughed. "Touché—so you'll stop working whenever the season ends?"

"Yes." She nodded.

"Is this a plan you can live with?"

"Yes."

"Okay." He moved back to his chair and leaned back. "Now I have to make up with my team, let them know I'm okay and ready to make baseball my priority again."

"I'm sorry. I'm sure that's my fault."

"This was something we had to weather together. Tomorrow, if they allow me to play, you'll come to the game with me? You'll hold your head high and talk about our New Year's Eve wedding? Kate has been working nonstop to make sure that the pictures are buried and no credible news source is running them. Although social media is harder, she's working with the other victims' publicists about putting a spin on the lawsuit against Russ. We weren't the only people whose photos were released, so there will be half a dozen of us inundating the public with the story of how he breached security and set up the hidden cameras. It's a bit of a scare tactic, making people focus on places where they might be getting caught on camera, instead of on us, but it's working."

"Kate's brilliant," Becca said, nodding.

"Will you go to the game with me?"

"Of course."

"I spoke to Jax earlier and he said Cyndi would meet you so you wouldn't have to sit alone. Emilie and Viggo will be there as well."

She nodded. "Okay."

"Kate is trying to get on a flight—it will be best if she can be here tonight. I haven't heard back from her and she was flying standby, so she may be on the plane as we speak."

"I'd love to have her here."

"There will undoubtedly be questions about the pictures. It's up to you whether or not you want to answer them." He met her eyes.

"I don't have a problem answering them, but I honestly don't know what to say." She frowned. "I don't feel like it's anyone's business what we do in the bedroom and without Jamie here...I refuse to speak for him."

"Then say 'no comment.' When the game is over and they come to me, I'll distract them."

She arched an eyebrow. "Dante...if you say something outrageous—"

"They'll forget all about our threesome!" He grinned at her. "Come, eat your breakfast."

S itting in the stands the following night, Becca had never been so grateful for friends. Kate sat on one side of her and Cyndi on the other, with Emilie, Viggo and Simone behind them. She'd sensed the stares of some of the other wives and girlfriends, but she pretended not to notice. At one point when someone had begun to approach her, Emilie promptly dumped Simone in her arms with a bottle. Becca had smiled as she fed her, glad to see the woman change her mind about talking to her once she had an infant in her arms.

"Hey!" A dark-skinned woman with a bright white smile and a fabulous hot pink scarf wound through her long braids leaned over Cyndi's seat and gave her a hug.

"Hey, Berry!" Cyndi grinned up at her.

"You haven't introduced me to Becca yet," the woman said, giving Becca a friendly smile.

"Becca, this is Berry Cordova—Fernando's wife. Berry, this is Becca Hernandez. Did you know she and Dante set a date?"

"You did?!" Berry sank into an empty chair and held out her hand, shaking Becca's warmly. "Me and Nando, we eloped! Biggest regret of my life, so don't do it!"

Becca smiled. "He wouldn't let me even if I wanted to! I don't know what we're doing yet but it's going to be in Las Vegas on New Year's Eve."

"New Year's Eve in Las Vegas?" Berry rubbed her hands together. "I'm down for that!"

"It's probably going to be low-key," Becca murmured. "I don't have any details yet. We've been kind of busy this week."

Berry shook her head. "People'll do anything for money—pisses me right off! Don't you worry, honey, it'll all blow over soon. I can't wait to see what Dante does to distract everybody."

Becca raised her eyebrows. "What do you mean?"

Berry just laughed. "Girl, I've been married to a player for ten years—and I've been watching Dante even longer than that. He's good, knows just what to say and do to put the focus where it belongs. He did it last year with Kate, and now he's gonna handle it for you. Don't worry."

Becca glanced out at the field where the game was tied 1-1. "I hate that he's always on guard, always making sure that his persona is a certain way…I don't know how he does it."

"It's what he does," Kate said gently. "It's part of who he became because of this life in the spotlight."

"I am so glad he didn't marry that Larissa bitch," Berry muttered. She had the grace to flush when she realized what she'd said. "I mean, I'm not glad she's dead—I just wanted him to dump her sorry ass. She was rotten to him."

"I know." Becca nodded. "I'm not perfect, but I'll never, ever treat him like that. I love him."

"That's good." Berry let out a whoop. "Yeah, that's right—line drive down the middle, baby!"

Becca turned to see Dante sliding into second base, the second baseman not even close to tagging him. She smiled, loving the way he moved, the muscles in his legs rippling as he got to his feet.

"He move like that in bed?" someone called out.

Berry snapped her head around and laughed loudly. "Damn, he better! What good would all those muscles be if he didn't use them in the bedroom?!" She nudged Becca and whispered under her breath, "Just keep your head up."

Becca stared straight ahead, taking slow breaths, in through her nose, out through her mouth. It was going to be a long game, but she could do this; she *would* do it for Dante because he'd been protecting her one way or another since the day they'd met. Even though he'd wanted to see her again, he'd respected what he thought were her wishes by staying away so that her reputation would remain intact.

When they got together at Christmas he came up with a story that explained their connection and kept her from feeling cheap for having a one-night stand. Then he'd called a lawyer and made sure that the raid on the club went away almost as quickly as it started.

Now he'd literally bought her the club, sued everyone involved with those pictures, and she knew deep down he'd convinced Jamie to leave the Sidewinders so she wouldn't have to. At the end of the day, Dante had done anything and everything to make sure she was okay and she wouldn't disrespect that by letting him down tonight. No matter how hard it was, she would have his back.

35

THE BOTTOM OF THE NINTH INNING HAD THE TEAMS STILL TIED AND AS DANTE stepped up to the plate, there were two outs and a runner on second base. He turned, his eyes finding Becca's in the crowd and he pointed at her. Then he turned back to face the pitcher, his bat over his shoulder in the way Becca recognized as his home run stance. It changed subtly each time he did it, but being so intimate with him now, she knew every nuance of his body and it told her he was going to do something big.

Sure enough, when he swung the bat, it connected with the ball with such a loud crack she jumped. Kate, Emilie and Cyndi were on their feet before she was, knowing before she did that this was going to be the home run they needed.

"That's what I'm talkin' about!" Berry yelled from a few rows behind them.

"Damn, girl, that boy loves you!" someone yelled out.

"Go, baby!" Becca whispered as she got to her feet with everyone else, tears puddling in her eyes as she watched him circle the bases. As he crossed home plate his teammates all surged forward to pick him up, but his eyes were on Becca, slowly inclining his head.

"God, he's good," Kate murmured, linking her arm through Becca's. "No one can even remember those stupid pictures right now."

"Can I go to him?" Becca whispered. "I don't know what I'm supposed to do!"

"Go down to the front—come on!" Kate grabbed her hand and pulled her down as close to the field as they could get, hanging over the rail.

"Stay here," Kate whispered. "I can go down there with my press credentials and I'll tell him to grab you." She hopped over the rail, and one of the security officers rushed to help her since everyone knew her.

Becca watched her stand off to the side, waiting to get Dante's attention and he slowly moved away from his teammates. Kate whispered in his ear and he smiled, not looking up at Becca immediately, but leaning over to say something to one of his teammates.

As reporters began to surround him, he held up his hand, indicating he wanted them to wait. He looked up, locating Becca at the railing, and holding out his hand to her. She swung her legs over the rail and he reached up to put his hands around her waist as she jumped down. He pressed his lips to hers and whispered, "I've got everything under control—just smile and don't act surprised by anything."

She smiled shyly as the cameras turned towards her but Dante's arm was around her shoulders, holding her close to him as he approached the press.

"Dante, is this your girlfriend?"

"My fiancée, Rebecca Hernandez." He kissed her forehead before turning back to the cameras. "Yes, she works for the Las Vegas Sidewinders. Yes, we're getting married later this year. Yes, she's in those pictures with me and we're not going to talk about them. Anyone goes out of their way to ask about them, I'll never answer another question for you—and you know me, so you know I'm not kidding."

The crowd of reporters got quiet until someone yelled out, "Why not, Dante? You usually love a good scandal!"

Dante chuckled. "I do, but that's when it's just me—Becca's only in the spotlight because of me and that's not fair. Period. What we do in the bedroom is none of anyone's business...does anyone want to talk about the game or am I going home early?"

A few questions came out about his ninth inning home run and finally someone asked the inevitable: "There are rumors that you're going to retire now that you're getting married. Is that true?"

"I'm thinking about it," he nodded. "I've been doing this for fourteen years and Becca and I want a family. I don't want to be gone all the time and miss seeing my kids growing up."

"Is she pregnant, Dante?"

He rolled his eyes at a reporter he'd known for years. "For real? Knock it off, Steve! No, she's not pregnant—I just don't know how many seasons I've got left in me. We'll see in the off-season how I feel. I'm not making any decisions now, but…"

The questions came one after another and they were solely focused on baseball. Becca smiled to herself as she recognized what he'd done and how effectively, once again, he'd deflected the media. The pictures had come up but he'd been the one to do it and the conversation had been so brief it didn't even register on anyone's radar.

By the time the postgame interviews were over and Dante had changed and met Becca, Kate, Emilie and Viggo in the limo, it was late and everyone was tired. They were quiet on the way home and it was finally Viggo who spoke.

"Do you know for sure when you're going to hit a home run?" he asked quietly. "How do you do that?"

"For sure?" Dante shook his head. "Nah. No way to know for sure, but the reason I make the money I do is because I can do what I do…since I was about fourteen, something about the bat in my hands has taken me somewhere else. I feel it, sense where the ball is going to be, how I need to hit it…I can't explain it. Always been that way; me, the bat and the ball. There's a few pitchers in the league I can't hit off—ever—'cause they got what I got, except with pitching. With everyone else I just get a feeling."

"I don't think I have that," Viggo admitted. "I love hockey, and I'm good, but you're a different level player, my friend. I'm a little bit awestruck." He held out his hand and Dante shook it.

"Thank you. That means a lot coming from another athlete." He nodded.

"Are you really going to retire?" Kate asked.

He laughed. "Nah. Becca's going back to the Sidewinders for another year and she don't want a baby yet, so what am I gonna do for a year if I retire? I just got them all going nuts. Now my agent will be fielding calls day and night with ridiculous offers to keep me in for another year. It'll be fun."

"Would you move if you got another offer?"

"Now? No, but after Becca leaves the Sidewinders, maybe. You want to live somewhere other than New York, baby?"

She looked surprised. "I hadn't thought about it. I think the big question is the club. If we keep it, we can't watch over it unless we're in New York."

"The club?" Kate blinked. "What are you talking about?"

"He bought me the club," Becca whispered, even though she didn't know why.

"He bought Club Inferno?!"

"More like he won it," Becca nodded.

"The owners knew it would never survive after I got through with them. Instead of suing them, they basically gave it to me and I put it in Becca's name." He looked at her tenderly, a smile playing on his lips. "She needs something of her own, something to give her the emotional power to never succumb to what people say or do—being rich gives you power and now she's rich."

She shook her head. "I don't need to be rich."

"You need your own power, *querida*." He kissed her and hovered, his lips close to hers. "You need to feel powerful without me so that you feel like my equal."

"I love you so much," she whispered.

He wrapped his fingers around hers and squeezed. "I know."

"So you're going to run the club?" Emilie asked in surprise.

Becca frowned. "I don't think so. I'd like to be involved, but with me in Vegas and the club in New York, I don't see how that's possible."

"Then what will you do with it?" Kate asked.

"I don't know," Becca said. "We're going to get some business consultants involved so they can tell us what went wrong—if anything—the way it was, and see what we can do to make it better."

"I might be able to give you some ideas," Emilie said slowly. "I've spent a lot of time at sex clubs over the years and there are quite a few things I can think of that I've always wished were available or done better."

"She's also a very experienced dominatrix," Viggo said with a grin.

"I'd love to hear about all of that," Becca nodded. "We're going to see if it's financially feasible to open it back up. If not, we can sell it."

"You," Dante corrected mildly.

"Me what?" she asked.

"*You* can sell it. It has nothing to do with me, legally."

She rolled his eyes. "You're helping me with this, mister!"

He just smiled, leaning back against the seat, the fingers of one hand twirling a lock of her hair.

"I think running a sex club would be amazing," Emilie said softly. "I mean, being in charge, you know?"

Viggo looked at her in shock. "*Really?*"

"Yeah." She flushed. "Designing clothes is my passion, but it's not something I can do full-time right now, not with a baby. Running a club would be something I could do and keep Simone with me."

"You can't bring our daughter to a sex club!" Viggo's eyes widened.

She just laughed. "She's three months old! For the next few years she'll have no idea at all about what goes on there, and anyway, I'm picturing an office where she sleeps in a crib while I…" She paused. "Anyway, I was just thinking aloud. Not like you asked me to run your club."

Becca cocked her head thoughtfully. "But you could. The only way we're reopening is if we have people we trust involved. What happened with these pictures will never happen under our watch—that's something that's going to be a top priority, after safety and cleanliness. If you want to be my manager, Em, I'd love it."

"Wait a minute…" Viggo looked confused.

"It would be a management position," Emilie said gently. "You know, making sure the staff shows up, security is where they should be, the DJ is playing the right music, the bar has the right permits…things like that. Right, Becca?"

Becca nodded as Viggo frowned. "We should talk about this."

Emilie quickly agreed. "Yes, of course."

The rest of the ride was quiet and they all separated as soon as they got to Dante's house. Peeling out of her clothes in the bathroom, Becca stepped under the shower and let the cool water wash over her. It had been hot and sticky at the game and it felt wonderful to clean up. Dante had showered at the stadium so she was surprised when she felt him slide in behind her, his hands moving around her waist.

"Hi." She leaned back against him.

"You were brave tonight," he said softly. "It made me really happy to have you there with me. Cyndi told Jax that you never batted an eyelash, no matter what was said."

"I probably batted more than an eyelash," she laughed. "But I hid it pretty well."

"Ah, *querida*, I love you so." He turned her so he could kiss her and their mouths mingled lovingly.

"It's going to be hard to go back to work," she said with a soft sigh.

"You know you don't have to."

"But I do." She looked into his glittering eyes. "You said you understood…"

"I do!" He put his hands on either side of her face. "I know how important it is for you to go back with your head held high and do the job you worked so hard to get. I simply wanted to remind you that you don't have to—I'm happy to have you live here with me and do nothing but get ready for the wedding."

"Dante, after the way Larissa used you—"

"No." He put his finger over her lips. "You aren't Larissa. You are ten times the human being she was. That never even crossed my mind. Larissa felt like I owed her, but no matter how much I gave her it was never enough. With you, I practically have to beg you to let me buy dinner. I don't compare you to her, ever."

"Okay." She nodded slowly. "I'm a little nervous about going back, though. Everyone on the Sidewinders saw those pictures, I'm sure..."

"No." He smiled. "I spoke to Karl, who spoke to most of the team. They agreed not to look."

She crinkled her forehead. "I know you're Dante Lamonte and you have these weird super powers related to your bat and making the press believe whatever you want, but you can't possibly believe that grown men aren't going to look simply because you told them not to—that's ludicrous!"

"If they're too afraid to admit it, what's the difference?" He was completely serious. "You're their friend. Yes, I'm sure some of the guys on the team looked or had already seen them, but you know what? The people that matter did not. I don't know if Karl did—he didn't say—but Kate obviously saw them since she had to deal with them, so he probably did as well. But think about the members of the team that you know best? Do you think Zakk looked at those pictures? Or if he did, simply so he would know what's going on, do you think he did it maliciously? Do you think in the midst of everything that went on this summer his priority was looking at you and me having sex with Jamie? I'd be willing to bet not."

She nodded slowly, biting her lip. "You're right—the guys I'm closest to —Karl, Drake, Cody, Zakk—they wouldn't because they care about me. If they did, like if Karl did because Kate had to see what she was dealing with, it's something he would never, ever bring up."

"And the others, well, like you said—I have super powers."

She giggled. "You *are* kind of scary that way."

"Not to you, I hope."

"No." She nestled closer to him. "I trust you more than anyone in the world."

"That's the greatest thing anyone has ever said to me."

EPILOGUE

Dante and Becca sat on the couch of their living room, smiling at their guest. Joe Westfield had been in love with Trey at the time of his death, and though he'd only met him a few times, Dante had a feeling he would have been the one Trey settled down with. Older, distinguished, and extremely solid —all the things Trey had longed for but hadn't been able to find until it was too late. They'd technically been broken up when Trey was killed, but he'd told Dante he was going to go to New York once the situation with Larissa was under control. That trip had never happened, but Joe knew Trey had changed his mind about them being apart.

"Lunch was excellent," Joe said, looking at them. "I enjoyed it very much. And now that we've moved past the pleasantries, I'm curious as to why I'm here."

Becca nodded. "You were close to someone we cared about and have an excellent reputation in the security world; we're in need of your services and thought this would be a good icebreaker."

Joe raised his eyebrows. "For Club Inferno."

Dante grinned. "You're aware that Becca owns it now?"

"Becca? I thought you owned it."

"No. I got it in exchange for not suing those idiots, and I gave it to Becca so that she has some financial independence."

"That's nice." Joe smiled and nodded. "Do you need me to provide security? Install alarms? Background checks on employees?"

"All of the above." Becca handed him a stack of papers. "We're moving the club to Vegas. I don't know if that will be problematic for you, but if it's something you think you can fit into your schedule, we'd be willing to put you either on retainer or make you a permanent, albeit part-time, member of the staff."

"Really?" Joe looked pensive. "I keep thinking I need to get out of New York, but I have so much business here it's difficult. This might be a nice compromise, though."

They talked numbers and responsibilities for a while and Joe finally leaned back thoughtfully. "I think I have the perfect head of security for you. His name is Darryl Carruthers. He's ex-MI6 and a serious badass, but he's also one of my closest confidantes. I trust him with my life, and as a bonus, he's dabbled in the BDSM world."

"Is he in New York?"

"Right now he's in Europe with a client, but he's planning to come back to the U.S. as soon as this security detail—rock band that's on tour—is over. He hates the cold so I think Vegas would be right up his alley."

"When can we talk to him?" Dante asked. He'd been quiet until now, but security was something he was going to have a say in. He knew Becca was perfectly capable of running a business, but this kind of security wasn't something she was familiar with so he planned to oversee it until he felt comfortable stepping back.

"Tour is over on Saturday and he's flying to New York on Monday. I can set up a meeting mid-week? Will you be in New York?"

"I'll be in Toronto next week—perhaps the week after?"

"Darryl's a good guy, I'm sure he'll be flexible."

"That's it then," Becca nodded. "If you want to draw up a contract, you can get it to us and we'll go from there."

"We could have done this on the phone," Joe said with a smile, his blue eyes twinkling.

"I wanted to see you," Dante admitted. "Perhaps seeing someone who was so close to Trey makes me miss him a bit less."

Joe looked away, nodded slowly. "The anniversary is next week. I'm thinking I have a date with a bottle of Jack Daniel's that day."

"I have a game," Dante said. "But Becca will be with me for that trip and we'll do something in Trey's honor."

"It's been hard to get past," Joe replied. "Some days I still can't believe he's gone. He wasn't my usual type, but there was something special about him. He would play the prissy little stereotypical homosexual just to get a rise out of people, and then a minute later he was talking about baseball like he played the game, you know?"

"He *did* play the game," Dante smiled. "Most people don't know that, but that's how we got to be friends. We had an English class together, but we both went out for baseball. Trey was tiny, but man, he could run. He'd bunt and be on first before anyone realized what happened. But he didn't love it the way I did. He just did it for something to do and because he liked to look at the guys in the locker room."

Joe snorted. "Sounds like Trey."

"I wish I'd known him," Becca admitted.

"Me, too." Dante squeezed her hand as he glanced at Joe. "But let's not make the same mistakes again. Let's keep our friends close—not take relationships for granted—and make sure they know what they mean to us every single day."

Joe nodded, his eyes somewhat misty. "I'd like that. I'm excited to help you get the club going and I think Trey would have been happy to see us working on a project together."

"He would have," Dante said. "He definitely would have."

Becca raised her glass of ice water with a smile. "To friends, family and Trey."

"Friends, family and Trey."

I hope you enjoyed Dante and Becca's story. Please consider leaving a review at the retailer of your choice—they mean so much to us.

The next book in the series is Jamie and Viggo's story—flip the page for a very steamy excerpt.

EXCERPT FROM "TEMPTATION'S INFERNO"

"Harder! Viggo, please!"

Shit.

Jamie grimaced. Emilie and Viggo were having sex and he was close to walking in on them. He was about to turn and go back to his room when he heard the sound of a hand slapping skin. Jesus, were they into spanking too? His cock twitched just thinking about it and he couldn't resist taking the last three steps to the end of the hall. He peeked around the corner feeling like a creep, but the moment he caught sight of them there was no way he was going anywhere.

Emilie was bent over the back of the couch, Viggo buried deep inside of her, one hand gripping her long blond hair, the other slapping her beautiful little ass. He watched in fascination as Viggo pounded into her, over and over, the muscles in his taut ass straining as he fucked her. She was panting, her long legs spread wide to give him deeper access, and Viggo's body was like that of a powerful animal as he took her. Jamie couldn't even blink as he watched. They were fucking *hot*, and he hadn't had sex in a couple of months, so he was already aroused.

"More!" she whimpered.

"Dammit, Em, I can't hit you any harder," Viggo grunted.

"Please!" She whispered something in Swedish that made Viggo groan, but he stopped moving and let go of her hair.

"Em, *I can't.*"

I could, Jamie thought, his hand unconsciously traveling to his erection.

"Viggo!" Emilie dropped her head, frustration practically oozing out of her.

"I'm sorry…" He seemed as unsatisfied as she was. "I just, it's not me. You know how I feel about this."

"But I like it," she cried. "You're not hurting me!"

"I'm sorry…" His voice trailed off.

"I can hit her." Jamie wasn't even aware he'd spoken until Emilie and Viggo jumped in surprise, their heads whipping around to stare at him.

"Jamie!" Viggo's face flushed slightly. "Damn, I'm sorry, we thought—"

"I don't have to do anything else with her," Jamie continued slowly, walking towards them. "I can just spank her while you fuck her—nothing else. If it would help. You both seem irritated and…it's kind of my thing."

"Oh, Viggo, please!" Emilie reached back to clutch her husband's forearm.

Viggo hadn't moved, his cock still buried inside of his wife, and he met Jamie's gaze with interest. "You're sure? You don't mind?"

Jamie let his towel fall away, revealing his throbbing erection, his eyes meeting Viggo's. "Watching the two of you fuck is hot as hell—I've always enjoyed watching—and I don't mind jerking off when we're done."

The two men exchanged a look of mutual appreciation as Viggo slowly nodded. "Em, are you sure?"

"Oh, yes." Her blue eyes were glittering with excitement.

"I'll be right back." Jamie turned and practically ran into his room, yanking open the closet door and grabbing the only belt he found. If she liked it rough, he'd give her rough; it was one of his favorite things when it came to sex.

Viggo's eyes widened when Jamie returned, and he glanced down at his wife. "Em?"

"Oh yes…" Her voice was a breathy whisper this time.

Jamie didn't hesitate, folding the belt into a manageable size and bringing it down on her left cheek, careful not to hit Viggo's crotch in the process. She yelped and he immediately did it again. This time she moaned, surging back to meet Viggo's hips.

"I hit, then you thrust," Jamie instructed Viggo, who nodded.

Jamie's cock got stiffer and stiffer as he increased intensity and Emilie bucked like a wild woman, her chest rising and falling in an almost rhythmic pattern as she begged for more. She was whimpering, her skin getting redder and redder. He paused, running his hands over the inflamed area gently.

"Okay, baby, I'm going to hit you twice more," he said softly. "Once on each side, and then you're going to come. You can't take much more—you understand?"

"Wait..." she was breathing hard, her cheeks flushed, body covered in sweat. "We should come together...all of us...not fair...for you to just watch."

"I don't think—" Viggo began.

"It's okay—" Jamie said at the same time.

"But it's what I want," she whispered. "Both of you on your knees, one behind me, the other in front. We come together..."

"Yeah, all right." Viggo looked conflicted as he gave him.

Emilie dropped to the ground on her hands and knees and Jamie knelt in front of her. Without hesitation, she took him into her mouth and he let out a long, low moan.

"I'm not going to last long," he muttered. "It's been a while."

"Em's on the verge too," Viggo murmured, positioning himself behind her and sliding in deep.

Jamie fisted Emilie's hair, using his hands to hold her head still as he pumped in and out of her mouth. "Can you deep throat me, Emilie?" he asked.

She nodded and he drove straight to the back of her throat, closing his eyes and enjoying the sensation of her warm lips and tongue enveloping him.

Viggo picked up the pace, holding her in place by the hips. He met Jamie's rhythm and they fucked her together, their bodies perfectly in sync, moving as though they'd done this a million times before. Viggo's big, muscular body was sheer perfection in Jamie's eyes; large, strong and pure masculinity. Emilie was the complete opposite, as feminine as any woman he'd ever seen with milky white skin, light blond hair, pale pink nipples and the softest skin he'd ever felt. Watching Viggo fuck her had gotten him excited; having her suck him off at the same time was more than he could stand. Jamie lost control first, growling as he pushed his cock down her throat, shooting deep. Emilie never even blinked, swallowing without so much as a cough, continuing to suck until he nearly collapsed. Viggo yanked her against him, rocking back on his haunches without breaking contact and pulling her up so her back rested against his chest.

"Put your mouth on her," Viggo growled at Jamie.

Jamie didn't hesitate, crawling over to them and gliding his tongue right between her folds. She was completely bare and her clit puffed up between his lips. He bit down lightly, one hand sliding underneath to cup Viggo's balls. He had no idea what made him do that but the urge to touch his large, sexy friend was suddenly irresistible. Viggo's reaction was all he could've hoped for too, a moan escaping him as he briefly met Jamie's cautious gaze. Unable to resist, Jamie ran his tongue from her slit to the base of Viggo's shaft and wrapped his mouth as far around it as he could. Viggo shuddered against him and thrust up hard, both he and Emilie coming together.

Jamie lay back and collapsed, still breathing hard. Emilie crawled off of Viggo and lay on the floor on her stomach. Viggo didn't move, simply watching both of them with heavy-lidded eyes. The aftermath of what they'd just done was heavy in the air and Jamie sat up first.

"She'll need aftercare," was all he said as he started to get up.

"Yeah, and you'll be the one to give it to her," Viggo rumbled, reaching over to run a hand over Emilie's bright red ass.

"I thought—"

"You thought what? You'd come in here, have sex with us and walk away?"

"I figured that's what you'd want," he said quietly, crawling over to Emilie and gently running his hand down her back and onto her behind. "I didn't mean to interrupt but when I heard you say you couldn't hit her harder…it's my thing so I…I'm sorry. I didn't mean to overstep the boundaries of our friendship."

Viggo chuckled. "Did you hear her beg you for more? I can't give her what you just gave her."

Jamie hesitated. "I'm, uh, I'm not sure what to do now."

"Take care of her," Viggo murmured, getting to his feet. "I'll clean up a bit and be right back." He padded out of the room without a backwards glance and Jamie leaned over Emilie, moving her hair back so he could see one side of her face.

"How're you doing, hon?" he whispered softly, one hand trailing along her cheek. "I went at you pretty hard. You okay?"

"Oh yes." She smiled faintly. "It was lovely."

"I, uh, didn't know you liked this kind of thing."

"I didn't know you did." She opened one eye and grinned. "I loved having you both take me."

He smiled and used his hands to gently rub her bruised behind. "Honey, I think you'll need a cool cloth for this. You're awfully red."

"I'm fine," she murmured. "My skin's sensitive, but I'm not hurt. I promise."

"Still." He got to his feet and bent to lift her. "I'm going to put you in bed and get a towel—"

"I've got it." Viggo met Jamie's eyes and motioned with his head. "Go on, take her to the bedroom."

Want to follow Jamie and Viggo on their journey? Click here for Temptation's Inferno.
Or flip the page for a list of all my books.

ALSO BY KAT MIZERA

Las Vegas Sidewinders:

Dominic

Cody's Christmas Surprise

Drake

Karl

Anatoli

Zakk

Toli & Tessa

Brock

Vladimir

Royce

Nate

Sidewinders: Ever After

Jared

Dmitri's Christmas Angel

Ian

Sidewinders: Generations:

Zaan

Tore

Anton

Alaska Blizzard:

Defending Dani

Holding Hailey

Winning Whitney

Losing Laurel

Saving Sara

Chasing Charli

A Very Blizzard Christmas

Tending Tara

Calling Cassie

Playing Peyton

St. Louis Mavericks (with Brenda Rothert)

Hard Fall

Hard Limit

Hard Pass

Lauderdale Knights:

Slap Shot

Big Shot

Rock Hard:

Play

Pause

Rewind

Fast Forward

The Royal Trilogy:

Nowhere Left to Fall

Nowhere Left to Run

Nowhere Left to Hide

Royal Protectors:

Sandor

Cocky Protector (book 1.5, part of the Cocky Heroes Club series)

Xander

Axel

Dax *(A Royal Protectors/Sidewinders crossover novel)*

Inferno:

Salvation's Inferno

Temptation's Inferno

Redemption's Inferno

Tropical Inferno (formerly "Tropical Ice")

Romancing Europe:

Adonis in Athens

Smitten in Santorini

Lucky in Lugano

Other Books:

Special Forces: Operation Alpha: Protecting Bobbi (Susan Stoker's Special Forces World)

Special Forces: Operation Alpha: Protecting Delilah (Susan Stoker's Special Forces World)

View Kat's entire collection of books at www.KatMizera.com

ABOUT THE AUTHOR

USA Today Bestselling author Kat Mizera was born in Miami Beach with a healthy dose of wanderlust. She's lived from coast to coast, and everywhere in between, but home is wherever her family is.

A devoted mom and wife to her wonderful and supportive husband (Kevin) and two amazing boys (Nick and Max), Kat loves to travel the globe with her adventurous, hockey loving family. Greece is at the top of that list. She hopes to one day retire there, spending her days writing books on the beach.

Kat is former freelance sports writer who now writes steamy hockey romance about her favorite fictional teams, the Las Vegas Sidewinders and the Alaska Blizzard. The library of novels she's penned also include sexy contemporary stories about baseball stars, alpha sex club owners, special forces heroes, rock stars and royalty. Regardless of genre, her books about bad boys with hearts of gold will steal your breath, rock your world and melt your heart.

WHERE TO FOLLOW KAT:

WEBSITE
FACEBOOK
TWITTER
INSTAGRAM
BOOKBUB
KAT'S PRIVATE FACEBOOK GROUP